THE BURNING PLANET

A FABULOUS AND FUTURISTIC NOVEL
FANTASY MEETS REALITY

The Burning Planet

A fabulous and futuristic novel
Fantasy meets Reality

Edmund Arndt

*We do not inherit the earth from our fathers, we
borrow it from our children*
- Inuit saying

TAMARIND TREE BOOKS
Toronto

Library and Archives Canada Cataloguing in Publication

Arndt, Edmund, author
The burning planet : fantasy meets reality / Edmund Arndt.

ISBN 978-0-9950538-3-0 (paperback)

I. Title.

PS8601.R646B87 2016   C813'.6   C2016-904031-3

*This book is dedicated to my friend Vlado
and I also want to thank Jacqueline Szorady for her
tireless and dedicated support.*

When I was a young man, I asked Joe Mandel if humankind was doomed to perish in an atomic war. I don't remember using the term "nuclear" back then.

"Atomic or not, our planet and humankind will eventually burn up! It might not be that far away, not all that long, and hell will come to visit and destroy us. Oh yes, we will burn. We all will burn in a fire so hot that everything on our planet will burn. Even the rocks and the soil and the sand will ignite and the sand will turn into glass," was his gloomy forecast.

"Unless, unless ... humankind will come to its senses!"

Do you believe it is possible?

Want to find out?

Since you are already a partner of the future, why don't you begin to read and become a partner of the fantasy?

— Edmund Arndt

Table of Contents

Chapter 1

The Accident

On a cold and snowy December day in 2000, Vlado had taken a shortcut, the Braden Road, on his return from Fort St. John. He would be home for Christmas, after he had spent the summer and fall months in this northern boom city of British Columbia, where he had built several houses in the recent past and had sold them for a handsome profit. The Braden Road was an unpaved link between the Alaska Highway and the John Hart Highway, cutting off about a half hour of travel time from Fort St. John to Prince George.

A grader had removed the heavy snowfall of the previous night. It was still snowing and the fresh flakes unfolded a new white blanket over the road and the fields on this windless day. It innocently covered the treacherous ice underneath and a deep rut that the grader had filled with soft snow just hours earlier.

The slow and lonely station wagon in front signalled for him to pass, and Vlado moved into the left lane to overtake the car. That's when he hit the hidden rut with his left front tire and lost control on the icy road surface. He tumbled down the steep embankment in his Dodge Dakota, rolling over and over four times.

The big strong man—who could effortlessly carry two concrete blocks, one in each hand, when others only carried one with both their hands—was not strong enough to overcome this horrific tumble.

No, he was not strong enough, and the weakest part of his body snapped right where his heavy head attached to his torso. He was lying there in the mangled pickup truck with his neck broken until help finally arrived two hours later at the remote accident site. He did not feel the terrible cold of minus 20 degrees, he did not feel anything anymore, and he knew that he would not be home for Christmas.

They airlifted him to the University Hospital in Edmonton and for the following days and weeks he would be fighting for his life.

I booked a flight on WestJet in early January. What an exerting trip that turned out to be. It took all bloody day to get to Edmonton. I probably could have driven the 800 kilometres in less time if only the roads would have been safer and my mind would have been less clouded with worry and anxiety.

First, I flew from PG to Vancouver in the morning, where I changed planes. After a stopover in Kelowna, the flight continued, crossing the spectacular Rocky Mountains on a perfectly clear day and landing in Calgary. There again, I had to board another plane, and finally I arrived in Edmonton in the evening.

My brother was waiting for me at the airport and took me straight to the hospital. Visiting hours were over for the day, but the nurse let me see him for a short while.

He had difficulty speaking, his windpipe and oesophagus were damaged and his lungs had collapsed.

"Shit, Herr Kamerad," he whispered. His voice sounded raspy and strangely hollow. "Look at me, I am a cripple! I will never walk again. I would be much better off if I had died and they would be better off, too." He tried to move his hand and then I saw Marika, his wife, and Ilona, his daughter in the back of the room. They cried; they had been crying for three weeks.

"They were waving for me to pass. Shit! Please, God, let me die."

"No, no!" wailed Marika from the back and rushed to him, but speaking had exhausted him and he closed his eyes for a moment.

Both women had taken a leave of absence from their employment. They shared a room in a small hotel nearby and visited every day, one to comfort her husband, the other to comfort her father and her mother.

I was shocked to see my friend in this helpless and miserable condition. Feeding and draining tubes ran through his nose, IVs were hooked up to his arms, cables ran from different parts of his body to monitors, and a large neck brace stabilized and immobilized his head. More hook-ups were underneath the bed covers.

His big brown eyes looked at me so immensely sad. It was a heartbreaking moment and I began to talk, just babbling gibberish, nothing important. Because, for what was important I could not find the words, and it remained unspoken. I talked about my drawn-out trip, the weather, about some news and gossip from back home in Prince George. Nothing important, nothing important at all. He listened to everything I told him and maybe just the familiarity of my voice brought a flicker of light and a splinter of hope to the dark thoughts of his mind.

The nurse appeared.

"I will see you tomorrow, my friend," I said and I saw in his sad brown eyes that he would like that.

Vlado stayed at the University Hospital for the next four months and Marika was by his side every day to give support to her often depressed and emotional husband, encouraging him to keep on living.

"Why? What the hell for?" he would groan. "There is not one good reason to live a life as a paraplegic. The only reason why I keep on going is to get enough movement back to the fingers of my right hand, so that I have the strength to hold my .45 and pull the trigger to end this misery."

"Hush, don't you talk like that!" she said. "I need you. I don't want to be alone, and the girls, they need their father. I shall look after you. Remember when we pledged for better or worse and in sickness and in health? You remember those words? I shall be there for you my darling. I shall always be there."

"I want to blow my brains out," he replied and his depressed mood prevailed. "It is the best solution for everybody. I do not want to live as a cripple, and I do not want to be a burden to all of you. The girls have their own lives anyway. They are both married. You are the one that will get stuck with me, you alone!"

"I don't mind."

"What do I have to offer? I have nothing, absolutely nothing. There is nothing I can give you."

"You know why I love you? Because of your mind, your humour, your decency, your valour, your spirits, your crazy ideas, your laugh, your sincerity, and your deep concern. You still have all those great attributes that I admire. There is nobody else like you in the whole wide world; there is no duplicate of my Vlado out there! I want you to be my companion for the rest of my life, just like we promised on our wedding day."

Vlado had tears in his eyes and tried clumsily to wipe them away.

"God, woman," he said. "I always knew you were the best thing that ever happened to me. But this is serious, really serious stuff. This is too big for you to handle. It's a commitment beyond your strength and it will ruin your life too. No, this is no solution, not an option."

"You can't kill yourself. Ilona might lose her baby!"

"Oh, my God," he barely moved his lips and then they just looked into each others' sad eyes for a long while and nobody spoke a word.

"Hold my hand," he whispered, "and squeeze it, not too hard, please, just a bit. Is it really true? My little girl will have a baby?"

"Yes, it is true," Marika nodded her head.

"I can't do it. I can't do this to Ilona. No, I cannot kill myself. You are right, my darling. I will not hurt my little girl. Looks like you get your wish after all—you will be stuck with me now!"

And for the first time after the horrific accident, they both tried to smile. It was not easy for them because they had almost forgotten how.

The new life that Ilona carried in her body would jumpstart her father's life. Vlado pushed his depression aside and embraced a new strong will to live and survive. But many medical hurdles had to be cleared before he could properly breathe, drink, and eat.

The next time I visited my friend, I came with my wife Ursula. It was in April that year, and we travelled by car through the magnificent Robson Valley, noticing only sparse signs of the new emerging season. Moose Lake still carried a solid sheet of ice and the Rocky Mountains in Jasper Park seemed adamant to cling to their wintry beauty and refuse to let it go. It was snowing on Obed Summit, but the snow did not stick to the road and the fluffy flakes were blown off the highway into the empty ditches. The countryside was barren and dull, clad in monotonous grey, still deep in hibernation. It looked desolate and overdue for change, a change to colour and life, sprouting fresh greens, exciting reds and yellows, blues and purples.

We refuelled in Edson and stopped at Smitty's for a late lunch and coffee. One hundred twenty more miles to go, 200 kilometres or so, or two more hours of driving. It was a long trip, but now I felt refreshed and was pushing to get to the big city of Edmonton. Ursula reminded me softly about the speed limit.

After four months at the University Hospital, Vlado was moved to Glenrose, a high-level care and rehabilitation facility. He was paralysed from his waist down. His upper body, although badly mangled in the accident, was functioning with limitations. He still had problems with swallowing and preventing food from entering the trachea and ending up in his lungs. His lungs had collapsed three times while he was in the hospital, but now he was stabilized and his breathing was normal. The use of both his hands was impaired, and special exercises several times a day were prescribed. Soon they brought results and he regained movement and feeling in most of his fingers of the right hand. His left hand, however, stagnated in the healing process and he only received partial use from it.

Vlado was in the pool when we arrived at Glenrose.

"Hello, Herr Kamerad!" he yelled in his booming voice. "Look, I can stand up!" he joked and pulled himself into a vertical position at the edge of the pool.

"The doctors say that the nerve strands in my spine have to grow back and this exercise stimulates the growth, one millimetre per day they figure. It will take longer for me of course, because I am so darn tall," he laughed. "But I'll get there and I will walk again, you watch and see, even if it takes me longer!"

When he returned to Prince George, after two months in Glenrose, he was full of optimism and progress was quite evident. He had built up his upper body strength, regained some weight, and showed an overall strong confidence. But the progress and the confidence faded fast when he and Marika were confronted with the financial reality.

The auto-insurance company was fighting the workers' compensation board, and neither of them was willing to dish out the money to remodel their home for his needs. No one wanted to pay for a wheelchair, the ramp, or the lifts. No one wanted to pay for his daily home care or for the prolonged physio treatments. The health care system reluctantly kicked in, but soon cancelled the visits to the pool after another therapist resigned from the skeleton group of specialized caregivers.

It took two years of legal wrangling until everything was settled and sorted out, but the damage was done. The long interruption of treatments would prove to be harmful to his recovery.

In the meantime, his daughters and his sons-in-law built the two ramps and were helpful in many other ways. Ilona visited her father almost every day and it was a long drive from her home.

Chapter II

Vlado Comes to Visit

Today is August 13, 2035, and I am celebrating my 95th birthday, and there are many other good reasons for celebration.

Our earth is not burning anymore; humankind has come to its senses and finally brought armed conflicts and global warming to a halt.

The sand has not turned into glass after all; yet there is considerably more sand in the Sahara and in all the deserts, even in the many new ones. But there is precious little of it to be found on the beaches. Most of the once famous and fabulous beaches are underwater now, ever since the devastating 'Scorcher Years' of 2022–2025. The sand has been reclaimed by the sea.

Temperatures shot up drastically to new and unparalleled highs all over the world. Every glacier on the globe began to melt and whittle away. Rivers, filled with the increased amounts of water to the brim, crested well over the banks and dykes and flooded the fertile low-lying areas.

The uncontrolled raging waters gushed ahead, taking topsoil and plants from the fertile grounds and carrying them to the waiting sea. Every so often, the angry, dirty waters surprised the farm animals, cutting them off from land, and many would drown. The bloated corpses of cows, pigs, horses, even chickens, were floating on top in the foaming murky currents.

Both the polar icecaps as well as Greenland and Iceland were shedding millions of tons of ice daily in the sweltering heat, and the level of the oceans began to rise, slowly at first and hardly noticeable.

"Happy Birthday, Herr Kamerad!" yells Vlado as he skilfully navigates his state-of-the-art wheelchair up the stairs and through the maze of cluttered lawn furniture in the backyard of my house. He grabs my hand and shakes it.

"Ninety-five years! Quite an achievement, Herr Kamerad. Congratulations! I have to wait another four months for my 95th birthday! Five more years and you'll have it made, you son of a gun! The golden 100! Then you will get a birthday card from our princess, or did you get one today?" and he laughs.

It was only eight months ago when Megan Prince was catapulted into the national political spotlight. She fast became the darling of the news media after finishing in first place in the general national elections.

Then the 308 newly elected members of parliament chose her with an overwhelming majority for the top job of the country. She became only the second female to be elected as Prime Minister of Canada and the first native female to do so. The people soon began to call her affectionately and respectfully "our princess".

"I can't get used to the idea that a woman is running our country now," says Vlado.

"You can't get used to it because you are a stubborn male chauvinist!" I reply.

"Well, not really. Maybe just a little bit, you know. I'll admit to a little bit. How did she get so far and so fast, anyway? I bet all the Indians, the Hindus, and the Muslims voted for her. It couldn't have been any other way. All the minorities suddenly became the majority."

"I believe it was high time for Canadians to have elected a female leader and the fact that she also is a native Indian just adds another overdue element to it. Hey, by the way, one does not say Hindus, it is East Indians, my friend," I am telling him.

"Okay, okay! I think you are just too liberal sometimes. I liked Stephen Hunter; he had a good head on his shoulders."

"Enough! Enough! No more politics today, please!" I am stopping him.

Vlado looks at me apologetically with his big brown eyes.

"Sorry, Herr Kamerad," he mumbles. "Sometimes I get carried away."

He has always called me "Herr Kamerad", for as long as I can remember. Both words are German but they are not found in this combination. It is almost an oxymoron and means something like "Sir Buddy".

Vlado is having a good day, I can tell. After every good day, a "not-so -good-day" follows. He never has bad days, only "not-so-good-days". This has been the pattern for the past thirty years or so.

"What a beautiful day, Herr Kamerad. We should be out there planting bananas, and you are falling asleep. What's the matter with you? Hey, wake up, wake up!" and he touches my arm.

"I am not sleeping," I protest weakly and yawn. "Can't plant bananas today anyway; we don't have the seeds," I tell him. He appears puzzled for a moment.

"I didn't know bananas have seeds? I've never heard of it. Or is the banana itself the seed? We could plant a bunch of bananas right into the ground and see what happens. But what is the right end up and what is the wrong end down? We would have to try it both ways."

"What a waste! They will rot, you fool! That's what's going to happen! Haven't you heard of seedless oranges? Well, if there are seedless oranges, why not have seedless bananas."

"But how do they plant bananas?" he asked worriedly.

I shrug my shoulders. "Beats me, never really looked into it!"

It is a silly game and we play it quite often, pretending we never done it before and that it is a new idea born at the spur of the moment. It started when Vlado declared we should rename British Columbia into Northern California and then we would be able to grow bananas here and I would answer: "Can't grow bananas here. It's too windy. Bananas don't like wind."

He touches my arm again and shakes me. I am startled. I must have dozed off and I apologize.

"Can't sleep on your birthday, no sir! You will miss the party!" he laughs.

"I was telling you how the world has changed but you probably never heard a word I said. I am sure it all started in 2011, with that big flood in Australia when all of Queensland was underwater. That was terrible; imagine an area larger than France and Germany combined. Yeah, and then bang-bang, one after another, floods everywhere, in Bangladesh, China, Germany, Poland, Rio de Janeiro, Bangkok, even Manitoba, and God knows where else. Yeah, and when the dead birds kept falling out of the sky by the thousands, I knew that was a bad sign and that humankind was in trouble. Big trouble, Herr Kamerad. It was a warning from above. I am sure of it now."

"Oh, it most likely started long before that," I tell him. "We always had natural disasters, earthquakes, tsunamis, floods, droughts, the plague, and other pandemics. The 'Boxing Day' tsunami in 2004 claimed over 200,000 people. In 2010 we had two major catastrophes, the deadly earthquake in Haiti, again 200,000 victims, and the devastating flood in Pakistan affecting over 10 million people. Maybe it all started already in 2010."

"I don't think so. I believe the real change came in 2011, because something new happened in 2011, the youth revolt in the Arab world. It started in Tunisia, and then it spread like wildfire from nation to nation in the Middle East. Millions and millions of young people entered the labour force, only to find there were no jobs for them. The demographics were the same all over; the population had doubled in the last 30 years, and the average age in Egypt, for instance, was 24. The new young generation demanded changes and demanded jobs. They wanted the changes and the jobs—now! Never before in history were there that many young people in the streets, in the squares, and on the barricades protesting. No, never before! Technology had brought them together, technology and social networking. Wasn't technology the root of all the labour shortages? Wasn't it technology that brought all of this about? Technology was so much in love with automation that they mated in 24-hour frenzies daily and bred little robots, gizmos, microchips, and God knows what else by the millions and they killed good jobs by the millions in the process. The robots, gizmos, and microchips produced switches, timers, solenoids, computerized milking machines, computerized sawmills, computerized banking, computerized government, and computerized war.

Everything had changed as fast-as-lightning with the advancement of technology.

When I came to Canada in 1973, there was so much work it was unbelievable. I am telling you, there was always more work than we could handle. No healthy man was unemployed, no sir, unless he was a no-good lazy bum. Everyone worked and there was lots of overtime to be had, lots of it. Well, you must know that because you came to Canada before I did."

I am nodding sleepily; after all, I am 95 years old today.

"Back in those days," he continues, "a good hand faller with a good chainsaw cut down 100 trees in a day. He got 50 cents per tree, which was good money then. A single chainsaw had already eliminated about 20 jobs. Imagine that for just a minute: 20 jobs gone with every chainsaw. What a fantastic tool!

Twenty-five years later the hand faller and his chainsaw were replaced by the feller buncher. One person and one feller buncher would cut, on a good day, 2,200 trees and stack them neatly in bundles, eliminating not only the jobs of 22 hand fallers but also those of the choker men, who were putting cables around the tree-butt and hooking them up to a line skidder. And the line skidders were replaced by larger more powerful and more efficient grapple skidders. They drove up to the neat log bundle, clamped the grapple around it, and took it to the landing. Here a de-limber grabbed a log and in one swift action removed the branches and cut the tree to length. There was no need to trim the butt because the feller buncher had cut the tree cleanly and very closely to the ground without any damage or splintering to the log.

This is just one example to show you how technology has revolutionized the forest industry. It took less than 100 years and one feller buncher was doing the work of a thousand men. Similar comparisons can be made in almost any other industry, be it agri-culture or manufacturing, commercial fishing or transportation. Working men were replaced daily by automation and by new and more efficient machines.

The young Arabian people demanded jobs from their govern-ment in 2011, but there were no jobs for them. They were denied their natural fundamental right to work and the government could not help them. The oil was flowing through the pipelines with the help of powerful pumps and in the coastal cities empty super-tankers were waiting to be filled, and again pumps per-formed that task. Big money, which in most cases powerful poten-tates received, was often used to build up the military and, to some extent, to line their own pockets in secret overseas bank accounts. Finding acceptance in the military was not that easy anymore. Egypt, for instance, proudly possessed the eighth largest army in the world. How big do you want to go? There is a limit to all that. Sure, that kept many hundreds of thousands employed, but not for the good of humankind. Learning how to kill and destroy and blow up things, what kind of a job is that, Herr Kamerad?" he asks and then he is shaking me violently.

"Wake up, wake up! What's the matter with you? You getting old or something? Sleeping on your birthday. I can't believe it, it's only 11 o'clock in the morning, for crying out loud!" He is shaking me again.

"Are you feeling okay?" he enquires with concern in his voice.

Chapter III

The Fishing Trip

It was a beautiful summer day in 2028, when I had the appointment with God, and now I was going to be late. I was frantic. No! Not now! This was my chance of a lifetime to meet God and I might miss Him. The traffic had stopped and I was stuck in the middle of hundreds of idling vehicles. Nobody was honking their horns; it would come soon. My pulse was racing. I could hear my heart pounding violently in my chest and then I broke out in an uncomfortable cold sweat. Please, don't let me be late!

Vlado had it all arranged.

"I talk to God all the time," he told me. "And sometimes He will answer me."

"I am curious to find out what ever happened to the Garden of Eden. Is it abandoned now? Has anyone ever returned and set foot in there in all those thousands of years since the Lord chased Adam and Eve from paradise? Nothing has been written or said about it ever since. That is so sad! I would like to go there and walk through the famous gates of paradise with God on my side as my guide."

"I will ask Him!" said Vlado, and a week later he came back to me.

"I have an answer. God will not take you to the Garden of Eden, but He will take you to a different part of paradise. He will explain things to you when the both of you go fishing at Carp Lake."

My hearing was gone. I saw Vlado smiling and his lips were moving, but I did not hear a word. Then I became light-headed and felt dizzy. I had to sit down. That's when I noticed that I could not speak either.

"You are in shock, Herr Kamerad! God can have this amazing effect on people, I know!"

"When?" I finally stammered. "When?"

"Your appointment is for tomorrow."

The delay lasted only 15 minutes and then the traffic started moving again. I breathed a sigh of relief, wiped my forehead, and tried to calm myself down. Highway 97 was in good shape and I reached McLeod Lake in less than two hours. I saw Him standing by the Carp Lake turnoff, just like we had agreed upon. He was of medium height, good physical posture, and of indistinguishable age, like some Orientals appear to Caucasians and vice-versa.

"When I chased Adam and Eve and their brood out of the Garden of Eden, I still left them in paradise. Actually, I chased them not all that far away. It was a much better place, but the fools did not realize it. Take a good look at your beautiful planet and you will see that the earth truly is a huge paradise! Even the most uninhabitable parts, like the oceans, the mountains, the deserts and the 'eternal ice' have their own wonderful beauty. What else does humankind need? It is so perfect with the genial balance embracing the contrasts of the seasons and nature's intricate laws of physics and chemistry, the flora and the fauna and their mysterious wonders. Add to that the intelligence and complexity of the humans, their abilities and curiosities searching for something new and exciting, on a daily basis.

"Well, I have to admit, that I separated humans from myself on purpose, of course. I limited all their senses in perception and their intellect to a mere three-dimensional rationale. They do not have the capability to comprehend beyond this limit and that also makes them mortal."

"I have so many questions for you and I am so excited that I forgot where to begin," I told Him.

He laughed, quite amused.

"Just ask me whatever comes to your mind, you have an exclusive today."

"Are you sure Carp Lake was once in paradise?" I asked.

"Yes, it still is in paradise because your entire planet earth is the paradise," was His short answer.

"Yeah," I replied dreamily. "The first time Ursula and I came to Carp Lake, we thought it was paradise, and we instantly fell in love with it. It became our favourite lake, and we tried to return here as often as possible. Each visit was very special for us, and we treasured many beautiful memories."

My old pickup truck pulled us slowly along and it purred contentedly like a kitten. "The Vortec engine is good for 500,000 kilometres," the salesperson had told me many years ago when I bought the truck. I glanced at the odometer. It read 435, 017 kilometres. "We are getting close to the expiration date," I thought. Well, and so was I with 88 today.

"They still let you drive, being 88 years old?" asked God. "How did you manage that?"

"Actually, as far as the driver's licence goes, I am not 88 for another month. They screwed up at a renewal, a long time ago. When I told them that my birthdate was wrong, they demanded I produce a birth certificate and make a formal application of change. Can you imagine that? It was their mistake; all they had to do was check my old licence. Ha-ha. I liked it! Ever since then I am one month younger. To hell with those guys!" I muttered.

"Careful, careful," He said.

"Oh, sorry, my Lord." I bit my tongue. "While we are on the subject, can you please tell me if heaven and hell really exist and if the promise of an afterlife is real?"

"Ed," he replied. "There is no heaven and no hell, and St. Peter is not sitting at the 'pearly gates'! I will try to explain it to you in simple terms. Your human body will die and it will rot away. 'Dust to dust and ashes to ashes', as the saying goes. Some of your genes will live on, but that was established during mating and conception already. Don't expect a rebirth or resurrection of your body. Once you are dead, you are dead; that's final. However, your soul is immortal. The human soul and the human mind are individually unique like other parts of your body, like fingerprints, your irises, your DNA and many other components you humans have not discovered yet. Your soul and your mind, although closely related, are two separate entities. They cannot be replicated; each one of them is a special single edition. You can clone the body but you cannot clone the spirit, the mind, or the soul.

"Your spirit, your mind, and your soul will undergo a process similar to metamorphosis and it will happen in several different stages. They will never die!

"Ed, I did not create you to understand the multidimensional structure of your soul and the purpose of your being. Enjoy what you have and suffer when you do not have it! Cry when you are sad and cannot grasp the immensity of the universe, laugh when you are happy and content. I created humans with feelings and emotions, love and hate, sorrow and delight, pride and humility, anger and gentleness, passion and abject ignorance, and so much more."

"Do You have feelings and emotions?"

"I am complete and I encompass everything. To be complete, I have to be both good and bad. I am perfection but I will also make mistakes. There is no perfection without imperfection."

"I like to have the good God, who I can pray to. When people pray to You, do you help them?"

"Not always."

"Can't you hear their desperate pleas?"

"Yes, I do, but I am neutral and not compassionate."

"How do You determine who to help or not help? Is it random or is it a lottery system?"

"It is neither. You cannot comprehend my explanation."

"Is that why we should fear You?"

He did not answer and we were both quiet for some time. Each of us seemingly occupied with deep thought. I finally broke the silence and asked:

"Why is there so much misery and evil in this world? Why is there so much suffering and so much pain?"

"Every individual is free to make the choice how to live his or her life. Yes, I know that circumstances can limit and interfere with those choices. They can also reward or punish. Humankind, as a society, is not capable to govern itself accordingly and to uphold the individual's right to choice and the right to a humane life. I agree with you, there are too many injustices in the world, too much brutality, and the inequality of human existence is utterly appalling!"

"Yes," I said. "It's terrible, it's atrocious! People get maimed and murdered every day. Please forgive my boldness: can You tell me how many 15-year-old girls were raped today on this planet?"

"Oh, this is a very sad statistic." He sighed. "In the last 24 hours, 11,537 girls aged 15 were raped; the number for 14-year-old girls is slightly less."

"It's disgusting!" I said. "These are the things that are still happening, and they are happening in our paradise. What a frightening paradox! Don't you feel some responsibility to rectify the shortcomings of your imperfect creations? Don't you feel the urgency to interfere right now and put a stop to this absurd mayhem?"

"You are a tough interviewer." He sighed. "You cannot understand. You cannot possibly understand."

"All I understand is, that this is not sweet paradise for those 14- and 15-year-old girls who were raped today, and the ones who were raped yesterday, and before that and before that. It certainly will not be sweet paradise for the ones who will get raped tomorrow and after that and after that! Life can be so beautiful and rewarding for some, and for others it will be a horrible and terrifying nightmare, just by circumstance and without any wrongdoing by the individual? Why is that?"

He did not respond again and remained silent. I concentrated on my driving and slowed to a crawl, when we approached a flooded part of the road. A beaver must have been at work plugging a drainage culvert. Now the backed-up water had found a new way to get to the other side; it flowed right over top of the road. I steered through the middle of the large and muddy water puddle without any difficulty.

"You must have a long list of all my sins." I restarted the conversation.

"Yes, there is a considerable amount of notations." He smiled.

"I can see that; the older one gets the more sins get piled up. Can I go to confession and erase them from my list?"

"No." He laughed. "That only works for the Catholics."

"So, is there a reward for living a decent and righteous life? And what about the sinners, will they receive punishment?"

"I can't reveal everything to you. Some things must remain a secret." Again He laughed.

"Do you ever feel lonely?" I asked.

"No, I am God, and I do not have feelings or emotions, but for today with you I make an exception. I am human for the moment and I am enjoying the emotions."

"Please, tell me about the angels."

"Angels, St. Peter, the Pearly Gates…"

"Okay, I get it. None of that! So, Heaven must be a pretty boring place. Who then is singing Hallelujah all day long?"

"You are forgetting the ten virgins." He was mocking me, quite amused.

We were rounding another sharp curve on the rough and narrow gravel road, just creeping along, and on a small brown sign I read: Carp Lake 11 kilometres. A few minutes later, we crossed the bridge over the McLeod River, and soon we spotted the blue waters of a small lake, sparkling through the bush to our left.

"Aha, this is Rainbow Lake already. We are getting closer. A few more minutes and we will be there."

We drove up a steep hill and then wound our way through a park-like pine forest with tall straight spindly trees and hardly any underbrush. I could see the low blueberry shrubs and a plentiful assortment of colourful mushrooms. Another sign appeared, this one commanding us to slow down to 10 km/hour.

"We have arrived," I told Him, and He just nodded.

"It is as beautiful as I remember," He declared enthusiastically. "Let's put the boat in the water and start fishing!" He was smiling now, and His voice had changed to a melodic baritone.

"Please, don't rush me. I am an 88-year-old man, with the emphasis on old."

"Don't worry. I will help you," He said, and then He jumped out of the truck. I started to back up, and He expertly guided me to the boat launch; in no time, the boat slid off the trailer into the calm clear waters of the lake. We tied the boat to the rickety wooden planks of the floating dock and loaded the fishing gear into it.

"Did you bring an extra life jacket for me?" God asked.

I looked up puzzled for a second and then I began to laugh and I could not quit laughing. My whole body shook and I kept on laughing. "That is so funny! Are you joking?"

He grinned sheepishly like a little boy.

"Well, it is the law, isn't it? I would not want to break your laws. Imagine the conservation officer's face when he writes a ticket to God. Now, that could be very funny!"

"I always keep a spare one behind the seat," I told Him and continued laughing.

Then we chose a nice picnic site overlooking the lake and set up camp. An hour later, we climbed into the boat and pushed off. The 9.9 horsepower Evinrude outboard puttered quietly and increased its decibels when I turned up the throttle. In a few minutes, we were out of Kettle Bay. I slowed down the boat and the quiet returned.

We were looking at a wide expanse of mirror-like water. Every island's reflection was dipped upside down into the lake with such clarity and motionless perfection. It was a stunning picture of enormous beauty.

Even God was speechless for a moment. Then He said, "We picked a fine lake, Ed, one of my jewels. Do you believe now that we are in paradise?"

"Yes, I do, but it is not the Garden of Eden," I answered.

"You don't want to go there," He said sincerely. "People have destroyed it. The garden is scorched, filled with blood and tears and mass graves, with poisons and pollution and disease, with hate and fear and desolation. Wars and killings have ravaged the garden until recently. It is the most desolate place on earth now. It is paradise lost. Let's stay here and enjoy the true paradise!"

"Is this the true paradise because it is in the middle of the wilderness and there are hardly any people here? People are the ones who destroyed the Garden of Eden, isn't it right?"

"You are sure onto something," He replied slowly. He seemed sad and I did not question Him about the Garden of Eden anymore.

"I hope you did not order any wind." I changed the subject.

"Well, that's not up to me to decide directly. I leave the earthly operations to my local manager, if you will. You probably know her by the name of 'Nature'. I am generally pleased with her handling of the complex tasks. She does a fine job—granted, it is not always easy. You humans are Nature's prime achievement and also the most disrespectful participants."

I threaded a worm on my hook and heard Him wince.

"Do you have to do that?" He asked.

"Worms on a Bolo work the best for catching rainbow trout in this lake," I told him. "Just watch me!"

"I will try to fish with a bare and barbless hook," He told me.

"Good luck!" I said a bit sarcastically. "You know how fishermen would answer to that, don't you? Luck has nothing to do with it; it is pure skill."

Then He yelled, "Whoa!" and His angling rod almost bent in half. "Whoa!" He yelled again when the fish jumped straight out of the water trying to shake off the hook. God reeled it in slowly and expertly. When the fish reached the boat, He gently removed the hook, patted and caressed the frightened trout and released it back into the lake.

"This is fun!" He declared. "I love the action of the fishing rod."

"Yeah, thanks to the marvellous invention of fibreglass and carbon-graphite fibres. These fishing poles are ultra light and almost unbreakable and they provide the ultimate in fishing pleasure," I said.

"I have to correct you. Sorry to do so, but you cannot invent something that is already there. You can only find, discover, or re-invent it. You cannot import anything new to the world because everything is here already. Absolutely everything! You can only search and find."

"Does that mean that you invented—pardon me, created—the first computer?"

"Yes, I did," He answered. "Take a good shovel full of soil, put it into a container, and add any plant seed. I mean any plant seed and add water. What will happen after a few days or weeks? They will sprout! The tiny carrot seed will bring forth a green feathered top with an orange coloured carrot root and its distinct flavour. The tiny birch tree seed will sprout into a micro birch tree with leaves and roots, and it will grow and grow and become a giant of a tree. The tiny onion seed will extract its unique building blocks from the shovel of dirt and produce the strong pungent flavour every time. I could go on and on. The seeds are nature's micro-chips loaded with information and bundled with a fantastic pack-age of controlled features that will open on demand. The demand is triggered by water, light, and heat. The eggs and the smaller sperm are pre-programmed as well, and their purpose is to recre-ate life."

"What will happen after man has found everything?" I asked.

"Quite a bold assumption! It will never happen, you know. I told you about mutant diversions, but there are simpler things like ac-cidents, catastrophes, disease, and the constant evolution, for in-stance. I know there is a short-lived confusion when the human mind capitulates and accepts humility and limits, but already the next day, the search resumes and it will try to circumvent the bar-riers to intellect."

God was enjoying himself catching and releasing all the beauti-ful rainbow trout.

"Isn't this fun?" He laughed.

He completely outfished me and I was getting a bit annoyed about that. Usually, I would have hooked a half dozen by now. I knew the lake, I knew where the fish hung out, and I knew how to catch them, but it did not work for me today.

"Not lucky today?" He enquired. "Why don't you try trolling a fly? You have to catch supper, you know!" He laughed again.

"Flies don't work in this lake. I have tried it many times," I replied a bit grudgingly. "But, what the heck, I will try it one more time."

I changed fishing rods and pulled out line from the fly rod and pretty soon—bang! There was an explosion at the end of line, a fighting airborne fish! The adrenaline shot through my body, and I shouted and yelled with joy when I slowly brought in the fish.

"Hey, it worked! Unbelievable! What a beauty! That's enough for supper for the two of us," I said.

"I am God," He reminded me, "and I do not require food."

"Oh," is all I could say at that moment.

We were silent for quite some time and somehow I felt guilty that I had killed the fish.

"It is quite all right," He finally told me. "I created you to eat meat and fish among the many other things from nature and to obtain meat or fish you have to kill animals, birds, and fish. When it is for food and sustenance, it is a good thing."

There was another silence. I felt uncomfortable and did not want to fish any longer.

"Do you have any more questions for me?" He asked and His smile returned.

"Was Jesus Christ really your son?" I wanted to know.

"You are all my children—every single one of you! I admit, some are very special and Jesus was one of them, so was Mohammed and many others before and after. Every day one very special person is born with an immaculate soul, and every day one very evil person is born with a dark soul."

"Why?" I asked.

"To maintain the balance between good and bad. There is balance in everything. Without balance, there would be no universe and balance is only two-dimensional," He explained.

I must have looked perplexed. "But how do we recognize these very special people? How do we know? Is it in their genome make-up? Can we test for them and weed out the evil ones?"

"You mean destroy or neutralize them? That would 'upset the applecart'. It would shift the scales. It is a good thing that humans cannot analyze the soul."

"I was just thinking, if there is a good planet, is there also a bad planet? Or are we the bad planet?"

"A very good question, but I have to keep you guessing."

"Do animals have a soul?" I continued my questioning.

"What do you consider a soul? Okay, I will tell you what a soul can be. A soul is the sound, the senses, the feeling, the mind, the mood, the expression. I think feeling is probably the main one; there are so very many variants: love and hate, fear and joy, admiration, devotion, sorrow and cheer, pain and relief, etc. If you can think of a specific animal that has any of these attributes, you will have your answer."

"Will humans ever be able to surmount the three-dimensional barrier and become time travellers?" I asked.

"No," He said, "that is impossible for mortals."

"Please, excuse me, but are there other immortals besides you?"

"Aha! Another human trait—curiosity disguised in diplomacy. You want to know if there are other Gods, how could you?"

"I am so sorry, I am ashamed. Please, forgive me," was my weak response.

"Logic will tell you that there can only be one God, who encompasses everything."

"Even the evil?" I asked.

"Yes, even the evil. I am the sum of all things! I am complete; there is nothing else."

"What about the devil? Is Satan real?"

"No, there is no devil, no Satan, no Beelzebub, or whatever you want to call it. The devil is a fictional character and hell is a fictional place born entirely from human fantasy. It is all fabrication!"

"Oh boy, this is heavy stuff. Can we go back to camp now? I am quite exhausted."

He nodded His head and I accelerated the motor, leaving behind a foamy wake as we headed back for Kettle Bay. The sun was well-established in the west and was sending the last warm rays our way. It was time to get off the lake. We didn't talk during the noisy 20-minute return trip to the dock.

Back at camp, God started a fire while I was preparing the fish. I had already cleaned it while we were still on the lake. Now I patted it dry, made cuts into the skin, and rubbed spices on the inside and outside of it. Then I filled the inside cavity with lemon slices, cut-up bacon, and a generous helping of butter. I double-wrapped the trout tightly in aluminum foil and put it on the metal grilling rack above the fire.

"Time for a glass of wine," I said and went to fetch a bottle and two glasses.

When I returned He looked at me quizzing. "Why the second glass my friend?" He asked.

"Oh, I forgot you don't require food or drink—sorry!" I mumbled.

"I remember Jesus Christ was very fond of wine. Maybe I'll try just a wee bit for company, you know."

We sat down, leaned back in the uncomfortable chairs, stretched out our legs, and let the warmth of the fire help us relax.

"Please, tell me about the Jews. Why are they the chosen people?" I asked.

He was quiet for a moment and then he began: "Moses knew already at the time that there is only one God. He was a strong and cunning leader of the Israelites who endured much suffering and hardship, trying to find good arable land, which was not already occupied by other humans. To keep his people united in the new 'Faith of the One-God' during this tough time, he told them they were the chosen ones, they were God's favourite people. They still believe it to this very day and their unshakable conviction has helped them time and time again to overcome adversities and some of the most unspeakable horrors on earth. To me, all peoples are equal. I do not favour anyone or any nation or race."

"Is the Holy Bible God's word?" I kept on asking.

"Moses and many others wrote the Bible. It contains many wise thoughts; however, it has acquired some misinterpretations over time. Let's not get into that now," He said without additional comment.

I removed the trout from the heat and opened the aluminum foil.

"The fish smells delicious with the fusion of all the lovely herbs and spices you used, and the fine smell of the smoke from the firewood rounds it off just nicely," He said.

"Another plate for you? Another splash of wine?" I asked.

He shook his head and laughed: "A bit of the devil in you, isn't there?"

I began to eat and I realized how hungry I was. It was so tasty and I finished the whole meal after awhile. There was a surprised look on God's face.

"It must be good. You haven't eaten that much in years!" He said.

"Must be the fresh air in paradise." I burped barely audible and wiped my lips. "Before I fall asleep, now, I want to tell you that I am deeply humbled to have been allowed this special opportunity of spending this day together with You. Nobody will believe me, but that is not important. What's important is that I know what I know. I do, however, have a very special request. It is not personal. Can you please intervene and help humankind to survive and not foolishly destroy itself and everything on the planet? Can't you just for a moment put your thumb on the scales and tilt them a wee bit towards the good without upsetting the 'applecart'? We are your mean and rotten children; please make us a bit better."

"I will talk to Nature, my manager. I don't know if we can change the sad situation on earth immediately. It will take time."

"You are God! You can do anything, and You can make changes in an instant if needed," I said.

"Yes, that's true," replied God. "However, there needs to be great human collaboration!"

"Thank You, Lord, and please don't forget get the girls—the innocent young girls!"

Chapter IV

Early Celebration

Vlado is shaking me furiously again: "Wake up! Wake up! You dozed off! What's the matter with you this morning? Looks like you were in dreamland."

"I was fishing," I smile.

"Oh, no. Not again! Did you catch anything at least?"

"Oh, yeah. I caught a real beauty on a fly," I tell him.

He looks at me deeply concerned. "I'll call Jason," he says and talks into his built-in voice-controlled telephone.

Jason is one of my personal MCC nurse's aides, assigned to me more than five years ago. When his mandatory conscripted time was up, he chose to stay on with me and the Health Department had no objection to that. Jason and I get along together just fine. My other nurse's aide is Angelika, a perky petite young woman, an exotic beauty of German and Filipino extraction.

After humankind had come to its senses and a unilateral global disarmament had begun, the world was faced with staggering unemployment, primarily among the young adults. Many countries introduced a mandatory civilian conscription (MCC). It covered a broad spectrum of new employment opportunities in community and social services, in medical assistance and home care for the elderly, in individual teaching methods for special-needs kids, in the environmental field (recovery and cleanup) or the option to go to underdeveloped countries to assist with house construction and the establishment of viable small agricultural projects. This drastically brought down the unemployment numbers. It made perfect sense.

Why put millions of our young people in uniform and teach them how to kill and why spend trillions of dollars on high-tech weaponry? Why?

It is a very sad statement that we, the sophisticated humans, are unable to manage the simple and basic affairs in the world. Simple things like providing adequate food and shelter for everybody. More than a billion people go to bed hungry at night, more than a billion people are without proper shelter, more than a billion people have no access to clean drinking water, and more than a billion people can neither read nor write. We can fly to the moon and we can intercept supersonic ballistic missiles, but we fail miserably in basic support for our fellow brothers and sisters, and we still fail miserably when it comes to respect and preservation of our environment.

Why not reverse the mandate? Instead of teaching killing skills, teach our youth how to save lives, teach them how to help maintain a dignified life for the poor and needy, for the elderly and the sick, and teach them how to save the planet. The freed-up trillions would easily cover the new costs.

The duration of a typical MCC period was three years. It was a supervised apprenticeship and generally combined hands-on training with courses at a college, university, or a vocational teaching institute. The courses closely paralleled the work in the field and aimed to complement it.

Jason appears. "What's the problem? What's happening?"

"There is something wrong with my friend. He can't stay awake; he dozes off all the time," says Vlado.

Jason raises his brows and looks quizzically at me. "That's strange. I read the medical printout this morning and it was normal. Let me have a look at the current data." He touches a small screen on my wheelchair. The screen lights up and instantly displays my current vital statistics.

Jason mumbles as he reads. "Okay, blood pressure 128 over 76, nothing wrong with that. Pulse rate is 74, temperature is 36.9—all that is fine. Blood sugar and cholesterol levels are unchanged and even your white blood cell count is normal. Let me double-check your blood pressure; sometimes I don't trust all this fancy automated stuff."

"I am fine, just a bit tired. You think I could have a second cup of coffee, today? Being my birthday and everything?"

"Let me check you out first."

He straps the blood pressure collar onto my skinny left arm and waits until it deflates.

"You are good; your vitals are normal. Say, you guys, you wouldn't have had a little nip, a nifty, by any chance, hey? Being your birthday and all?"

"Maybe, just a little one," says Vlado. He laughs and produces the bottle of Pelinkovac, an herb-infused stomach bitter from his native Croatia.

Suddenly Angelika is there and with one swift move she wrestles the bottle away from Vlado. "That's enough of that!" she declares loudly and with authority.

"Sorry, but we can't fly on one wing," protests Vlado.

"There will be no more flying today. He is already high enough!" snaps Angelika.

"Oh, you little devil, you!" I complain.

"Little devil, now. Little devil, is it? You always told me 'Angelika' means 'little angel'." She laughs.

"The name really befits you," I say. "Make sure you stay the way you are. Sometimes little angels can become little devils."

"Ed." She smiles and looks deeply into my eyes. "What do you think of me?" She leans over and gives me a hug and a kiss. "Happy birthday, my dear friend!" she says, and then she goes over to Vlado: "Still mad at me?" she asks, and she hugs and kisses him too.

"Not anymore, not anymore! You made my day, now!" Vlado is happy.

Jason brings the coffee.

"Half and half," he says. "But there should be enough caffeine in it to sober you up."

He offers coffee to Vlado, but Vlado declines vehemently, as if he is about to receive poison.

"Let's get you guys out of the sun." Angelika unclips the remote and directs me over to the shady side of the house. Her silk white blouse is tightly drawn over her protruding large breasts.

"Why did you dress up so sexy today?" I enquire.

"I want to be pleasurable to your eyes!"

I give her a thumbs up!

Vlado is following us in his state-of-the-art wheelchair.

"You are pleasurable to my eyes, too," he says and whistles.

I must have dreamed. Now I remember, it was seven years ago when I went fishing with God at Carp Lake. It was in August, 2028, and a couple of months later, Masoud Abbasi, the President of ULIN, the new United League of Islamic Nations, phoned Jonathan Oliver, the President of the United States and the telephone call would change the world drastically for the better.

"Thank you, God!" I whisper. I tilt my head back and look up to the sky. "Thank you, God!" I whisper again and smile.

Chapter V

The Big One

The Big One struck at exactly 4:43 p.m. PST on Monday, October 30, 2028. It hit with such an incredible cataclysmic force that it sucked out the tectonic plates from under the city of Seattle and spewed them sky-high in a gigantic fiery ball of molten rock and lava into Puget Sound.

The Pacific was boiling.

It had to happen. It was predicted many, many times. But people had forgotten about the prediction and were lulled into their daily cluster of minuscule problems about family, friends, fun, and finances, about school, social networking, sports, and sex, about careers, politics, and health.

When the Big One struck, it surprised everybody in the Pacific Northwest and in coastal British Columbia. Millions perished in the greatest disaster ever recorded in the history of humankind, be it oral or written. Millions survived a very close call and Toby Zwosdesky was one of them.

It was not just an earthquake! No, it was a volcanic eruption and the earth opened up and displayed its horrific inside. Toby Zwosdesky had looked straight at the intestines of hell, just for a brief moment, but it was long enough to change his life forever and to leave a repulsive imprint of raw terror on his mind.

He saw the earth's crust buckle just a short distance ahead of him and he slammed hard on the brakes, as hard as he could.

The light pole to his right wavered only for a second and then it smashed down directly in front of his Toyota. He heard the sound of squealing brakes and tires and then the thud when another car hit him from behind.

"Fuck!" he yelled, and then, "Jesus Christ!" but he did not mean anybody in particular, especially not the Lord and Saviour.

He scrambled out of the Toyota, registering subconsciously that he was not injured. Cars and trucks in the other lanes were whisking by him like bullets obsessed with speed. He watched in horror as the speeding cars and trucks disappeared from sight, as if there were a giant hole in the earth swallowing them. He looked at the opposite lanes of the freeway and they were empty, completely deserted of any vehicular traffic.

"Oh, shit!" he yelled this time. Shit, there was a hole now where the earth had buckled just a few seconds ago. His senses cleared up; this was for real!

Tsunami! He thought. Big mother! The mother of all tsunamis! And he was right.

All of a sudden he was concerned about the person or persons who had crashed into his Toyota. He rushed to the back and saw that the hood had sprung wide open and steam began to rise from the demolished radiator, but that was not important now. The alarm was blaring and that was annoying.

Before he could reach the driver's door, it swung open and a naked leg appeared. He was already holding the door when the second naked leg followed and she stepped out barefoot.

"Are you hurt? Are you all right?" he wanted to know.

She just glared at him. "You idiot!" she shouted. "Why did you have to stop in the middle of the freeway?"

"Didn't you see the light post crashing down in front of me? Don't you realize we are having an earthquake and the earth has opened up and there is a gigantic hole ahead of us? That's where the freeway ends and all the cars and trucks are falling into it."

"You're kidding, right?"

"Look straight ahead and see for yourself! See, how the brake lights come on and then disappear all at the same spot. The poor devils still have their foot on the brake when they are plunging to their fiery deaths."

"Oh, my God!" her pale face changed to a lighter shade of pale and she held her hand to her mouth.

"Get your shoes and your purse! We have to get out of here, fast! A tsunami is on the way. Rush, rush, rush! Get into my car!" he urged her on.

As soon as she had closed the door behind her and put on her seat belt, he slammed the Toyota in reverse and rammed her car forcefully, moving it back a few feet. Then he shot forward into the next lane, nearly missing the toppled down light pole. He knew there was an opening in the concrete divider to his left, just ahead of them. Emergency vehicles would use this opening all the time to get across to the opposite side of the freeway.

"Holy shit, this is an emergency," he thought. The unmarked spot was coming up, he slowed down a bit, swung into it, and completed the U-turn.

"Where to now?" she asked after she caught her breath.

"To the highest point," he replied. "To the Fidelity Towers. We have no time to look for any better places farther away."

"That's where I work," she cried out. "Isn't that cool? I am just coming from there. I left at 4:30 today. It gets dark so early with that time change yesterday."

"I work there too, and I also left a bit earlier today. Right now, we have to hurry!" He was speeding and taking a right turn on screeching tires.

She looked at him with curiosity. "I think I've seen you before. I am pretty sure of that. My name is Lori Bishop, by the way."

"I am Toby," he said and brought the Toyota to an abrupt halt at the main entrance of Fidelity Insurance Company.

"Glad to meet you, Toby," she stretched out her hand.

"There is no time for formalities. Get out and follow me!" he shouted rudely. They jumped out of the running car and rushed for the huge revolving door. Once inside, he noticed that the elevators were still working. Power was still on! That was good, but they were not going to use the elevators. They raced through the enormous and pompous lobby to the wide marble stairs and did not stop until they reached the third floor.

Here things became congested. Hundreds of people were milling around, leaving the large hall, where a promotional seminar had just ended. They were all chatting and seemed to be waiting for something. The next announcement would get this herd stampeding, Toby thought. He did not want to stick around and find out in what direction it would take off.

Lori's face had lost some of its pale colour to a pink blush. She was holding her high-heeled shoes in one hand and her purse in the other.

"Okay," he said. "Let's go! Next stop, tenth floor!"

"Are we going to die?" she asked.

"Not yet! Not if I can help it!" he answered.

He grabbed her by the arm and calmly steered her through the crowd and towards the stairs. Grey concrete steps were leading up from the third floor. There was no marble anymore and the staircase was much narrower. It was also plugged up with people descending to the third floor. Toby stood by the metal fire door and held it wide open for the crowd to exit faster. They were spilling out through the narrow opening and were adding to the waiting herd in the hall.

"We have to wait until this traffic clears up," he told Lori. She stood very close behind him and Toby could feel her presence.

There was a loud united, "ahhh!" and some shrieks when the lights went out. It was pitch-dark in the windowless stairwell. An almost complete silence followed the "ahhhs" and shrieks. The people were moving slower and more carefully now, negotiating each step, and when they spoke, they spoke in hushed voices. The herd became mute.

Toby was still holding the fire door open.

"Lori," he called out hoarsely. She was right there and he could feel her warm breath.

"Yes," she said.

"We have to move up higher. It's very important. Give me your shoes and hold onto my hand. Are you ready?" She nodded and was feeling for his hand. Toby stayed hard to his right and gained stair after stair fairly quickly. Then everything became gridlocked and nobody could move.

"Watch out, we are coming up!" he shouted. "Get over to your extreme right. This is an emergency! We are coming up, make room, please! Move to the right! Thank you!" He was constantly shouting. It was tough, but somehow he managed to get ahead, pushing and shoving bodies out of his way in the eerie darkness. He only heard curses and no flattering words, but he didn't care. Higher—get up higher! But it was almost impossible. He held on tight to Lori's hand and pulled her with him. She cried.

"Lori, please. Come along, I don't want to lose you," he urged her on. She nodded her head again, but he did not see that in the darkness.

Why haven't the generators kicked in to activate the emergency lighting? he wondered. "Not a good sign, not a good sign," he mumbled. "Generators are usually in the basement, basements get flooded. Oh, shit!"

"Tsunami!" he yelled and that was the magic word. The downward movement stopped and reversed in an instant. Everybody was yelling "Tsunami!" It was amazing how fast they began to move upwards now. The crowd almost lifted them ahead. When they reached a platform of what he believed might have been the ninth or tenth floor, they stepped aside. With their bare hands, they were probing and touching the concrete wall, trying to find the metal fire door. Luck was on their side, and Toby found the door and pushed it open. They inched ahead very cautiously in the darkness, and the door slammed shut with a bang.

All of a sudden, they were alone.

"Where are you?" he whispered.

"Right here! My God, this is so scary." She sobbed and reached for him. Their hands touched. At that moment, a thunderous jolt hit the building. It swayed and swayed, it creaked and groaned, and they almost lost their balance. She was clinging to him, and he put one arm around her. God, did she smell good. He steadied himself with the other hand on the wall. Her shoes hit the floor.

"We are going to die!" she wailed. "I don't want to die! Please, dear God, let me live. Please, please, please! I am not a bad person, and I don't want to die."

"Lori, please, don't cry. Hang in there, baby! We are still alive, and that's the main thing. We are alive and that's important!" He babbled and he stroked her face and her hair. And then, he realized that the swaying and the creaking and the groaning had stopped.

What they didn't know was that the first tsunami, or the first waters rushing in to fill the gigantic hole in the earth's crust, had already flooded the basement and decommissioned the backup generators. The second tsunami, the real one triggered by the mega thrust of the volcanic eruption, was on its destructive way.

The 80-foot killer wave hit the Fidelity Towers with stupendous force. The first tower took the brunt of the hellish assault. It shook and it swayed and then it toppled over, consumed immediately by the raging waters, while the second tower remained standing like a beacon in all the turmoil.

Lori and Toby were on the ninth floor of the second tower.

"Don't cry, baby. Don't cry," he kept telling her and he held her firmly in both arms. "We are okay. We survived the first one and that was massive! I am telling you, baby, that was out of this world! Hey, and we are still here!"

"Don't call me 'baby'," she said and stiffened. "I do not like that!" She freed herself of his embracing arms and he reluctantly let go of her.

"What do you want me to call you?" he asked.

"My name is Lori Bishop. I told you that before," she replied.

"Welcome to the survivors, Miss Bishop," he mocked.

"I wish we had a light," she mumbled. "Hey, wait a minute. I think I have one of those mini flashlights in my purse."

"Wouldn't that be nice," he mused. He felt euphoric somehow, light-headed and lighthearted, almost happily delirious.

She was rummaging through her purse, touching and probing every object carefully if it had the right shape. It seemed to take her forever, but then with a triumphant "Ha!" she turned on the small light and shone it directly into his blinking eyes.

"Ha," she declared. "It's good to be prepared and organized!"

"You are a lifesaver," he said.

"No, you are the lifesaver, and I want to thank you for that." She put her arms around his neck and kissed him long and deeply on his lips. "You are the real hero!" And she kissed him again. The flashlight fell to the floor.

He picked up the flashlight and her shoes off the carpeted floor and they followed the corridor to an open area. It was probably a waiting room with a reception desk, several modern chairs, a sofa, and a credenza with a coffeemaker and cups on top of it. They walked over to the large window and tried to look outside. All they could see were rain droplets on the windowpane. Beyond that was an impenetrable grey semidarkness, not a single light was visible, not even a sliver of the moon. It had been a typical fall day in the Pacific Northwest—damp, dull, and cold. It started with heavy fog in the morning and a persistent drizzle that lasted all day. Not even the wind in the afternoon could break up the eerie cluster of grey low clouds.

"Shouldn't we get to the roof? Maybe, they will come and save us with a helicopter before the building collapses?" she asked.

"No helicopter will come out here tonight; visibility is very poor and is becoming worse by the minute. It's just too dangerous. They will not jeopardize their own safety. I believe they are actually forbidden to do so. They prefer to do these rescue missions in daylight because the pilot needs to maintain good visual contact with the rescue proceedings below him. We will only get cold and wet if we go up there. Pray the building holds out and we get saved tomorrow."

"Do you believe in God, Toby?" she asked.

"I really don't know. I am not sure about God, but praying in a situation like this is definitely the right thing to do." They knelt down, folded their hands, and Lori began to pray.

"Dear Lord, I am very sorry that I am not a good Christian and that I have never prayed before. I have only been to a church service twice—first time when I got baptized and the second time when my sister Megan got married. I am a good person; please, dear Lord, let me live and also my friend Toby. He is a good person, too. I am pretty sure of that. Please let us live; we don't want to die! I cannot promise that I will become a better Christian. I can only promise to continue to be a good person. Please have mercy and help us! Amen."

"Amen!" said Toby hoarsely and rose to his feet.

There were six doors leading to offices from the reception area and at its end another hallway branched off with more doors and more offices behind them. The first five offices were locked, but when he tried the sixth door, it swung open. He checked the number on the door. It was 911. Oh no, he thought. Is it good luck or is it bad luck? They entered the room. It was a spacious executive office with leather chairs and a leather couch. It also had a bar, a fridge, and a bathroom.

"Look at this, Lori! We have momentarily landed in heaven!" He grabbed her and swung her around.

"That was not called for, Mr. Hero!" she complained when he let her down.

"Sorry about that, but Mr. Hero suggests we get settled in for the night and lock ourselves in before the mob returns. I have the feeling things could turn rough and ugly. We should try to avoid contact or confrontation with the agitated crowd."

"But then we need another couch for the night. Let's get the one from the reception," she added.

They wrestled the second sofa inside and locked the room with the key dangling from the coat rack. She took the flashlight and disappeared into the bathroom. He just stood there in the dark and couldn't do a thing.

"Idiot! Stupid, stupid! How stupid can you get?" He hit himself on the forehead. His old cell phone used to have a built-in flashlight, he just remembered. Although he had never used it, he knew that it was one of the features. He fumbled for his new super slim ISS-pad, wondering if it had a built-in light source. As soon as he touched the screen, it lit up and displayed the time. It was exactly 5:12 p.m. Only 29 minutes had elapsed from the time Lori rear ended his Toyota. He thought it had been a lifetime.

Messages were flashing across the screen. Massive earthquake hit Seattle and Pacific Northwest at 4:43 p.m. local time, 10.8 on Richter scale. Early estimates, casualties could surpass a million. Tsunami warnings for all countries of the Pacific Rim. Tsunamis could hit 80 to 100 feet in height. Local telecommunication services interrupted. Watch for emergency messages via satellite feed.

"Holy shit!" he mumbled to himself and navigated his way over to the bar. The pale screen of his ISS-pad gave off just enough light not to bump into things. He found the fridge and extracted a Coke and some ice cubes. An opened bottle of rum was on the counter. He had spotted it when they first entered the room. Glasses were within easy reach and he began making two drinks. Then he shut off his ISS-pad, slid it back into his coat pocket, and waited in the dark for her to reappear.

"Where are you?" she was pointing her little flashlight in all directions, but she could not find him.

"Over here, by the bar," he finally said. "I made us a couple of stiff drinks."

"Oh, thank God. There you are!" she seemed relieved. "I wouldn't want to spend the night alone in this spooky place. It gives me the creeps and I am scared as hell. What kind of drinks did you make?" she asked, changing the subject.

"Rum and Coke," he replied.

She took her drink, sat down, and turned off the flashlight.

"Actually, I hate rum but tonight it tastes fantastic," she said after awhile.

"I'll make us another drink. Please, turn on your light."

"But how—"

"Sssh," he interrupted. "I must have had night vision for a moment, I guess."

She let it go at that. They sat quietly in the dark, sipping on their drinks for the longest time. The silence was oppressive.

"Say something, please!" she begged.

"I have to confess that I am also very, very scared, and I don't want to spend this night alone either," he admitted.

"I believe you, but can we talk about something else other than this shitty situation, please?"

He cracked his knuckles and she did not like that sound.

"Okay then. So you work for Angus MacMillan?" he asked.

"Yes I do. I have been his personal secretary for the past twelve months."

"What kind of a person is he?"

"Very bossy and very horny. He always wants to get into my pants."

"Well, have you ever let him?"

"Are you crazy? Then the fun would be over. I am stringing him along, you know, telling him that I am committed, that I am engaged to this guy Toby. He is so jealous, it's absolutely crazy. He always wants to find out who this Toby is, but I am not telling. I am getting a pay increase almost every month. It's absolutely insane but it's also real fun!"

"I am jealous about this Toby myself, who is this guy?" he wanted to know.

"Is there more than one Toby?" she asked flirtatiously

He was completely taken off guard.

"You! You!" he stammered. "You knew me all along?"

"What do you think of me? You think, I would jump into a car with a complete stranger?"

He was speechless and seemed to have forgotten to exhale. "You! You! Boy, you're something else. I'll get back at you on that one. I promise!"

She smiled.

"You were the Toby of my fantasies from the first time I laid my eyes on you," she confessed.

He still had a hard time controlling his emotions and he decided to remain silent.

"I guess I surprised you—ha! Now, it's your turn. Tell me your secrets, what kind of women you like and stuff."

"Oh, I like them all—all the beautiful women. As for preference, I would say my preference is redheads. Their skin is so smooth and creamy, their breasts are silky mounds with freshly opened flower buds, and their vagina is a soft jewel hidden in a marvellous bush of rose petals. Shall I go on?"

"Oh, I wish I was a redhead," she sighed dreamily.

"But you are a redhead," he objected.

"How would you know, Toby?" she asked teasingly.

He had lost his concentration and was lost for words again. She did not wait for him to speak and she shocked him once more.

"You know, we are going to do it tonight, right?" she said.

"Do what? Are you talking about the same thing I am thinking about?" he asked and his mind was racing.

"Yes, and we are going to make love, my darling, like neither of us has ever made love before! I promise you that!" And she kept her promise.

Chapter VI

The Morning After

It started out as a confrontational morning for the president and it looked like it might continue this way for the rest of the day, but it would get worse. Two men in hospital garb woke him at six o'clock in the morning, just allowing him a short trip to the bathroom and then they were all over him with their damned cold instruments, especially the stethoscope.

"Well, his vitals have greatly improved," said one of them. "How are you feeling this morning, Mr. President?"

"Ask me in half an hour. Hell, it's the middle of the night. Gimme a few minutes to wake up!"

"You sound much better this morning, sir. You sure gave us quite a scare last night, sir!"

Now it was slowly coming back to him—the botched campaign speech in Chicago yesterday, the constant booing of the angry crowd, and the exhausting trip to Cleveland in the evening. He had been under the weather all day, just not feeling right, fighting off an oncoming cold, he thought. Then, after dinner when he stood up, he felt a sudden weakness, and his knees gave out from under him. He almost hit the floor, if it hadn't been for the quick reaction of DeVries, his alert campaign manager. They rushed him to the hospital and that was the last thing he remembered.

"So, what's the verdict—I mean what's your diagnosis?" he asked.

"Basically, sir, it is exhaustion, burn-out, and stress related circulatory issues. What you need is rest, lots of rest!" volunteered one of the doctors.

"Bullshit!" replied the president. "What I need is a good breakfast. I am hungry!"

But they denied him his bacon and eggs for breakfast and tried to stuff him with low-calorie muffins, prune juice, and yoghurt. He protested to no avail.

Jonathan Oliver was a grumpy man these days. The re-election campaign was not going so well and had entered the final week of the drawn-out process. That bitch from the Republicans was way ahead in the polls and caused him more than one headache. Actually, she was a constant pain in the butt. She must be drinking snake oil for breakfast every morning, he thought. No matter what he said or did, the witch would turn it around and interpret it to her own advantage, every time. She was a fucking spin doctor without a degree. However, she was very smart and very sharp and had a devilish poisonous tongue.

They had waited until breakfast was over before they brought the news to him, and when they entered the room, he knew that something big and bad had happened.

"Spell it out for me, guys! I can take a whole truckload of shit this morning. Don't worry about my blood pressure. Let me have it!" he commanded.

They told him about the horrific disaster on the west coast and that Seattle was almost completely wiped off the map. They told him about the massive loss of life. There could be millions—nobody knew numbers yet. Reports were sparse and sketchy because it was still dark in the Pacific Northwest and many of the communication towers were down.

Oliver was quiet and composed at first. However, the loss of blood from his face was clearly evident, and then the devastating news really hit him. He slumped over for a few minutes and held his head with both hands.

"My God," he sobbed. "What a dark day for America and what a dark day for humankind! Oh, my God! America has been brutally hit again, only three weeks after that terrible superstorm Lucinda ravaged our east coast. Crews are still out there in full force, restoring services, mopping up debris, and helping the displaced and homeless people. Now, another new disaster—oh my God! This new disaster seems to be so much worse. A thousand times as bad and a thousand times as many dead Americans, by the millions, by the millions!"

The president wept.

"Are you all right, sir?" someone asked him after awhile.

"No, I am not. Just give me a couple of seconds and I will be okay. I have a job to do, you know! May God help me and may God help America!"

With that, he straightened up and looked at everybody in the room. They had come the night before to Cleveland for some serious campaigning today. It was last night when the earth shook.

"Why did you wait until now to inform me?" he asked in a calm voice.

"Mr. President, you were hospitalized and sedated last night. Furthermore, you deserved a good and sound sleep because we need you well and rested and with a clear head for the enormous task that awaits you today, sir," said a small man with yellow-tinted glasses.

Oliver looked at him quizzically. Most members of his campaign staff were different from the accustomed faces in the White House.

"What is your name and what are your duties?" Oliver asked the small man.

"My name is Jackson, sir, and I have been assigned to assist you in this crisis."

"But what happened to DeVries? Where is he?"

"Mr. DeVries is better suited for issues regarding your re-election. He will resume his duties when a new date is agreed upon. As of right now, the scheduled election for November 7 has been cancelled and postponed indefinitely. In the meantime, we will deal exclusively with the crisis on the west coast."

"Does the vice president know what happened?"

"Mr. President, the whole world knows what happened, and the world is waiting for a statement from you. We have prepared a short address and have arranged a nationwide TV broadcast for 10 a.m. Sir, are you up to it? Will you talk to the American people?"

"Of course, I will. But first, I need coffee, a whole pot of the real stuff and none of that caffeine-reduced shit," said Oliver. "Number two, Jackson, get a plane ready. We are flying to the west coast."

"Yes sir, Mr. President!" saluted Jackson.

"A catastrophe of sheer unimaginable proportions struck our nation last night. The entire sphere of destruction is unfolding right now, as daylight approaches the Pacific Northwest. Yesterday, the 'American Dream' was rudely taken away from us and replaced by a nightmare. Today, I am crying with you as a nation, and I am not ashamed of my tears. Today, we are in mourning and the whole world mourns with us. Today, we shall go to the Pacific Northwest from all corners of this nation and begin with rescue operations. Today, we shall also begin to count our dead. Tomorrow, we shall start to rebuild the American Dream! It will be a monumental task."

The president turned off the microphone and stepped away from the TV cameras. A limousine was waiting for him outside his hotel and they rushed him to Cleveland Hopkins International Airport. When the airplane lifted off the runway in Cleveland, a new dawn broke in Seattle.

Oliver had been elected in the fall of 2024 and took office early in 2025. He inherited an America quite different from the one of 2012, when he was a high-ranking general in the U.S. Air Force. He had quickly become a public figure with great prospects for a political career. His criticism over the war in Iraq and in Afghanistan, and the foreign policies in the Middle East in general, led to an early dismissal and stopped his political ambition abruptly in its tracks. He was blacklisted in Washington, he was blacklisted in all of America, but his strong personality eventually surfaced again.

Oh, yes, America had changed, and not for the better!

The first signs of public discontent were strongly evident already as far back as 2011, when the first "Occupy Wall Street" movement began in New York, and then quickly spread to other cities. It was a protest by the impoverished 99% of the population against the 1% of the super rich elite.

Barack Obama struggled to implement his policies on health care and tax reform. He finally did so, only with limited success. The expensive wars in Iraq and Afghanistan had drained U.S.' financial resources. The public purse was empty and the mountain of debt had spiralled to dizzying heights. He wanted to increase taxes on the super-rich, but he kept running into solid opposition.

In 2016, the American people wanted change and they received change. They wanted jobs and they believed the promises from the new contender, and they did not believe in Obama and the Democrats anymore. The new Republican president was sworn in and took office in January of 2017.

In very short order, the new administration abolished "Obama care", rescinded the tax increases to the super rich, drastically cut social and government services, and hiked-up fees on the already overburdened middle class. The promised jobs did not materialize; on the contrary, the unemployment rate shot up sky-high, and the American people felt cheated. A massive outcry of discontent reverberated all through the great country.

Then the riots and mass uprisings began and they rose to chaotic levels and brought the whole country to its knees and to its ruin. Some of the worst human rights abuses in history were recorded. A brutal police force and the even more infamous Interior Security Forces, which was the new name for the U.S. Army, tried with a heavy hand to secure law and order in the land. They accomplished only the opposite and the United States was out of control, no longer united anymore. The army just incited hatred, like they had done before in Iraq, in Afghanistan, in Pakistan, in Libya and other parts of the world. This time they incited hatred among their own countrymen.

Angry Americans retrieved their guns in defiance and took the law into their own hands. Trigger-happy rebels and independent militia armed with rifles and automatic weapons roamed the streets and the countryside. There were daily clashes with the police or the ISF all over the U.S., and thousands were killed every day. There were bombings, shootings, looting, fires, and wilful destruction of property. Murder and other capital crimes were rampant throughout the country.

The lawlessness of the Wild West had returned to all of America. When rumours of ethnic cleansing against the Chinese minority surfaced, a massive exodus of ethnic Chinese Americans to Canada and Mexico started. Hundreds of thousands fled across the borders in a very short time. Both neighbouring countries were completely overwhelmed and had to close their borders to the U.S. They joined many other countries in denouncing the U.S. and imposing a total trade embargo.

China acted quickly and called for immediate payment of the $6.5 trillion it was holding in U.S. Treasury Bonds. The United States of America defaulted and the once mighty financial empire collapsed. The U.S. dollar was now a worthless currency and nobody would accept it; American Express credit cards were refused and spat upon. The once invincible fleet of nuclear-powered aircraft carriers returned home from strategic stations around the world because they were unable to buy food and supplies for their crews. Not one country would extend credit to the U.S.

Finally, the American people graduated from 18 long months of looting and rioting, of curfews and martial law, of police brutality, military oppression, and of international isolation. The new military government, headed by a quintet of generals, firmly established law and order. Food stamps were printed and the shelves in the distribution centres slowly began to fill up. There was talk of brand new dollar banknotes being printed in distinctive colourful designs. It would soon replace the worthless "greenback".

Canada was the first country to reopen its borders, re-establish diplomatic relations, and relinquish the trade embargo with their southern neighbour. Other countries slowly followed and started to accept the new dollar, but it had lost its status as world currency forever.

Oliver served on the military junta for almost three years, until his election to president in November 2024. He also inherited an America at the height of global warming, later notoriously called the "Scorcher Years". A time when the entire world was suffering in sweltering heat, when the world's glaciers and polar icecaps were melting, when ocean levels were increasing, when floods and drought, crop failures and wild fires occupied the daily news.

Most of the many elaborate and high-tech flood prevention structures withstood the rising ocean waters, but all the low-lying areas without adequate protection eventually succumbed to the brutal sea. Sometimes, as if in slow motion, the waters would seep in gradually and begin to claim the ground inch by inch. Other times, surging tidal waves whipped up by strong winds would rush towards the shore and take immediate and destructive possession of the lowlands, often breaking up dykes and other protective barriers.

People were forced to move to higher ground. The growing world population had to share the ever-shrinking landmass, often in confrontational and bloody transition. Some new and attractive real estate emerged from the melted ice. Beachfront properties in Greenland became a particular hot commodity, and the first settlements were being built in ice-free regions of Antarctica. Arable and extremely fertile lands freed from the claws of ancient permafrost in Canada's Northern Territories and in Russia's Siberia were soon touted as the new bread baskets of the world.

The Northwest Passage through the Arctic Ocean was now reality, and during the summer and fall months, it was the busiest shipping lane in the world. The Panama Canal had lost its importance and ship traffic was down by 60 percent.

Americans suffered under the oppressive heat in those four years, and thousands of the elderly and the weak fell victim. Temperature records were broken day after day, not only in America but also in most parts of the world. In many regions, severe drought conditions had forced farmers to abandon their farms and their livestock. Water was a sought-after and scarce commodity; wells and ponds, creeks and rivers had dried up. Yet, other parts of the country were drenched and flooded by extreme downpours. Water, water everywhere and way too much of it! There was hardly a place in the nation where water had not become an issue. Nobody debated global warming because by then, everybody knew that it was not a theory anymore.

Then in early 2026, the rains returned to the parched lands and snow fell that winter in many parts of America. By some miracle, the weather had reverted back to its former state. Data collected from around the globe confirmed that a general cooling trend had ended the four-year extreme hot-weather phenomenon. There were different opinions floating around, trying to explain the reverse in weather pattern. Some saw the cause in extraordinary activities on the sun's surface; others pointed to orbital changes of our planet.

Oliver liked to lean back in his seat and reflect on the past. They were now two hours into the flight when Jackson approached him.

"Mr. President, I would like to update you with the newest information. Sir, if I may, please?"

Oliver nodded.

"The news is not good. Most of Seattle has now disappeared and sunk to the bottom of the Pacific Ocean. First indications are that basically three things happened and are still happening. Unimaginable underground pressures built up over time under the greater vicinity of the city of Seattle. They vented at the weakest point in the earth's crust in a horrific eruption in the Pacific Ocean, approximately 40 miles away from the city's core. An enormous mass of molten magma, which is shooting up sky-high into the atmosphere, is being sucked out from underneath the city of Seattle. The sudden vacuum created way below the city has caused the protective upper crust of the earth to buckle and collapse. The result is a 'super hole' of several miles in diameter and it is still growing in size. Half of Seattle has been swallowed up and has disappeared into this 'super hole', and it's consuming more and more of the city.

"The third element is the tsunamis, of course. The first one rushed in from the ocean to fill the 'super hole' initially and then followed the 80-foot killer wave that caused untold damage along wide stretches of the Pacific Coast, well into British Columbia. Vancouver and Victoria, the two major Canadian cities on the Pacific Coast, took the full brunt of the killer tsunami. They too suffered an incredible amount of destruction.

"The human death toll is staggering. First estimates are well in excess of 2.5 million in the U.S. alone; add to that another million in Canada. Countless more perished at sea and in the coastal regions of all countries on the Pacific Rim, when gigantic tsunamis surprised many people. There are still tsunamis rushing across the Pacific and clashing forcefully into anything in their destructive path.

"The powerful eruption is of cataclysmic proportions. It's creating a new landmass in Puget Sound. Lava continues to spew out in such large amounts—never seen before. The sea surrounding the new island is boiling for several miles and is killing all marine life. A complete geological and geographical transformation of the entire Seattle area is taking place, as we speak."

"But at what cost? It swallowed Seattle and annihilated its population. Oh, my beloved America, when I look at you, I weep!" wailed the president. Jackson silently retreated and left him alone.

Oliver's deep thoughts were soon interrupted by the captain's voice announcing their descent into Bellingham International Airport.

"Why are we landing in Bellingham?" he asked Jackson who had reappeared at his side.

"Sir, Sea-Tac Airport and Boeing Airfield are completely destroyed and inoperable; planes have to use alternate airports nearby. A helicopter is already waiting for us on the tarmac in Bellingham. It will take us right away as close to Seattle as possible, where Hernandez, the FEMA operative in charge, will join us," he informed the president.

"It will be necessary to attempt a fly-pass over the city to assess the indisputable damages in order to determine rescue operations."

Chapter VII

The Rescue

They did not sleep all night. They made deep and passionate love until they were exhausted. Then they lay in each other's arms, kissing and hugging and whispering intimate words. When she aroused him, they would continue their deep and passionate lovemaking.

"Please, give me your flashlight. I have to look at those sweet and lovely lips of yours. I have to see with my own eyes what gives me so much pleasure," said Toby.

"I want to see your lips and your face first," she answered huskily and kissed him again. Her hands were groping around in the dark until she felt the familiar shape of the flashlight and she turned it on.

"You are so beautiful and I love you so much!" she said and let the light glide over his body.

"Now, it's my turn. Hand over the light," he demanded.

But Lori backed up fast and shut it off. She dressed quickly in the dark.

"I know what you're up to, Mr. Hero. You want to check if I am a redhead or not—naughty, naughty! But I won't let you. I'll keep you a bit longer in doubt and suspense," she giggled.

"How long do I have to wait?" he asked.

"Just until we are safely rescued and are in an appropriate place," she promised.

They sat in the darkness. Toby sulked, but it didn't do him any good.

"I am hungry," he finally said.

"I was waiting for that," she laughed and moved towards the fridge. She found some fruit and melting ice-cream and they ate it all.

Approaching daylight moved the darkness into shadowy corners and soon there was enough light to see. They stood by the window and looked down at an unbelievable scene. It was like watching a news broadcast on a giant television screen, without sound. As far as the eye could reach there was total destruction; not one building could be seen. Everything was turned into rubble. What they saw in the floating fog was rubble, rubble everywhere, with mangled cars, ripped-out trees, and standing water, lots and lots of water. It was completely surreal. They could not yet see the bodies. For those details they needed more daylight.

Toby saw the rising steam coming from the "super-hole" and he pointed it out to Lori. They were scared now. She cried and he held her firmly in his arms.

"Is our building the only one still standing?" she asked, hardly audible, and he could feel her anxiety and her worry. "What will happen to us, Toby?"

"I don't know. Nobody does. Will there be another eruption? Will we have aftershocks and more tsunamis? Nobody knows."

"Are you afraid of dying?" she asked.

"I'll tell you what! Actually I am kind of content and happy that we had last night. If my life should end now, I have no regrets and I am not scared because last night I found true love and happiness and absolute fulfilment. I want to thank you for that, my darling!" and he kissed her.

"But I don't want to die, and I don't want you to die!" she sobbed. "I want the love, the happiness, and the absolute fulfilment to last forever and ever, and I want you to make love to me again and again."

They heard the distinct clattering noise of a helicopter. Her sombre mood vanished instantly.

"I can't believe it! It's happening. They are coming to rescue us, my darling. Let's run up to the roof. We are saved! Isn't that wonderful?" she cried excitedly.

"Cool it, baby," he said, but she interrupted him right there.

"Listen, mister, if you want this relationship to continue then stop calling me 'baby'. I hate that. I told you that once already and I don't like to repeat myself."

"I am sorry. It just slipped out," he apologized.

"But rushing up to the roof now isn't a good idea. I think that the roof is overcrowded and the helicopter can't land there and probably wouldn't dare to set down on it anyway. That means plucking each person up one by one, and as you know, a helicopter has very limited space. It is not built for mass evacuation. So, imagine what will happen? People will be jostling for position. There will be pushing and shoving, a downright stampede, and bodies will be flying off the roof."

The glass of the large window was thick and soundproof. It filtered out most of the noises, but they still could hear the shrieks of the people when they tumbled down 60 stories to their certain death.

"Toby, can you foretell things?"

"No, not really. But it doesn't take much to figure out things. It's human nature! In times like this, people shed their proper manner, their courtesies and politeness, and return to their animalistic heritage. Survival of the fittest, they call it. I say, it's survival of the meanest son-of-a-bitch. The ones who keep their human decency will lose. Those are the ones flying off the fucking roof!"

"Stuff like that makes me shiver and my skin crawl. I hate brutality; there is no place for that in a civilized society. And by the way, please add the four-letter f-word together with 'babe' and 'baby' to the list of unmentionables in our household."

"What do you mean by 'household'?"

"Well, we are going to be married, of course," she said.

"Gee, that's my line. I am the one who is supposed to ask if you want to marry me," he told her.

"So, why don't you ask me then?"

"You are something else, you know," he laughed and knelt down. He took her hand and looked up. "Lori Bishop will you marry me and live and love with me forever and ever?"

"Yes, I will," she answered in a throaty voice. "Take me!" she said and blood shot to his head and to his penis, and they forgot their surroundings.

"Yes, yes!" she screamed in ecstasy and he exploded inside her.

"Toby, you made a baby, you know?" and she smiled. "Toby, we made a baby!"

"How do you know?" he asked.

"Don't worry, women know about these things and I know," she said.

Actually, he was not satisfied with the answer, but decided not to pursue the matter any further.

"I agree with you on the four-letter f-word. It was taboo in my family home. Let's keep up the tradition," he said.

Helicopters had come and gone and the shrieking of the falling bodies had stopped.

"Do you think it's safe now to go to the roof?" she asked.

"It looks like it. Okay, get ready. We are leaving this cozy place. I'll never forget it, Room 911 and all."

Climbing 51 levels in a high rise tower demands good conditioning and they were young, but exhausted from the sleepless night and the continuous lovemaking. It was no Olympic sprint by any means and no records were broken. Actually, it was more like a pathetic crawl with many stops, gasping for oxygen. When they finally reached the roof, it was completely deserted. Not a single soul could be found up there. An eerie silence was the first thing they noticed and then the wind. The wind was not strong and made only soothing noises, but it was loaded with moisture and shivering cold.

Lori was scared, again.

"Everybody is gone. Do you think the helicopters will come back?" she asked in a frightened voice.

A short and heated argument erupted before the president

boarded the helicopter in Bellingham. He was adamant about sitting in the co-pilot's seat and getting the full bird's eye view from there. Both pilots, Jackson, and the rest of the entourage protested vehemently, but to no avail. Oliver pulled rank and authority. "I am your commander-in-chief and I order you!" he declared. When he was safely strapped in, he added with a sly grin: "I am also an Air Force General and a helicopter pilot."

"Welcome on board, sir!" said the pilot and lifted off. They were only a few minutes in the air when he spotted the first signs of the devastation the killer tsunamis had left behind. Evidence of destruction was everywhere.

He saw the black-and-white bodies of a herd of Holstein dairy cows swept together and piled up behind the remains of a concrete wall. He saw the catastrophic results of nature's awesome super forces unleashed, the tragic results after they ravaged and destroyed, killed and maimed. Another pile of bodies came into view, stacked up in similar fashion to the dairy cows, but this time they were human bodies.

"What a terrible tragedy!" Oliver said to himself.

He saw thousands and thousands of human and animal corpses floating in the water among the debris. He saw men, women, and children huddled together around smoky fires trying to warm their shivering bodies.

A crackling in his headset preceded Jackson's voice.

"Sir, I have Stephen Hunter, the prime minister of Canada, on the line!"

"Go ahead, patch him through," said Oliver.

"Hello! What a sad day for our countries and what a sad day for the world. My sincere condolences to you and the Canadian people!" said Oliver.

Hunter replied, "Mr. President, I want to express my deep sorrow to the American people. Canada mourns with you, Canada weeps together with America. Today is the darkest day in the history of our nations. We bow before God in humility."

Just like Oliver, his Canadian counterpart had flown to the west coast in the morning to survey the disaster-stricken areas first hand. He was now hovering in a helicopter above the scattered remains of a Vancouver suburb.

"I am lost for words," said Oliver. "I was just here last week campaigning. Now look at this. The destruction is of apocalyptic proportions! Just out of this world!"

They agreed to meet in the evening and ended their conversation.

Jackson received many more telephone calls from other world leaders. He took the condolences and the messages and promised to relay them to the president. Every single world leader who phoned also offered help; many wanted to send over first response rescue teams immediately. "Say the word and we are on the way!" Needless to say, Jackson politely declined each and every one of these offers because it was U.S. policy. A proud policy, where Americans look after themselves—always did and always will, no matter what it takes. This is what made America! We pull together and help our fellow countrymen. When the going gets rough, we get going, without outside help!

When they reached the outskirts of Seattle, Oliver was stunned at what he saw. It numbed his senses. He imagined himself on another planet in a faraway galaxy. This could not be the city he visited just a week ago. This was an unrecognizable and an unidentifiable pile of debris, rubble and ruins of corpses, cars, and boats, all violently smashed up into garbage. What a mess! It was revolting and sickening.

Hernandez, the FEMA operative in charge, called and excused himself. It was impossible for him to leave his command post and join the president on his fact discovery tour. He was completely overwhelmed.

They proceeded farther on and then he saw the "super-hole" and the gigantic steam cloud rising from it.

"According to the coordinates, downtown Seattle should be straight ahead of us, sir," said the pilot.

"Look, there is nothing there, just one lonely giant ruin sticking out like a sore thumb in a sea of mist and junk and shit and water. It's absolute devastation," said Oliver.

"My GPS confirms that Seattle is right below us." He heard the co-pilot speaking behind him.

"Get closer to the tower. I think I saw some movement on the roof." Oliver was pointing to the lonely giant ruin.

Lori had taken off her bright yellow sweater and was waving it frantically above her head to attract the helicopter. It worked! The chopper changed course and was coming straight for them. They were ecstatic, both screaming at the top of their lungs, but nobody could hear them because there was nobody around who was still alive. Lori kept yelling and waving her sweater even when the helicopter was in clear sight.

"Put your sweater back on. You're half naked, girl," said Toby.

"Okay, okay!" she was panting.

"We are not going to rescue that young couple. I absolutely forbid that!" said Jackson. "We cannot jeopardize your safety, sir!" declared Jackson with emphasis.

"And I say we start the rescue operation right now! I am the president and I am a soldier and a general, and who the fuck are you?"

"I am responsible for your safety, sir."

"Keep in mind, I am responsible for each and every American and those two on the roof need help. The building could collapse at any time. Let's go and get them!"

The pilot lowered the aircraft within a few feet of the roof and they flung out a rope ladder. "Just hang on tight! We are pulling you up!" they shouted to Lori. She hung on for dear life and when she reached the cabin, Oliver pulled her inside and flung the rope ladder back out for Toby. It was only a matter of a few minutes and the successful rescue operation was over.

Oliver felt good about himself. He had accomplished something positive in all that gloom and doom. He suddenly smiled because he could see tomorrow's headline: "Our President the Hero! Oliver single-handedly rescues young couple!" Let's see if the bitch can top that, meaning his Republican opponent Mary-Lynn Krocher.

The adrenaline high quickly subsided and Lori and Toby began to shake and shiver.

"Cry, baby, cry. It's okay, you are safe, baby!" Oliver was stroking her hair and Lori was too weak to protest. Months later she was in conflict with herself if she should vote for him because he had called her "baby."

The pilot changed course and headed for the next rescue shelter. News spread fast and when they arrived, TV cameras and microphones were set up for an interview and reporters had forgotten all common courtesy. They rushed ahead towards the chopper like a pack of hungry wolves and they had to be held back forcefully by security guards.

Stephen Hunter, the prime minister of Canada was already waiting on the tarmac in Bellingham when the president's plane touched down in the evening. He had arrived in the morning at Abbotsford Airport, which was quickly becoming Vancouver's main air transportation outlet. YVR, once the proud international showcase, with only 14 feet of elevation back in 2011, had a history of dyke building and runway lifting to prevent the rising sea levels from flooding it. When the disastrous tsunamis struck, they completely destroyed the whole infrastructure.

Gigantic airbuses and Boeing 747s were floating out to sea with the powerful suction of the first returning tsunami. Then came the second one, the third, the fourth, and the fifth—each one of them large and powerful. YVR was swept clean of all buildings and airplanes, of all people and all cars. What remained were flooded fields and runways.

Hunter moved forward and embraced the president when he stepped off the plane.

"Glad you could make it Jonathan. I hear you had quite an exciting day," he said.

"Quite so!" replied Oliver. "Only one wonderful highlight in all that misery; the young couple we saved almost died of hypothermia. I spotted them, you know. She had taken off her yellow sweater and was waving it around above her head. I caught a glint in the corner of my eye. Pretty good eyesight for an old guy like me, I'd say. You should have seen her eyes, Stephen. She did not have to say a single word. It was all in her eyes; they told me the whole story. I saw a frightened girl, who was thankful and awestruck. I am not sure if I had anything to do with it or if she even recognized me. I saw a woman who could not hide her strength and determination and her unashamed female pride. She displayed her sexuality with a superior casualness, like it was her God-given right. What a woman! I'll never forget her compelling green eyes!"

"Well, she must be an extraordinary woman to leave such a strong impression on you!" laughed Hunter.

"One of a kind, I can tell. You meet them once in a lifetime. That is, if you ever do. Now, enough about her! Stephen, tell me about your day."

"I have to say that today is the saddest day of my life and it is the saddest day in my country. I cannot begin to fathom the extent of the catastrophe. It is totally overwhelming and mind-boggling. I cannot begin to express my deepest sorrow and my regret over the countless millions of Canadians and Americans who succumbed to this super-sized tragedy. I am reaching out for words to describe and express my feelings and how to deliver solace and hope to my people, but I cannot find these words."

Hunter's eyes filled with tears and he was choking back words. It was the second time that day he was overcome by emotion. It happened earlier in the afternoon during a hastily arranged press conference in tsunami-ravaged Victoria, British Columbia's wonderful capital and Canada's pride and joy on Vancouver Island's southern shores. Some crude reporters crafted attention-grabbing headlines: Surprise! Stephen Hunter is not a robot! Our prime minister is human after all!

Oliver moved closer to him and said with genuine concern in his voice:

"I want to convey my deep regret and my sincere condolences to the Canadian people. Your losses are also tragically high. This is a very sad and trying time for both our countries."

They climbed into a black limousine and were swiftly taken to the "Excelsior", Bellingham's newest and finest hotel complex.

The two statesmen met half an hour later for a simple dinner in the presidential suite. They continued to talk about the day's events, about their individual shocking observations, and about the deep and traumatic impressions of the horrendous catastrophe. They skipped dessert and the after-dinner drink.

"Let's go downstairs and listen in on the joint meeting of the top emergency chiefs from both of our countries. Hernandez must be here by now. He is a very busy man—a good man!" said Oliver.

Hunter was consulting his ISS-pad and stood up.

"Yes, I also have word that Roy Watkins, the newly appointed head of Canadian Emergency Services has just arrived."

When they entered the conference room, everyone rose from their seats.

"Please sit down. ladies and gentlemen, I want to introduce the prime minister of Canada, the honourable Stephen Hunter. May we interrupt your meeting for a short announcement?"

Oliver handed the microphone to the Canadian. Hunter cleared his throat, stepped forward, and then he addressed the assembled men and women.

"You are the experts, the trained professionals, and you surely don't need our advice. The catastrophe has not only devastated and transformed many parts of the U.S. Pacific Northwest, it also has brought destruction and death to the coastal communities of Canada's British Columbia.

Two major cities, Vancouver and Victoria, received the full impact of the killer tsunamis. We are dealing here, just like you in the United States, with the largest natural disaster ever. Nothing of this magnitude, nothing on a scale like this, has ever occurred on our continent or in our countries.

"The president and I have decided to evoke our Emergency Measures Act and declare the borders between Washington state and British Columbia open for 30 days. We also agreed to combine our rescue and recovery and relief efforts for this period. I thank you all! Men and women like you are deserving of my highest regard!" Hunter relinquished the microphone to the president.

"I suggest you list your most urgent priorities and examine the immediate cooperation and coordination between the rescue and the aid agencies of our countries. Please check if unused or excess resources in one place can be deployed in other parts of the disaster areas. We have to work together, hand in hand. Human misery does not know national boundaries," said Oliver.

He rose from his seat and walked over to Hunter.

"They are calling me, Stephen. Some other fucking emergency! I have to go! I'll talk to you tomorrow."

They shook hands and Oliver returned to his suite.

Chapter VIII

The Adult Prank

"What?"

"I think the whole world shook when the Big One struck."

I am shouting at Vlado. He is adjusting his hearing aid.

"You bet it did!" he says. "I even fell out of my wheelchair. Did I ever tell you about that? What a commotion it was. They had to call the paramedics to lift me out of the rose bushes."

"Yes, you told me about it, at least once or twice, but probably more than that."

"They were picking thorns from my butt and my back for weeks. Ha ha ha! I can laugh about it today, but back then, it was terrifying. There I was lying spread-eagled on my back, like a giant beetle, helpless and unable to move. Horrible feeling—absolutely horrible, I tell you."

"We sure have seen great changes in Prince George since the Big One struck, haven't we?" I am changing the subject.

"Yes, our chickenshit politicians abandoned Victoria and fled north to the safe interior haven of BC. They brought the whole government up here. No tsunamis in Prince George, you know! No, sirree! They had to govern out of pretty cramped quarters for quite a while until we built 'em that fancy palace on Cranbrook Hill. Have you been up there lately and seen all the lavishness and luxury? What a waste of taxpayer money! Some things never change!"

"Look at the many positive changes the relocation of the government has brought to our city. Modern housing developments in the bowl area at the confluence of the Fraser and Nechako rivers have attracted a good mix of people. Now we have a vibrant and completely new and different commercial community meeting the needs of the rapidly increasing population."

"You are right," he says. "Downtown has turned into a great place nowadays. No more homeless vagrants, panhandlers, and dope addicts to molest you; no more hookers and pimps. I like to go there in my wheelchair. I always go with Adrian, my caretaker, and we always have a cappuccino at Lilly's Cafe. I enjoy sitting by the sidewalk, sipping my cappuccino and watching the flow of the pedestrian traffic. I can sit there for hours, just watching. There is an atmosphere of relaxation, curiosity, and mystery in the study of the human individuals passing by."

"Let me guess! I bet your favourite study subjects are gorgeous young women," I tell him.

"How did you figure this out?" He laughs.

Angelika is back buzzing around us like a mother bee, making sure we are comfortable in our wheelchairs and we are watching her with delight.

"Do you speak German, Angelika?" Vlado asks her.

"No, not a word," she answers.

"But your father was a German, wasn't he?"

"My father was a terrible man; he passed away when I was a baby. I grew up without a father and my mother was without a husband to support us. I'll never forgive him for that!" she says.

"Why are you so angry at him? How did he die?" I ask her.

"Well, he just went out one day and never came back. They found him three days later floating in the canal. Nobody knows how he drowned."

"That's a very sad story," says Vlado. "How did you end up in Canada and, more specifically, here in Prince George?"

"There is no mystery about that, not after I accidentally found his Canadian passport. That was nearly ten years later. We were playing a game like hide-and-go-seek with a bunch of kids from the neighbourhood. I cheated a bit, you know, and hid in the tiny shed of my father's, where I locked myself in. There I was sitting quietly as a mouse, not even daring to breathe. I could hear the other children calling my name over and over again. I kept quiet and finally they gave up and went home.

"By then, my eyes had become accustomed to the shady semi-darkness in the shed and curiosity replaced boredom. Everything was so disgustingly filthy, everything was covered in dust and mould. It was gross but it did not stop me. I lifted containers and boxes and moved them over to one side. There were tools and wooden boards of all kinds, from rough short blocks to finely finished planks. I didn't want to move all that wood—no way!

"Then I spotted a mouldy cardboard box under a dust-covered stack of polished mahogany pieces. I removed the mahogany and opened the carton, ceramic tiles, the same as our kitchen floor. Hmm! I took out the top one and then the second one and when I lifted the third tile, there it was—the treasure, double wrapped in aluminum foil, my father's Canadian passport and 5,000 U.S. dollars, all in 100 dollar bills. I knew right away that I had found a treasure and I kept very still and I stayed in the shed until my mother came home from work.

"The rest of the story is pretty straightforward. My mother went to the Canadian Embassy in Manila with my father's passport and his death certificate. The Edmonton address in Beverly turned out to be a small, older house my father owned. We also inherited a modest sum of money in a savings account at the CIBC bank.

"An elderly Ukrainian couple were at the house when we arrived in Edmonton. They had lived there all those years since my father had left on his Far East voyage. They had taken good care of the house and the large garden and had paid a low monthly rent to the lawyer my father had hired to manage his affairs.

"This was quite something! We were the owners now, but we just could not go ahead and evict the old Ukrainian couple. Well, what to do? We just moved in with them. We were used to cramped spaces and it was the best decision my mother ever made.

"Imagine the language issues when we arrived at 'their home' in Edmonton? We spoke Tagalog, a bit of Spanish, and very little English. They spoke Ukrainian and broken English.

"You wanted to know if I speak German, Vlado? I told you no, but my Ukrainian is pretty good, and I am proud of it! I am also proud of my adopted Baba and Gido. Actually, I am proud of my father as well, because of him and his arrangements, we are now in Canada. Still, I missed not having a father."

Angelika loses it right there and begins to cry. Emotion has completely taken over and she is sobbing uncontrollably.

"Come to me, I will hold you in my arms," says Vlado and I immediately feel jealous when she moves over to him. Vlado is holding her and clumsily strokes her beautiful black hair. He is talking to her in such a low voice that I cannot understand a single word he is saying. She continues to cry and big tears run down her face and her whole body is shaking with spasms.

I am furious by now. This is all wrong. This is my birthday and she is my caregiver and I should be holding and consoling her, not Vlado.

"That's enough now," I am telling them and my face must be red like a tomato. They just ignore me. Vlado keeps on stroking her hair and he keeps on whispering to her. Finally, what seems an extremely long time to me, she calms down and quits sobbing. She gets up and with a few quick strokes with her hands, she removes a strand of hair from her face and straightens out her blouse and skirt. She turns around and smiles at me.

"I feel much better now," she says. "I guess I needed this talk. Thank you, my friends!"

She disappears inside the house again. Vlado tilts his wheelchair back a fraction turns his head slowly and looks at me with a big grin.

"Boy, that was nice, that was exquisite. First class! What a wonderful feeling to touch and to smell a gorgeous woman like her at my age. That is a dream come true! I was thinking, would you mind parting with her, so she could switch her job and take care of me?"

If I was tomato-red a minute ago, I am a few shades darker by now. I am so upset I can hardly speak.

"You—you no good conniving and deceiving bastard, you are not stealing my Angelika from me!" I am screaming. "You want to put our friendship on the line over a woman? Over my woman?" I am still screaming.

Angelika is back. It is amazing how fast she can appear out of nowhere.

"Stop it, you two old fools! I am nobody's woman, Ed, remember that! If the two of you don't make up right now, I will quit my job, and neither one of you will ever see me again!"

She takes my wheelchair and pushes it closer to Vlado. He still has the big grin on his face.

"Hey, Herr Kamerad, we need to have a bit of fun once in a while, that's what keeps us young. Humour and laughter are the best medicine! Just settle down, simmer down, my friend!"

We shake hands.

"I think you are an asshole and that was really shitty what you did to me!"

He keeps on grinning.

"I enjoyed every minute of it!" he says and starts laughing louder and louder. "This was really funny. I really got you going, you jealous old goat!"

Then he stops laughing and asks me right out of the blue, "Hey, if you could clone yourself, would you do it? Would you make a copy of yourself?"

"No, I don't think I could stand another one of myself," I answer.

"Ja, ja, I like your honesty. I know how miserable you can get sometimes and imagine what I had to put up with all these years. It wasn't easy, I tell you. Sometimes, you can be a real pain, you know? But if I would clone myself, would I still be paralysed then?" he continues his questioning.

He catches me off guard.

"I have to think about that one. Yeah, I believe you will remain paralysed after cloning. Sorry, my friend, but your clone, the other you, will not be paralysed," I answer.

"Does that mean that my clone is not a perfect copy?"

"It will be a perfect copy without your injury, that's what I believe will happen," I tell him again.

"So, if my clone, my other self, is a perfect copy, why can't I become the new me and discard the old crippled me?"

"Whoa, whoa, we are treading into some complex territory. Let's leave it for some other day! But tell me, why has modern medicine not worked wonders on you? Why are you still paralysed and wheelchair bound?"

"I will answer you with another question. Why are you sitting in a wheelchair today and every day? Answer me that one, Herr Kamerad!"

"Well, I am just too old and too weak. My knees and my hips cannot support me any longer. I will collapse if I get up, and I will topple over and fall to the ground."

"There is your answer, although I am four months younger than you. We are just too old, Herr Kamerad. They can perform absolute miracles now with spinal cord injuries. They can fuse damaged or severed cords in a matter of minutes, but when it comes to older—or in my case ancient—injuries with completely dead matter, it is a different story. It is possible to initiate re-growth, but the process is extremely tedious and takes forever. They have not come up yet with a formula to speed it up. Modern medicine has helped me in other ways, mainly in the area of pain management and I am very thankful for that!"

I am not completely relaxed yet, my hot blood is beginning to cool down a couple degrees; it was at the boiling point just a few minutes ago. I am trying to control my breathing and to bring down my pounding pulse rate. I am still very angry, but I cannot show my feelings openly, not to him. I have to attempt to hide them and I know that I am not good at disguising my emotions and sensitivities. He probably can read them in my face because he often says that my face is like an open book.

We are sitting there quiet for awhile and again he surprises me with a total change of subject.

"I never read a book in all my life because I did not receive the proper schooling, not in Croatia, not in Italy, and not in Germany. I speak the languages but reading is difficult for me. Your face, Herr Kamerad, is like a book and I can read it well and I know that you are still angry with me. It was a cruel joke, please forgive me."

"Okay, forget it! Tell me again how you escaped from Croatia when it was still under Tito's communist regime."

He lifts his head and looks into the blue sky. His facial expression gradually changes, but he remains quiet, still forlorn in deep thought and memory and when he starts to speak his voice changes to a demure tone.

Chapter IX

The Telephone Call

At first, President Oliver did not want to speak to his Iranian counterpart. The small man with the yellow lenses was waiting for him in the presidential suite and was holding the telephone.

"I'm tired and I've had enough excitement for one day. I don't want to talk to that moron. Can't you get rid of him, Jackson?"

Jackson was shaking his head.

"I have done it already; that was about four hours ago. But now he's back and very determined. He is adamant to speak to you in private."

"Oh, Christ! I don't even know if he speaks English. What the hell does he want—the holocaust denier and nuclear opportunist, the menace to the free world? We should have bombed the shit out of them when we had the chance," mumbled the annoyed president.

A second aide entered Oliver's suite carrying several papers.

"Mr. President, sir, we have urgent messages for you from four important world leaders: Igor Popov, president of Russia; Mr. Lin, president of China; Mr. Singh, prime minister of India; and Isabella Elegante, the Brazilian president. All four implore you to talk to President Abbasi. They say it's in the very interest of humankind."

Oliver swore. "Sometimes I hate this job," he muttered and depressed the green button on the telephone. "Yes," he snorted.

"Hello, is this Mr. Jonathan Oliver? I only want to speak to him and no one else." The voice carried urgency and authority, the accent was strong but did not take away from the clarity of the pronunciation.

"Yes, I am Jonathan Oliver, the president of the United States of America. Just wait until the video comes on and you'll recognize me."

"Oh, thank you. I am waiting on this line for quite some time. Thank you for taking my call, dear friend."

"Let's make this perfectly clear, Mr. Abbasi, I am not your friend and I am not interested in talking with you. My time is limited, so speak your mind, say what you want to say, but I warn you, if you start insulting me and my country or the state of Israel, I will hang up."

"Mr. President, nothing is further away from the thought of insult! On the contrary, I want to express my deep sorrow and convey my sincere condolences to you and all the American people. No other nation has ever experienced this horrific level of death and destruction; no other nation has ever endured so much hardship and suffering, as you are enduring right now! The people of the United League of Islamic Nations, whom I represent, also convey their heartfelt sympathy and offer help and support. Hundreds of skilled aid workers are ready to be deployed at a moment's notice, and two airplanes are on standby, fuelled and loaded with emergency shelter materials and supplies. Just say the word and help will be on the way in the matter of minutes."

Oliver replied stiffly: "Thanks, but no thanks! The American people and I have a long tradition of managing our own affairs. We have overcome many adversaries and challenges in the past and also severe natural disasters—always without any outside help. My people are proud and dedicated and committed to stand up for their country when in need. Therefore, I will not accept your offer."

"I am sorry to hear that, sir, but your understandable pride, commendable as it might be, could on the other hand, delay rescue and aid efforts due to a shortage of manpower. To a great many victims help simply will arrive too late. Please, think it over and do not make a hasty decision. Millions of Americans have perished already, and we do not want to add more casualties to that long list."

"You speak darn good English, mister. I am really surprised. My sources have not informed me accurately of your English-speaking ability, I have to admit."

Abbasi chuckled. "There are some things the CIA and NSA do not know or are misinformed about. I have studied and practised the English for the last two years and strive to become fluent in it. Thank you for your compliment! The second reason for my call is of a totally different nature. My friends, the leaders of the BRICS nations (Brazil, Russia, India, China, and South Africa), have expressed a very strong interest in my plan to save our planet and also ensure the survival of the human race. They have urged me to contact you and start preliminary talks with you. The plan calls for the speedy implementation of a global government. Only a common and united approach to the enormous global problems has a chance to succeed. The plan asks for concessions from every nation. It calls for the complete elimination of all nuclear arms and the closure of all nuclear power-generating facilities. It also proposes, among many others, a reduction of the global human population to sustainable levels by way of voluntary birth control. Unilateral cash incentives by government can be one way to speed up the process, for instance."

"That's nothing new! All this has been discussed and has been tried before in the UN. It failed miserably on agreement and implementation."

"We are not the United Nations. We are only a handful of concerned and responsible world leaders, who are prepared to act alone. We cannot waste precious time on procedure squabbles in some useless and toothless UN committee. It's a farce—a gong show, you Americans would say. We have to try to stop the threatening destruction of our environment and the poisoning of our air and water. We have to try to stop the climate change and minimize its disastrous effects. We have to try to save humankind and our beloved planet. Mr. Oliver, do you want to become a part of our team and work for the betterment of our world?"

The president looked bewildered and surprised. "Is this an invitation?" he asked.

"Yes," answered Abbasi. "We would like you to join our team as the representative of the United States of America. We want you to become involved in the global decision-making, the forming of a global government, and the creation of a new world order. We value your strong voice and your input!"

"Well, first of all, you should go ahead with good example and clean up your own house and get rid of all your own nuclear junk!" stammered Oliver.

"Do I still detect that frosty hostility, Mr. President? Of course, we are willing to shut down and destroy our entire nuclear inventory and our nuclear power-generating installations. The ULIN Government passed the anti-nuclear resolution in the house with a large majority just two weeks ago! I guess it did not make the world headlines. Yes, we are fully prepared to follow an earlier lead by the United European Nations and rid ourselves immediately of the devilish and deadly nuclear menace. We guarantee full cooperation with the International Atomic Commission and their inspectors. Mr. Oliver, I would like to invite you to a top secret summit two weeks from now in Oman. The sultan has graciously offered his palace as a meeting place. The leaders of Brazil, Russia, India, China, and South Africa will be there. I also invited Maxima Müller, the chancellor of Europe and President Sadikin of SEPA, the new South East Pacific Alliance, which as you know includes Korea, Vietnam, Thailand, Singapore, Malaysia, Indonesia, and the Philippines.

"I know this is short notice and a very inopportune time for you. The horrific disaster on your Pacific Coast requires your full attention, but then you have very qualified personnel to take charge of the situation. What can you do personally? Be a hero and rescue another person? You can give speeches of solace and hope to a few of the countless victims. You can address the American people on a national broadcast and promise the best of help that is humanly possible. But after two weeks, you are done with it. Political issues and rivalry will surface again and dominate the news. Then you will be ready for a change, the escape to Oman, I hope. That's why I urge you to attend the summit. It will be for the good of humankind!"

Oliver's head was spinning.

"Mr. Abbasi, sir, I must say you are full of surprises. Thank you for the interesting conversation and for the invitation. I will advise you of my decision soon. Goodbye!"

Oliver swore after he ended the video phone call and he wiped the perspiration off his forehead. He knew that at least six other people had listened in on the telephone conversation and he summoned them to his suite.

"What the hell is going on?" he demanded to know, but nobody could give him an answer.

"We are as surprised as you are, Mr. President!" one of them volunteered.

"How can this no good son of a bitch cook up something like this with the major world leaders and nobody here knows a fucking thing about it?" He fumed. "Get me Doyle from the CIA on the line at once! Then I want to talk to the vice president. In that order! Prepare a meeting in the oval office for tomorrow. I want the Security Council, the Joint Chiefs of Staff, the foreign secretary there and whoever else is important. You guys know the drill."

"Should we call the leader of the Republican Party?" they asked.

"Oh, for Christ sake, no! Don't call that bitch. I am in no mood to start sparring with her again!"

Oliver finished his telephone calls, and then he joined the group of his four trusted advisers discussing the conversation with the Iranian. They watched the video-replay several times and tried to analyze every single word Abbasi had spoken.

"What do you think about his emergency aid offer?" asked the president.

"It's a first! Abbasi appears quite sincere about it and his motives seem genuinely noble. I don't believe he plans to send us a couple planeloads of terrorists," answered the only woman in the group.

"Our resources on the east coast are stretched to the limit, sir," said Jackson. "I just received an update from Dan Spooner, the Chief Operative for FEMA, East. As you all know, we had a relatively quiet hurricane season this year with no major storms to report. Then all this changed. Our hopes of riding out the storm season on the same calm wave it began were completely dashed when we were taken in by a nasty surprise: Superstorm Lucinda.

"It made landfall three weeks ago on an extremely wide front and it was pounding the entire Atlantic Coast relentlessly with 150-plus mile per hour winds and dumping massive amounts of rain on the affected area. The whole system was colossal, and some assessments have it surpassing Superstorm Sandy in size and ferocity. The destruction was so enormous that insurance estimators still cannot put a dollar figure to the total damages. Thank God that the elaborate and expensive dyke and pump-out system in and around New Orleans withstood the savage powers of the hurricane. It was bad, but it could have been worse.

"Ladies and gentlemen, today, three weeks after Lucinda's wreckage of our eastern shores, there are still thousands of aid workers involved in mop up and rebuilding operations. Spooner told me that the last of several remote residences will be hooked up to electric power by tonight, but there are still an estimated 200,000 who lost their homes and housing and are living in community or makeshift shelters now. Federal funding is starting to get to them and damage claims are slowly being processed. Spooner figures he can spare the first response teams and members of the medical staff. He has already made arrangements to have them send to the west coast. So, we have another catastrophe in the making and it couldn't have come at a worse time. FEMA will have a real struggle out there."

They conferred for two more hours discussing a variety of topics, from Abbasi to the immediate disposal of human bodies in mass graves, when Oliver finally said: "That's enough for one day. I need my beauty sleep. Tomorrow comes early and we want to leave for

Washington in good time. Don't forget we are losing three hours. Jackson, can you please get me Stephen Hunter on a secure line? I want to talk to him before I retire for the night."

"Hello, Jonathan! Are you watching the news? What an impressive act of heroism, dear friend. Your rescue caper is headlining every news broadcast. Congratulations on a job well done!" The Canadian prime minister had picked up the telephone after the second ring.

"Oh, gee, I missed it! Well I am sure I'll see the replay tomorrow. I'm calling to tell you that I received the strangest phone call today from none other than Mr. Abbasi, the self-proclaimed king of the ULIN," began Oliver.

"I believe he was elected in fairly proper fashion, Mr. President. UN observers did not find any fraud or wrongdoing at all," interrupted the prime minister.

"Oh, whatever! Anyway, he offered to send two planeloads of emergency response teams with supplies. They are on standby, loaded and fuelled, ready to go, he says. Just waiting for my okay! What do you make of that?"

"Many countries have contacted us and offered assistance and support. The British and the Germans are sending large contingents, and many smaller groups are coming from various other countries," said Hunter. "We have also accepted the offers from the Indian and Chinese governments. Teams from both countries are on their way and arriving soon. They will be setting up field hospitals. We have a huge Chinese and East Indian presence in this area and a large number of them do not speak English. I think this is a good solution to circumvent the language barrier. It will expedite the examining process for the medical staff, instead of being bogged down by the awkwardness and clumsiness of unqualified translators."

"I wonder if our guys thought of that?" mumbled Oliver. "I mean Iranians in the U.S.? There can't be that many, I guess. Most of them are well educated and speak English."

"So will the members of their emergency response team, I am pretty sure of that," remarked Hunter.

"But that was not the full extent of our conversation," continued Oliver. "Ah, may I remind you, Stephen, that the following is highly confidential for now? Okay, now listen to this! He claims to have come up with a rescue plan for our planet and a survival plan for mankind. I would say there must be some credence to his claim because it attracted the interest of some high-level personalities. Listen to this, Stephen: All five leaders of the BRICS countries and this guy, Sadikin from SEPA have agreed to meet at a top secret, top-level summit on November 19th. Even Chancellor Müller of Europe confirmed her participation."

"And Abbasi invited you to the summit?" asked Hunter.

"Yes, he did," said Oliver. "I haven't decided yet. I would like to go there more out of curiosity than anything else. I would like to find out what he and the BRICS guys have dreamed up."

"Do you want to share the intelligence your people have gathered?"

Oliver shifted uncomfortably in his chair. "My boys have very little to report and most of it is speculation. As I said, I have to find out for myself."

He put down the telephone and sighed: "Yes, I have to find out for myself."

Doyle, he hadn't been any help. Complain, complain, complain! Like an old woman. He should learn how to work with his limited resources and be innovative, like others do that spoiled brat!

But Oliver had to admit, the CIA was still having a rough time. It never fully recovered from the "Chinese blowout" during the time of the uprising in America when the Chinese struck. They blew out the NSA and blew it off the map! And they crippled the navy and the air force. Doyle did not let an occasion pass by to remind the president again and again of the dismal state of the CIA, and he had done so again last night.

America once held 792 military posts, strategically placed around the globe. Today we hold less than a dozen in Britain, Germany, and Canada. During these infamous months, the Chinese and Russians used the opportunity to destroy and disable our surveillance satellites; they called them spy satellites. Our "eyes in the sky" are gone; electronic listening stations were jammed with new virus-infested technology and brought to a standstill. They are not recording and they are not transmitting anymore.

A massive security leak to the Chinese enabled them to tie into our code bank and retrieve every code for every single drone, for every single piece of nuclear and ballistic weaponry, and for every one of our fighter jets. They used the self-destruct command for the drones and blew them all up. Our missiles, the nuclear arsenal, and our fighter jets were decoded and recoded with their alien technology. Our scientists cannot crack the new codes and the whole military hardware is relegated to a pile of expensive useless junk!

We still can use our Navy fleet, the submarines, and aircraft carriers. They left them untouched. But we can't fire a single missile or fly a single jet, except rescue helicopters and transport planes. They have us by the short and curly ones, and they darn well know it. The drastic budget cuts to the CIA have crippled operations and reduced them to a bare minimum."

The president's plane touched down smoothly at Joint Base Andrews in mid afternoon. Waiting limousines took him and his entourage directly to the White House.

Everyone rose when the president entered the oval office.

"Good afternoon, ladies and gentlemen, please take your seats," began Oliver. "Many thanks to all six of you for coming on such short notice. All of you, who made yourselves conveniently available via direct video link, get your sorry asses over here right now. This is a confidential in-camera meeting!" snorted an annoyed president.

Reporters who were scanning the airwaves picked up the wireless transmission and instantly started crafting tomorrow's news headlines: What pissed Oliver off? Does America have a secret agenda? Temper, temper Mr. President! Cool Oliver turns red hot! Why was the president so rude?

The meeting at the oval office was rescheduled for the evening hours. A group of 17 was assembled now and they settled comfortably in their chairs after having finished a light but tasty dinner.

The president had cooled off somewhat and his anger had subsided. He glared at the CIA director.

"Mr. Doyle," he began, "please tell me, why is it that so many world leaders share a secret that I don't know a damned thing about? And why is it that Mr. Abbasi speaks perfect English while you have been telling me all along that he has only little knowledge of our language? Please, tell us!"

Doyle apologized and repeated almost word for word the same excuses from the night before when he had talked with Oliver on the telephone. "We are still the laughing stock of the whole world when it comes to gathering intelligence. The Chinese, the Russians, even the Brazilians are playing with us and feeding us misinformation on a 'wholesale level' every day. The Europeans don't trust us anymore and our reliable and faithful ally Great Britain was ejected from the European Union and is totally isolated now. Their spy installations were also completely destroyed by the Chinese, so there is no intelligence forthcoming from the Brits. Our other allies, like Canada, New Zealand, and the Aussies, are still mistrusted and cut off by the world community because of their historic intelligence ties with the U.S. The CIA has been paralysed for years now. It has not been able to rid itself of the darn Chinese curse. The Chinese already know about any action or initiative before we even start it. Our resources are extremely limited and our budget requests are automatically denied year after year.

"Mr. President, ladies and gentlemen, I know you are expecting answers and results. Sorry, I am afraid I can't give you what you are looking for." Doyle sat down.

"Why doesn't he just resign?" thought the president.

"The budget for the defence department is a mere trickle of what it once was. It is sad to note that our neighbours, Canada and Mexico, spend more money on defence than we do—" declared one of the generals.

Oliver interrupted, "We do not want to discuss budgets tonight. We want to examine the possible need for outside help and how to cope with the two natural disasters that struck our country."

"If we get all these planeloads of foreigners with their equipment and supplies, they will have to be treated as high security risks to the U.S. God knows what they might smuggle in on their own airplanes to blow us up. On the other hand, we can't invite them in and then use the third degree and sniffer dogs on them. That would create an international uproar again while we are trying to repair some diplomatic ties," said a TSA official.

"Anybody read yesterday's Teheran newspapers?" asked the small man with the yellow lenses. They all looked at each other dumbfounded and shrugged their shoulders; some did not know where Teheran was, but they did not admit to it.

"Well, the headline reads as follows: Allah spoke to Abbasi! Apparently Allah told him: 'You are all my children, you are my sons and my daughters! So act like brothers and sisters! You love and respect each other! If your brother or sister has a different opinion or a different religious belief, respect their opinion and respect their belief. Exercise tolerance. Remember Allah loves all his children! Go Masoud and make peace with the Americans. They are punished enough. Forgive the Americans and go and help them because they need your help!'"

"Where the hell did you find that information?" asked Edward Doyle, the CIA director.

"On the internet," answered the small man.

The director of FEMA raised his hand and stood up. "Mr. President, ladies and gentlemen, I want to talk to you about the two most horrific natural disasters that ever occurred in our country. The timing could not have been worse! Just three weeks ago Superstorm Lucinda ravaged the east coast with destructive force, and the day before yesterday, all hell broke loose in Seattle. I want to talk to you about the millions of Americans who perished and the millions who survived but are out there shelterless, freezing, and braving the elements. I want to talk to you about the millions who are out there injured and bleeding without medical help, and all those who are hungry and without drinking water. We need all the help we can get! Denying entrance to foreign volunteers out of security reasons is pure frivolity and a tragic joke. It was not the foreigners who destroyed our country and caused the 'collapse', it was our own homebred ignorant imbeciles who grabbed their guns and rifles to occupy Wall Street. Do you remember the thousands who were gunned down that day by the military? It was slaughter, the greatest mass killings in U.S. history! The enemy was within our borders, right next door, neighbours, friends, brothers, and cousins; they had gone berserk! It was not the foreigners who brought harm to our country. That's why I strongly recommend acceptance of the generous offers of aide from all countries!"

Jackson applauded and soon others joined in. The TSA official, the CIA director, and the four generals were stunned.

Within 24 hours, hundreds of first response teams arrived in the U.S. from all parts of the world, eager and dedicated to help. They began their formidable work of rescue, set up durable tents, and provided first aid, food and water, warm clothing, and a source of heat. Others faced the grim task of recovery.

Corpses were piling up. Wherever electricity was restored, morgues and commercial cooling storage facilities filled up fast. Specialized identification teams worked around the clock, but they could not keep up with the overwhelming volume. Boatloads of human bodies were coming in steadily, waiting to be unloaded, until Hernandez ordered not to pick up any more floating bodies. The tides and the waves deposited thousands and thousands onto the shores, and the seagulls, the ravens, and the eagles were in a feeding frenzy, fighting amongst themselves to see who could pick out the eyes of a body that was turned face-up.

Huge excavators were digging mass graves, and dump trucks filled with cadavers were waiting in a long row at the burial sites for their signal to turn around and back up to the gigantic elongated hole in the ground. Then they lifted their box in the front and the carcasses would slide out through the back gate in one swoosh. Sometimes a body was snagged around the hinges of the backdoor and the truck driver would jerk the hydraulics, trying to bump it off. It was a God-awful noise and a God-awful scene. A bulldozer at the north end was starting to backfill. It was spreading the excavated dirt in heavy layers over the mangled human corpses and packing it down hard and tight with its enormous weight.

Chapter X

On The Run

Jeffrey Brockerhoff was a young medical student and an aspiring surgeon, when a ruthless gang blackmailed him. They had captured his sister and threatened to do despicable things to her and kill her unless Jeffrey joined them. As he would soon find out, they needed his surgical skills for their disgusting criminal activities; they were a reliable international trader of human body parts. On the surface they appeared legit: a company that received orders and enquiries and arranged speedy worldwide deliveries for a hefty price. Trans-Part Inc. had pioneered a revolutionary storing system of human body parts in a web of banks around the globe. The bulk of the inventory came from registered donors, from people who had made prior arrangements while they were still alive to donate parts of their body after they died.

Trans-Part Inc. soon discovered that the demand was overwhelming and they could barely fill three out of five orders from their limited supplies. Each day they checked their computers and tallied up the missed business opportunities and the potential money they were losing. The amounts were staggering.

Nobody knew at the time that the corporate owners were also high-ranking members of the East European mafia. Then greed entered the evil and twisted minds of the corporate owners and they devised a devilish plan to boost their inventory by means outside the law.

The company acquired a large chain of funeral homes and a string of crematoriums. Many illegal acts were performed behind those closed doors quite regularly. Corpses released to be cremated were often detoured and rushed to a backyard "collection agency". Here is where Jeffrey was forced to spring into action. With skilled hands and a scalpel, he had to quickly remove organs and eyes, tendons and ligaments, veins, skin, and bones. The remainder of the corpse was then delivered to the crematorium to be incinerated.

Trans-Part Inc. kept their approximately 1,000 employees on a very tight leash via a highly sophisticated surveillance and tracking system. It was the newest in ultra spy technology and was superior even to the one the NSA was using.

Every new potential staff member had to agree to a mandatory medical checkup. During the examination, the individual was secretly inserted with a nano ID implant without their consent and knowledge. But soon a strong suspicion surfaced among the coworkers that they were under 24-hour electronic surveillance, and persistent rumours pointed to some secret transmitter on their bodies.

When Jeffrey confronted his supervisor, Stefanek, the burly Czech grinned and freely admitted the existence of such an implant.

"We have you by the nuts, asshole, and we can squeeze them anytime. Hell, we can even cut them off if we have to. You can't fucking move without us knowing it. We watch your every move. We know everything! There are no secrets for us. That's why we watch! You fuck up, we'll kill you—just like that, boom boom!" and he moved his index finger like he was pulling a trigger. "The implant is untraceable, except for us. Only we know where it is and it tells us everything! Ha, ha, ha!" Stefanek was laughing now. He spoke with the hard accent of the Slavic people.

"How is my sister? What's happening with her?" Jeffrey asked.

"Your sister is a piece of shit and a lousy fuck! I even had her myself. Not worth the effort, I tell you. She is a fucking junkie, just garbage. Maybe we should get rid of her too, and you can cut her up next time around." He started to laugh again.

Jeffrey's boot caught him hard in the genitals and the burly Czech doubled over. In a swift move, Jeffrey was behind him, grabbed his silly ponytail, and yanked his head up, holding the razor sharp scalpel to his throat.

"Don't even breathe hard, you bastard, or your head will roll off you to the ground. I am an experienced meat cutter, as you know, and pigs are my speciality!"

Stefanek groaned, obviously in much pain.

"Where is my implant?" hissed Jeffrey and increased the pressure of the scalpel. Blood began to trickle from the Czech's throat.

"Don't jerk me around! I am extremely impatient. You have five seconds, compadre! Where is my implant?"

"It's in your left earlobe," the Czech said frantically and coughed. Jeffrey cut his throat and pushed him forward. A fountain of blood gushed from the lifeless body when it hit the floor. Jeffrey retrieved the dead man's ISS pad and wallet and put it into his own pocket without even looking inside. He left the room unhurriedly and locked the door. Then he went to get his surgical bag from the main room and took it to the small bathroom of the makeshift clinic in Chicago. The scalpel was covered with blood and he carefully cleaned and sterilized it; then he looked into the mirror and slowly proceeded to sever his left earlobe. It bled profusely at first, but soon he had expertly administered a pair of clamps and reduced the bleeding significantly. Then he collected the detached earlobe and shoved it into a plastic bag, together with the paper towel he had used to clean the blood from the sink.

"Double check! Double check!" he told himself. A last scanning look around and then he quickly left the building and hailed a taxi.

"Take me to the Hampton Inn," he instructed the driver and leaned back into his seat, pressing a small towel to his left ear.

"What happened to your ear?" asked the cabdriver.

"Just some stupid accident. I don't really want to talk about it," said Jeffrey and that ended the conversation right there.

When they pulled up at the hotel, he placed his plastic bag on the floor behind the driver's seat, paid the fare and exited the taxi. Jeffrey remained standing on the sidewalk, still holding the towel to his ear as he watched the cab speed off in the distance. And then it just blew apart in a fiery explosion.

"Holy shit! That was close; that's efficiency!" he thought and looked at his watch. "It only took them 39 minutes since I cut that bastard's throat. Their automated red-code-alert system must have immediately dispatched one of their deadly mini-drones. There goes my earlobe!" He laughed out loud, entered the hotel, and took the elevator up to his room. He was in no hurry now because "officially" he was dead, terminated by the company. He was dead for them, blown apart into thousand pieces and burned to a crisp. They were not looking for him any longer. But he had to leave Chicago before the police became involved and established a link to him.

There wasn't much to pack. He put some clean underwear and socks, a couple shirts, a spare pair of pants, an extra jacket, and a toque into his backpack. He always wore the toque in the early brisk and damp mornings when he went for his half-hour jog.

"No, I won't pack my toque," he decided and put it on his head instead, carefully covering both ears. And again he gave his surroundings a thorough looking-over before he left the room. His suitcase, the dirty laundry, and the shaving kit he was going to leave behind because he had no intention of properly checking out of the hotel. Then he shouldered his backpack and was carrying the surgical bag in his left hand when he rode the elevator past the lobby to the downstairs garage. There he exited the garage on foot at a side street and proceeded to walk for a few blocks away from the hotel. When he spotted a taxi, he flagged it down and ordered the driver to take him to the airport.

Back at the hotel, he had rummaged through Stefanek's wallet and found a driver's licence with a blurry picture and a Houston address, a social security card, a medical card, and four credit cards, Visa, American Express, Sears, and Walmart. It also contained $647 in cash.

Jeffrey had used Tadeusz (Ted) Stefanek's Visa and the ISS pad to book a flight to New York and also a room in a four-star hotel for two nights. At O'Hare, he checked in his backpack, wound his way through the clumsy security, and walked straight to his gate. There he sat down in the waiting area and pulled Stefanek's ISS pad from his pocket; 45 minutes until boarding: enough time to write an e-mail. For a short moment he relaxed, leaned back, and concentrated; then, he began to compose a letter to the Federal Bureau of Investigation. After he finished typing, he read the letter one more time and hit the send button. Then he disabled Stefanek's ISS pad and discarded it unnoticed into a trashcan.

His letter sparked one of the largest international police actions ever, and three days later Trans-Parts Inc. was no more; it had ceased to exist. Every one of their worldwide 47 branches was raided by Interpol in conjunction with local police and then shut down. All employees, managers, and associates were locked up behind bars to be sorted out on their day in court. The judges would decide then if they had to remain in their cells, if they were allowed to post bail, or if they were innocent and able to be released.

He had no problem boarding the plane. The yawning attendant scanned his boarding card listlessly and hardly glanced at the driver's licence he was holding in the same hand. When he landed in La Guardia, he walked directly to the baggage carousel and waited for his backpack to arrive on the belt.

Somebody tapped him on the shoulder while he was retrieving his bag. Jeffrey spun around so fast that his backpack went flying. He almost knocked down the bewildered little old lady behind him. She seemed to tumble and he lunged for her and grabbed her at the last moment before she lost her balance.

"Whoa, whoa, hold your horses, young man!" she managed to say completely surprised by his spontaneous reaction and freed herself slowly from his unprompted embrace. "Are you all right? I noticed you are bleeding, young man. Do you need some help?"

"No, no…" he mumbled, but he never finished the sentence and collapsed right in front of her. She did not have to ask him for a second time if he needed help and sprang into action. Actually, she just screamed, and in no time there was a crowd assembled around the unconscious Jeffrey. He was out only for a few seconds, and when he came to, he was looking straight into the bespectacled washed-blue eyes of the little old lady. Her eyes had the colour of faded jeans and her pleasant face looked familiar.

"This is my son," she declared. "He is having one of his spells. It's been a hectic day for him, a bit too much excitement, I guess. Please, get me a wheelchair! I'm taking him home."

Jeffrey closed his eyes and once again exhaustion flooded through his entire body, and he was too weak to fight it. Two young men tried to lift him into a wheelchair when the first-aid attendant arrived and right away an argument started. The first-aid attendant was trying to pull some authority, but the little old lady would have nothing of that sort and told him to shut up and help the other two lads with the lifting. They hoisted Jeffrey into the wheelchair and pushed him towards the exit and then followed the little old lady's directions to her parked vehicle.

Jeffrey was stirring in the backseat of the car where they had strapped him in. Finally his head began to clear and the overall weakness began to leave his body. He tried to orient himself in the darkness and soon realized he was in a car motoring down a busy freeway. Traffic was heavy and the oncoming headlights were offensive and blinding to his eyes. He blinked a few times and tried to look at the driver. He saw the long grey hair of a woman and then he remembered the little old lady from the luggage carousel at the airport. It must be her.

"Who are you and where the hell are you taking me?" he asked hoarsely, surprised by the strange sound of his own voice. She turned around for a split second and he could see the enormous tinted glasses she was wearing.

"My name is Nadine and we are headed west to your mother's place. Relax, enjoy the ride; we should be there in about 30 minutes."

"My mother's place? My mother lives in Ohio, for Christ's sake! Where the fuck are we?"

"Don't swear, Jeffrey. Watch your tongue, young man. Your mother moved to New Jersey almost two years ago. When is the last time you talked to her?"

"I don't remember," he mumbled embarrassed. He was quiet now but his mind was hyperactive. Strange and obscure images were chasing wild thoughts through his convalescent mind, trying to make sense of the bizarre situation, but he couldn't.

"You, you! You know my name?" he asked almost accusingly. "You knew that I would be at the airport at luggage carousel 8 at 7:20 p.m. and you came there to intercept me?"

"Yes," she said.

"Who are you, lady, and who sent you?"

"My name is Nadine. I am a close friend of your mother's, and I am a psychic. I promised your mother to help find her two lost children."

"But how could you possibly know where to find me?"

"It's a long story. It was very frustrating and I almost gave up because I could not connect to you. I've been trying for over a year, and day after day I was drawing complete blanks, beginning to doubt my own ability. The breakthrough came this afternoon. It knocked the socks off me. I was totally overcome by the strongest vibrations I ever experienced. Surprising and so powerful they moved me into a new and unknown phase of psycho-kinesis and para-telepathy. I could see a room and I could hear two men arguing and I instantly realized that one of the men was you. It was like watching a movie."

"Oh, my God! Oh, my God! Oh, no! This is not happening. This can't be. It's unbelievable—it's impossible!" blabbered Jeffrey and then he asked, "What all did you see?"

"I saw and I heard everything. I saw the killing, the self-mutilation when you cut off your earlobe. I saw the taxi blow up, and I saw Ted's credit card when you booked the flight. I even jotted down the credit card number and the expiration date. I can show it to you later. Right there and right then, the movie ended very abruptly. Well, this is my story in a nutshell."

If his mind had been hyperactive before, it was rapidly accelerating now. His head was spinning. The oncoming headlights really began to bother him now and he closed his eyes.

"Very strange," he said after awhile. "Very strange. I've never been unconscious in my entire life and now all of a sudden I totally blacked out at the luggage carousel. It is a complete mystery. What happened to me? Did you have anything to do with it?" he asked suspiciously.

"Oh, just some tricks of the trade and my trusted micro-slim hypodermic needle. I bet you didn't feel the little prick when I touched your shoulder," she laughed.

"You are a very talented and a very dangerous little old lady," he concluded.

"I accept that I am talented, but I do not agree that I am dangerous. I very much object to you calling me old!" she replied.

He apologized and then he asked her, "Isn't clairvoyance another one of these shady occupations, along the line of fortune telling, hypnotism, faith healing, black or white or whatever colour magic, reincarnation, after-death and out-off body experiences, intergalactic communications, and God knows what else?"

"You tell me!" she said hotly. "You just can't lump everything unexplained and everything out of the ordinary together and throw it into one pot. Some of these subjects have become recognized sciences in the last century. Those 'hidden disciplines' have escaped their closet of obscurity and come out of their dark past. Some new and some good light has been shed on them. I am thinking primarily of psychiatry and psychology, which have been lifted out the hazy shroud of mystery and are being taught at many universities around the world today.

"But other than these few exceptions, the scientific community in their almighty wisdom is still reluctant to promote or sanction any studies of the many subjects regarding the psyche, the obscure, the unexplained, and the paranormal.

"Weather forecasting is another exception. It was rather hastily elevated to the science of meteorology with the introduction of thermometers and barometers. Actually, I believe that weather forecasting or meteorology has failed as a science because it's so darn popular. Everyone can do it, and it does not require a university education and degree to practise it. Some self-professed amateurs have a remarkable gift of foretelling the weather and they often outperform the experts."

"Are you looking for some credibility for your own profession?" he asked.

"Actually, I don't. I am well-known and well-respected as a psychic detective. I get called quite often by the FBI to assist in some of their investigations."

"Did you ever find Elsie?"

"No, Stefanek lied to you. He killed your sister over a year ago. Her body was never found."

Soft sobbing sounds were coming from the backseat and she knew Jeffrey was crying.

"The many videos of her, the many recordings of her, and the pictures they gave me: They were all lies? All my sacrifices were for nothing? Life must have been hell for her."

"Life must have been hell for you too," Nadine answered.

Chapter XI

Secret Meeting in Muscat

Oliver had disappeared and so had his press secretary. Just vanished into thin air or swallowed up in the deep, dark underground. There was a short press release from the White House announcing the president had taken a respite for a few days.

No explanation, no other details! The usual reliable sources remained tight-lipped and dried up. The news media was in frenzy. Speculation was running high and information was cut off!

Some sharp investigative reporters started to retrace Oliver's recent movements and found that he had flown late last night, via private charter, to Ottawa, the Canadian capital. That's where the trail mysteriously ended. Was he still in some secret meeting with his northern colleague? And if so, what was it all about? They had met just a few days ago in Bellingham for crying out loud! What could be so darned important for another hurried get together?

"There is something big in the air, something mega-big. I can smell it!" said a seasoned chap from CNN, and others nodded their heads in agreement. A senior government official denied Oliver's presence on Canadian soil.

"You guys are speculating. Sorry, nobody by that name in Canada!" But the smirk remained on his face.

Oliver had stayed only 10 minutes on Canadian terra firma, long enough to get transferred to a regular scheduled DHL freight plane to Frankfurt. The entry on the shipping manifesto read 'VIC: very important cargo, Crown Royal, Oman'. Many people in the industry knew about the Sultan's weakness for Canadian rye whiskey. The Secret Service, who was commandeering the plane, was using it as their code: 'Operation Crown Royal'. They touched down in Frankfurt, where they refuelled and filed a new flight plan; then they continued their long trip to Muscat International Airport in Oman.

All airplanes arriving with travelling dignitaries were diverted at the last moment from Muscat to a nearby air force base. From there a military helicopter took them on a short but overwhelming scenic flight to the Al Alam Royal Palace. Even from the air there was evidence of splendour and glamour, and the immaculate setting in one of the world's most spectacular pieces of real estate.

The sultan welcomed every one of his distinguished guests on their arrival at the heliport. He greeted Oliver with open arms and embraced him like a friend. They chatted as they were strolling towards the palace, followed by a group of servants and Oliver's own personal staff.

"Mr. Abbasi has a packed agenda. We will see you at dinner in about an hour, Mr. President."

After a delightful dinner, the Iranian rose swiftly and made his way to the podium.

"Your royal highness, honourable and distinguished guests! First, I want to thank everybody for accepting my invitation and for coming here today. I know that for most of you it was inconvenient to take time out of your hectic schedules and it was difficult to make this long journey in total secrecy. I also want to thank our royal hosts, the sultan and his lovely wife, for making their gorgeous palace available to us for our important meeting.

"I welcome you to an open and frank discussion about a possible new world order. In the next three days, we shall exchange and examine new thoughts and new ideas, as revolutionary as they might be, to change the world for the betterment of humankind and for the sustainability of our planet.

"Everything is on the table for re-examination, for re-evaluation and for rethinking. We have to start thinking outside the box! Yes, we are boxed in by centuries' old customs, rules, and religion, by prejudice and narrow mindedness, by laws, limits, and boundaries, and of course we are misguided by power, by money and greed, and by mistrust of thy neighbour and thy politician. Collectively, as humans, we have a very dismal record: population growth is still out of control, food and education contribution is totally mismanaged, and the desirable and more equal distribution of wealth is moving fast in the opposite direction. What a sad predicament! All thanks to the vile viruses of capitalism.

"Furthermore, we have almost destroyed our planet, poisoned the atmosphere, and brought imbalance to our ecosystem. I declare without a doubt that we have the most beautiful planet in the entire universe and all the other planets envy us. So, why are we out there in full force, hell-bent on ruining it?

"We cannot continue raping our environment and wrecking our beloved earth. Remember, it's the only one we've got! We have to start to reverse things. We have to begin to undo the damage we created. Of course, not everything can be repaired, replaced, or redone; much is gone forever!

"We do, however, need to begin somewhere and create hope that humankind comes to its senses; we need a new way of thinking and new priorities, a new way of living, a new way of treating nature and people with a new respect for God's creation. We have to combine our efforts on a global scale! Only then, will the human race have a chance to survive!

"The time for action is long overdue! It has been delayed and deferred too often. We cannot stall any longer! The time for immediate and consolidated action is now! Ladies and gentlemen, cast aside your divisions and embrace cooperation!"

Everybody applauded and Abbasi continued after a short break.

"Again, there are others who think we are painting a far too gloomy picture of our future. They strongly believe in the triumphal salvation through technology and science, and they propagate: 'Long before this planet becomes uninhabitable, we'll have found a new planet and we'll have found a way to get there.'

"What does this mean? Does it mean when we have wrecked and ruined our lovely planet earth, we are off to a new world with the same destructive demeanour and attitude and the same rotten lifestyle? Please, think about it for a minute. Wouldn't it be an easy way out, leaving all our serious problems behind? What kind of dreamers are they these irrational people who want to shed all responsibility and rely solely on a fantasy? We have to dismiss fantasy and come back to reality and we have to believe in ourselves to manage our current situation and find a solution together."

Abbasi paused for a moment. He looked up from his notes and surveyed his audience attentively.

"I have chosen quite a revolutionary theme for our meeting," he said with a grin. "I call it: 'Visions of A New World Order!' At this time, I would like to share some of my many thoughts for a better world with all of you. I am cautiously expecting that my thoughts will trigger an invasion of new ideas and will spawn a multitude of new suggestions with workable solutions. Ladies and Gentlemen, let me address two important subjects this evening:

global government and universal birth control.

"Earlier this year, the world population eclipsed the eight billion mark and it continues to rise. Again, the news set off alarm bells, but only temporarily, and then it disappeared from the radar. Although the increases have moderated in recent years, the trend still remains upward. Conservative think tanks have determined a much lower sustainable population number for our planet and pegged it at about three billion. The figure has been confirmed by study after study and by countless computerized analyses. Of course, others claim the exact opposite to be true and maintain humankind can produce enough food to feed everyone on earth and even a few more billion on top of it. They strongly believe it can be done with the assistance of genetic engineering.

"Ladies and gentlemen, the reality is different! The effects of global warming and climate changes have led to the direct loss of millions of hectares of arable land. Natural food producers and their counterparts of artificial food substitutes are under extreme pressure. They can barely meet the global demand. Prices have become unaffordable for many, and inefficient logistics often fail to reach the world's poorest inhabitants. The excessive waste in the so-called rich countries could probably feed the estimated 1.5 billion who are starving if we had a perfect distribution and storage system. But we do not have the perfect system. For one, getting perishable foods to the long-distance consumer still creates enormous challenges, and the high costs associated with it make it a non-profitable exercise.

"No profit is a bad topic in the business world and the private sector bows out quickly from such money-losing endeavours. If there is no profit, why do it? Unless government pays for it, but if there is no government responsible for the situation and willing to fork over enough cash, the project dies before it gets started.

"That is why hunger is still a grim reality for millions, not only in Africa but on virtually every one of our continents, and the daily search for food is often brutal and tragic.

"Water has also become a scarce commodity in many regions and thousands die every day of dehydration and the direct causes of contaminated water. In spite of these facts, leaders of the major world religions hang on to their orthodox doctrines and deny the right for effective birth control to their followers.

"The 1994 International Conference on Population and Development in Cairo received worldwide publicity and expectations were high. For the first time, a panel of top international medical experts, scientists, researchers, and religious leaders were discussing the possible reduction of population growth and birth control on a world stage. The outcome was very disappointing; some powerful religious leaders vetoed any form of birth control. Nothing was really achieved there other than a handful of minor recommendations and the resolve to meet again.

"Case was deferred, and then again, and again.

"Ladies and gentlemen, we cannot postpone the issue of birth control any longer. We have to act and we have to act now. We are done with all the fancy and fruitless talking. What we need is action!"

Abbasi stopped for a drink of water.

"As you all know, most major problems in our world have no geographical boundaries. Their implications are universal and global, and they can only be addressed and solved internationally. I believe it is time to form a world government based on democratic principles. Only then, with a combined and united effort and with the redirection of our resources, will we be able to ward off impending doom. Only then can we start to save lives from famine and disease effectively, only then can we begin to save our planet with an organized and purposeful approach."

"How do you propose we establish a world government?" asked Oliver.

"This, of course, is a great subject for discussion and a subject that invites ideas, interest, and vision. Personally, I see a rough structure of all existing countries in peaceful cohesion, where the famous slogan of the French Revolution should apply: 'Liberty, Equality and Brotherhood'. The individual statehood of all countries and their boundaries shall remain and their governments will manage internal affairs. New global laws and regulations, however, will override existing state laws where and when applicable. Once approved, a global law shall be binding and cannot be subjected to legal appeal.

"Let's take education as an example. My suggestion is as follows: (a) Every child completes a minimum of eight years of mandatory schooling. (b) Every English-speaking student has to learn a second language. (c) Every non-English-speaking student has to learn English. (d) Attendance at schools, colleges and universities is absolutely free for everyone in the whole world!

"This example shows how global law would override any state law, if and when it differs. I can see other changes to our laws, the human rights code, and the criminal code. Our diverse societies, often guided by tradition, religion, or ideologies have developed rules to regulate living in the human community. Some of the rules or laws have wandered into the extreme and are not acceptable for everybody. We cannot have ultra libertarian western views practised together with ultra Islamic sharia law, for instance. Here we have to find a workable and sensible solution.

"Now, back to the subject of universal birth control: Never before in history were there this many humans, this many cattle and sheep, this many pigs and chickens on our planet. Never before has our planet been subjected to the daily monstrous output of poisonous emissions from factories, from the enormous consumption of gasoline, oil, and coal, from the careless use of ozone-depleting agents, and from the millions of tons of garbage deposited daily into our soil or into our oceans, rivers, and lakes.

"Never before did our oceans encounter mile-long floating plastic garbage islands and floating nylon nets that trap and entangle many of our precious sea animals. So many things are out of control in nature's vulnerable places on our planet.

"I strongly believe that further population growth will bring more harm to all of us. Trust me, it will do irreversible harm. We know it will negatively affect our environment, our oceans and waters, the air we breathe, and the protection of our atmosphere. We have already witnessed climate changes and the results, the drastic increases in severity of hurricanes, droughts, floods, and wildfires.

"We already know that further population growth will add to the food and water shortages, and it will add to the misery of billions of the poorest among us whose lives are already just a pitiful sub-human existence.

"So, how do we stop population growth and how do we reverse it without killing a single human being?

"We cannot do it with tough legislation alone. I know that legislated birth control will meet strong defiance from the populace and the patriarchal society. Defiance will also be boosted through interference from a multitude of fanatical representatives of the powerful and persuasive world religions.

"So what would persuade people to change hereditary views and customs, and what would be persuasive enough to defy religious beliefs? I think the simple answer is money—the old capitalistic trick: 'You can buy anything with money! You can even change people's minds with money'.

"I propose a voluntary universal sterilization program that will have cash rewards or tax incentives for both women and men who decide to undergo sterilization. I envision something like this: If a woman decides to have no children or have the sterilization after her first child, she will receive the equivalent of 20,000 Euros. If she decides to have the procedure done after having borne two children, she will receive the equivalent of 10,000 Euros. After having borne three or more children, she will lose her eligibility for a cash reward. A male will receive the equivalent of 10,000 Euros at the time of his sterilization.

"Yes, 'impact', is the word.

"The immediate impact on the world's economy would be tremendous. People will stand in long lines to get sterilized and to collect the money. How will they spend their money? Most of them will rush to spend it right away. We, as the government, will have to try to slow down the spending and find ways to direct the flow of these enormous sums. We have to put brakes on the frenzied spending and make housing or proper shelter a priority.

I can imagine a dramatic rise in demand for all sorts of consumer goods. If the markets react in the traditional way, an economic boom will erupt and inflation will flare up to unwanted highs. We may need some kind of controls and price protection. A mad rush and spiralling boom will likely lead to an early end with an eventual collapse of the ballooning economy. It is desirable to decelerate and prolong the economic activity because the day will arrive soon when the next impact will surface: the immediate halt in population growth.

"Well, is this enough food for thought for tonight?

"Tomorrow morning, my friend Omar Sadikin, the president of SEPA, will come to the podium and take over the microphone. He has the most interesting views, numbers, and statistics on how a global government may be established."

The delegates rose, exchanged some pleasantries for a short while, and then retired to their rooms. Jet lag syndrome and fatigue overcame most of them, and soon the distinguished rulers of the world succumbed to a deep sleep.

Chapter XII

Vlado

"I was three years old when my mother died. The British were dropping bombs on suspected Ustasha and German hideouts. My mother and her brother were killed that day while they were out in the nearby woods collecting firewood. I don't remember any of it. It was 1944, towards the end of the Second World War. When the war was over, they took my brother to a state-run orphanage in Mostar and he attended the Tito School. He became a fine communist and always had good paying jobs and important positions. I hated him, the traitor.

"They let me stay with my grandmother in the tiny mountain village of Vrapcici. I loved my babalula and helped her with the goats and the sheep. We even had a donkey and chickens.

"'What about my father?' I would ask her and she always answered the same way. 'Oh, you don't have a father, Vladili. Forget about your father, Vladili!' Then she mumbled something angrily and walked away. I could see that she really became upset every time I asked about my father, and after awhile I did not ask her anymore.

"We prayed often and every day and my babalula told me how important it was to communicate with the Almighty.

"'Don't lose touch with God, our Saviour. He must become a part of your life and you have to invite him to your soul. Then it will be a good and satisfying life for you, Vladili.'

"I spent most of my days outdoors, tending to the sheep and the goats. These amazing animals always found their own sources of food in the barren and rocky terrain. Sometimes they would wander off in different directions and I had to herd them back together again by the end of the day. That was the hardest part of my job, but usually it was quite lethargic and relaxing. I would listen to the unique sounds of nature and look into the sky, watching for airplanes.

"When I heard the train's steam whistle blow in the distant valley, I knew it was calling me. It was calling me to come down from the mountains and down from our desolate village that was baking in the heat of the sun every day. Here the bare and burned rocks dominated the landscape and formed an almost inhospitable environment.

"The calls from the train whistle would reverberate up from mountainside to mountainside and echo their luring messages into our tiny village and up to me. There was an obvious irregularity and no sure way of foretelling when the whistle would blow. Sometimes I waited for hours, listening for the enticing sound and it would not happen. Disappointed, I went to bed, only to wake up in the middle of the dark night to hear the train's happy whistle. I knew right then that it was happy and not demanding like at other times. But it only happened once. All the other times there was a clear urgency to that sound and the urgency increased with every year.

"One day my babalula said, 'Vladili, I think you should get instructed in the word of God and you should learn how to read and write, now that you are six years old', and she took me by the hand and we walked to Bijela Poljana, which means white field and where the nuns lived in a convent.

"The nuns were strict teachers. They were not entirely pleased with me and frowned on my 'undisciplined and carefree' behaviour. The frowning soon made way to annoyance and anger when I deliberately interrupted the class and the other children laughed and I laughed. But the nuns did not think it was funny.

"They didn't laugh and brought out a willow switch and I received my first lashing.

"My behaviour gradually improved and I accepted most of the rules, but they could not curb my wild fighting spirit. There was no way I was going to back down or walk away from a challenge; my hot blood would rush through me with a roar and the fisticuffs were flying. The other boys used to tease me and knew exactly how to provoke a fight. We were not comparing the length of our penises, we were comparing our stamina in bloody raging battles, to find out who was the strongest and the toughest of us.

"I was tall and skinny and they used to call me pop. Oh, I hated it! 'I am not a priest and I don't want to be a priest!' I yelled at them. 'I am going to be a pilot, you wait and see!' The kids ignored me and kept on chanting pop, pop, pop.

"'Why don't you want to become a priest?' the nuns asked me. 'It is such a wonderful way to do God's work here on earth and it is so rewarding!'

"'No, no, no!' I cried. 'I want to be a pilot and I want to fly big airplanes and I will have a nicer uniform than my brother has.'

"The nuns must have been talking to my grandmother because she knew everything.

"'Vladili, Vladili, what are we going to do with you? The nuns are giving up on you. You have been a very difficult student and now you told them that you don't want to be a pop. My God, my God, there goes my dream!' she sighed

"'I want to be pilot, babalula,' I said and she looked at me with tears in her eyes.

"'But then you will have to go to Tito School,' she cried, 'and I will lose another one of my precious grandchildren to the evil communists.'

"It was a lot farther and it took a lot longer to walk to Tito School than to the nuns' convent. But by then, I was older and much stronger and I easily covered the distance on bare feet in both directions. We were poor and I had no shoes, only some crude homemade foot covering made from dried animal skin. These galoshes were very uncomfortable, yet my babalula insisted that I wear them during classes.

"We did not pray at Tito School and there was more emphasis on sports and physical activities. The boys were bigger and meaner and I fought them all, lost many a fight, but I also won quite a good number of them. Then came this terrible day that brought the greatest disappointment of my young life.

"'You will never be a pilot, Vlado. During the medical examination the doctors discovered you have a birth defect, a rare medical anomaly. Your heart is on the wrong side of your body. It is called dextrocardia.'

"I ran out of school screaming and did not care if I had permission to leave or not. I was screaming and crying all the way to Vrapcici, and I did not stop running until I was high above our hut. Eventually the sobbing abated and I wiped the tears from my eyes. A deep anger crept up in me and I became furious and annoyed at God and the world and the communist teachers at Tito School.

"'Why me? Why me?' I shouted into the mountains and clenched my fists. The echo returned my wailing cries completely distorted and it sounded so ridiculous, that I started to smile after a while.

"My grandmother was waiting for me. She looked very concerned.

"'I am not going back to Tito School!' I said and told her about my physical abnormality and my disillusion with God and the rest of the world. 'I can never, never be a pilot. Why is this happening to me, babalula?' I sobbed again.

"She took me into her arms and just held me for a long time before she said anything. 'Maybe God had a reason to put your heart on the right side of your body and make you special and outstanding from the rest of men,' she whispered.

"The next school I went to was the Gimnazija in Mostar. Again I walked the ten kilometre distance to and from the high school barefooted almost every day. At odd times I would get a ride on someone's wagon or I would double up with a friend or a neighbour on a bike.

"Then came the glorious day when I received my own bicycle, and that made things quite a bit easier. I loved the swoosh of air in my ears and the exhilaration of the increasing speed when I was flying down the mountain road in the mornings. Of course, I had my share of wipeouts and crashes, and I limped into school with bruises and scratches more than once.

"My proud ownership of this speedy transportation device ended abruptly when my drunken uncle destroyed my bicycle in a violent fit of alcoholic stupor. He was completely out of control and kept on smashing my bike into small pieces of useless trash. Two days later, he apologized and said he was sorry. I just screamed obscenities at him and ran out of the hut. He came after me enraged and tried to catch me, but I was too fast. I could run like the devil and he had no chance in hell.

"I never believed the world was going to change. There was high unemployment among the Croats and much excessive drinking and the many problems that go with that. I always hated the Serbs; they were the communists' elite and they were in power. They divided the good jobs and the good positions up among themselves. I also hated the Muslims because they were different and they always seemed to manage on their own somehow. That is the way I was brought up: a good catholic Croatian boy in Yugoslavia and already a young political activist.

"Once a year, the Tito School held a summer camp for boys, and it was mandatory for all male students of the other high schools to participate. I did not mind the sports and physical exercises and even some of the military drills, but I hated the communist brainwashing sessions.

"When I returned to the Gimnazija in Mostar after the summer break, one of the Croatian teachers singled me out and took me aside. He had realized that I had become a passionate nationalist and that I was headed for trouble. My political views were not concealed at all; on the contrary, I made my dislike of the ruling communist regime known quite obviously.

"'What were you thinking when they asked you at Tito School who is the prime minister of Yugoslavia and you answered Ante Pavelic? Are you nuts? You know darn well that Marshal Josip Broz Tito is our prime minister and not Pavelic, the fascist leader from the past. Stupidity, envy, defiance, and hotheadedness will take you nowhere; they are destructive. Trying to change or overthrow the government is very dangerous; don't even think of it! It could cost you your life. You are creating too much controversy in our school and you have raised the attention of the political overseers at the Polit Bureau. They have branded you as a troublemaker and are watching you extremely closely right now. You make any more waves, they will pick you up and make sure that you will never surface again. I know for a fact you would be expelled from our school before graduation. If they do have plans for additional punishment, I wouldn't know about that.

"'Political change will come here in time, but it may be bloody and brutal. Major changes and improvements to individual rights and freedoms are taking place all over Western Europe now. In many parts, economic activity is gradually picking up, except for Germany where the rebuilding of the destroyed country has begun in full swing. Their economy is red hot; they call it das Wirtschaftswunder, the economic miracle. They have already full employment and need many, many more workers. Thousands of Italian construction workers have gone to Germany where they found good paying jobs and generous social and medical benefits. I know of a few men from our area who have secretly escaped from Yugoslavia into Italy and then gone north to Germany.

"'I am telling you, Germany is where it's happening in Europe now and there are unlimited opportunities for a young ambitious man like you. My advice to you is, leave our country and go to Germany. If I was 20 years younger, I would come with you.'

"It was in August 1955 and I was still 14 when I said goodbye to my beloved babalula. I knew I would never see her again. She was the only reason I was so sad when I walked the train tracks leading out of Mostar. About two hours into my brisk walk, I came to a sharp curve. That's where the train had to slow down, I figured, and that's where I planned to jump on it. I laid down in the tall grass nearby, in the shade of a large tree, and waited for the next train.

"The whistle was loud and very close, and then I spotted the giant locomotive coming into view, belching enormous clouds of steam from its chimney. It was a scary sight. I was hiding behind the tree trunk and let the decelerated train slowly pass by. My target was the very last car—what a mistake that was!

"He was grinning at me when I opened the door and tried to climb inside. 'Get off my train right now, you son of a whore!' he yelled. 'Jump or shall I push you?'

"'Okay, okay. I will jump,' I said and turned around. His boot caught me just below the shoulder blades and I went flying completely unprepared towards the moving ground.

"The night was cold and dark and my whole body was hurting. I doggedly stumbled ahead in the dark, closely following the train tracks. They would eventually lead me out of the country and bring me to Trieste but that was going to take another eight months.

"It was an arduous and adventurous time. Often, I was hiding during the day in the woods. Under the cover of the night, I began to move around, seeking out garden plots, cornfields, fruit trees, and berry bushes to steal something to eat. One thing that remained persistent was the constant nagging hunger.

"I was chased by dogs, by police, and by angry garden owners. I was caught and incarcerated and beaten. And I escaped because I could still run like the devil. I jumped on trains and I jumped off trains before any irate conductor had a chance to push me off again.

"Once, they shot at me—ping, ping, ping, like mini shots from an air rifle. That was scary, I ducked and ran zigzag like a rabbit. Why would they shoot and try to kill me? I don't know; it was just bad stuff. And then a machine gun went ra-ta-ta, ra-ta-ta. Just bad stuff and I kept running all night.

"With the oncoming of winter, it was harder to find food outdoors. I took on small jobs here and there, gathered firewood for a poor elderly couple and shared the simple meals with them. I repaired fences, cleaned the mortar of old used bricks, helped farmers bring in their crops, and did many other odd little jobs in return for food.

"I met many wonderful and fascinating people who were good

to me. I also met some bad people who were very mean to me.

"When I reached Trieste, it was springtime and everything was blooming and clad in refreshing new green. The old port city-state had just been divided up between Yugoslavia and Italy. Thousands of people were in the refugee camp and I felt imprisoned in misery. The conditions were absolutely deplorable.

"'We have to escape tonight', whispered Augustin, the elderly Slovenian I had befriended. 'Word is that they are shipping a whole train load of us back to Yugoslavia as early as tomorrow. We have to get over to the Italian side. It won't be easy; the border crossing points are heavily guarded, but I have a good and reliable lead. Be ready after midnight and don't fall asleep before that!'

"It was a cakewalk, so easy. We were delirious when we surrendered to the Italian authorities. They took us to one of their refugee camps and checked us in. There we received a numbered tag with campo profughi #1 printed in bold black letters on it. We had to wear it when we ventured outside the campground. The food was basic and sufficient, but camp life was dull with limited activities, especially for a young energetic juvenile like me, rapidly approaching adulthood. That didn't mean maturity, which came much later in my older years and completely alienated me for the longest time.

"Some mornings we had to stand in a row outside the gate with our backs to the fence. The local farmers came by and inspected us from head to toe before they took their pick. I felt like a slave on the auction block in ancient times.

"'Hey, you and you,' an older farmer pointed at me and my friend. 'You come!' He drove us to his farm and we worked all day side by side with him. He was a nice man who treated us fair. We liked him right away. He was also a very funny guy and we laughed a lot. We stopped several times that day to rest and his wife brought us food and water. In the evening, he drove us back to campo profughi #1.

"'You want to come back tomorrow?' he asked and we nodded our heads. A new trend then developed, and more and more work groups were shipped out for weeks at a time, to mainly agricultural areas of Italy. We spent a couple of months in Latina, south of Rome, and when we returned, they shipped us to Bari just in time for the fruit-picking season. But we always returned to campo profughi #1 in Trieste.

"My friend and I were looking for ways to get out of Trieste, to go to some other places, see the world, do something different. We were bored and craved some excitement.

"'Let's join the Foreign Legion. Then we will go to Africa or Indochina,' I said. My friend loved the idea and we decided to escape from our camp and travel to Nice in France by train and enlist with the Foreign Legion. The adrenalin was flowing again when we jumped on the first train. It was only a short ride to the next station where the freight train terminated. That did not deter us; we boldly climbed into a waiting passenger train. This ride did not last too long either and we were escorted off with a warning at the next city.

"'Well, shit, we can handle that! Let's just sit tight and wait here. There is another train leaving in 45 minutes,' I said, after studying the departures schedule and we both laughed. That was fun! No more train-jumping. We travelled quite sophisticated now, we were boarding passenger trains, and we were being escorted off them, always at a stop a bit closer to our destination. It took us a few days to reach Nice, so what? We had all the time in the world and every day brought fresh adventures.

"They chased us out of the Foreign Legion's office. 'Go back home to your mummies, kids. This is a place for men and not for little boys!'

"We were totally pissed off. We were mad. We were angry and full of rage. It took awhile until we started to simmer down. Actually there was this boat, and this boat helped us to finally rid us of our temper, or did it? Anyway, there was this boat tied up to the dock with nobody around.

"'Would you like to go for a boat ride?' I asked, and my friend was very willing. It turned out that the boat was not tied to the dock—matter of fact, it was chained to the dock and secured with a lock. I found a rock and hammered away on the lock until it broke.

The motor started with the first pull and away we went. This was exciting, something totally new, none of us had ever been in a boat before, let alone manoeuvring it around on a big body of water. It was exhilarating and we yelled and screamed as we bounced over the small waves. Suddenly, the waves were much larger and we became scared and did not know what to do.

"Meanwhile, the boat owner had alerted the police and they were out looking for us. They brought us safely back to shore and put us in jail for two weeks. I'd been in jail before a couple of times during my eight months of escape odyssey from Yugoslavia. The jails over there in no way compared to the French version in Nice. Here it was almost luxury, and after the two weeks were up, we really didn't want to leave, but the police gave us train tickets to Trieste and escorted us to our reserved seats on the train. It was the first time that we travelled via rail legally with actual tickets.

"To get into Germany wasn't quite as easy as my teacher in Mostar had told me. Lots of red tape and proper documentation was needed for the complicated application process. But before I was going to leave for Germany, I wanted to see Rome, the ancient city I had heard so much about. Especially now that I was so close. My chance came a few weeks later during an interrogation with the youth employment review board.

"'What are your plans for the future young man? What kind of trade would you like to learn, son?' they asked me, and out of the blue I stammered shyly,

"'Pop, I would like to become a priest,' I lied. But it raised their interest, out of the many hundreds of refugee boys, I was the first one who wanted to become a man of the cloth. They looked at each other, talked very quietly among themselves, and nodded their heads a few times. Then the older one of the trio addressed me.

"'Vlado, is it? Are you serious about this? Can you at least read and write?'

"'I am very serious about it! I went to school at the convent of Bijela Poljana,' I answered proudly.

"'Well then, the best place for you would be in Rome. There

is the Pontifical Croatian College of St. Jerome that has schooled many Croatian priests over the years. Okay, we will give you a pass and a train ticket to Rome. Once you get there, you go directly to the College and see Monsignor Krunoslav Draganovic.'

"I could hardly contain my jubilation. I thanked every board member personally and then I rushed outside to find Augustin and tell him the good news.

"'You sly son-of-a-gun.' he laughed and then he became serious. 'Okay, here is what I know about Rome. You listen carefully! Wear your profughi dog tag at all times; it allows you to ride the subway and most city buses for free, and there are other advantages. You can go to any church, for instance, tell them that you have just arrived and that you have no money. They will give you 1,000 lire, just like that!'

"'First things first,' I thought, when I arrived in Rome and I entered the first church I saw. A half hour later, I exited the church with 1,000 lire in my pocket. Thousand lire was not much money, but for me, who had never owned any money before, it was like a small fortune. I had to try it again.

"'Where is the next church?' I asked somebody and was told that it was just around the corner, take a left, and then a short right. It took only 15 minutes this time and I was holding another 1,000 lire in my hands. There are over 500 churches in Rome and in the following four weeks I visited over 200 of them and collected 1,000 lire every time. I was in a daze. I stayed at shelters and refugee camps at night, but during the day, I was busy visiting new churches. But all good things come to an end. All of a sudden I was red-flagged and the churches denied my request for monetary assistance.

"It was time to visit the College of St. Jerome, but first I had to get rid of my enormous bundle of money. I carried two paper bags full of lire to the post office and arranged a money transfer of an even 200,000 to my grandmother. It felt so good I almost cried. My poor babalula was going to be very proud of me.

"At the college I had a very short visit with Monsignor Draganovic. 'Sit down, son,' he said and made an inviting gesture with his hands. My attention was immediately drawn to the compelling eyes of this man. His measured and long scrutinizing stare irritated me, and I moved nervously in my chair.

"'You've been stealing from the Church!' he said accusingly and wagged his right index finger at me.

"'No, no, I did not steal. I just asked for money and they gave it to me!'

"He cracked a smile and then asked me where I was from and what I had done with the money, and I told him.

"'Well, you sent the money to your babalula, that was a good thing to do, I suppose. We do not have a job opening at our college and I presume you don't want to study for the next five or eight years to become a priest.'

"I shook my head vigorously.

"'That's what I thought!' He tapped his fingers on the desk and then leaned back in his chair, while his long scrutinizing look returned.

"'You do need a job,' he finally summarized and started writing something on an official looking piece of paper. Then he took a large stamp, depressed it on an ink pad, and ceremoniously administered it to the official paper.

"'Here,' he said, 'is my recommendation of you. You take it to St. Peter's Cathedral. I know for a fact that they are short of janitorial workers. You might find a job there,' and he dismissed me.

"For the next three months I scrubbed and cleaned, I swept and dusted, I waxed and polished in the holy sanctuary of the famous cathedral. A few times I even stood in as an altar boy when there was a sudden shortage of them. Then one day a priest took me aside and said: 'Go to the College tonight and see Father Draganovic.'

"'I have a letter from the nuns in Bijela Poljana. They verify that your grandmother received the money you sent to her. It also says: We all love you and we all miss you and we all thank you for the generous donation to the convent. Good luck to you, Vladili, and may God bless you!'

"My babalula had shared her good fortune with the nuns. I cried and Draganovic watched me. He smiled, and this was the second time that I remember him smiling.

"'Isn't it ironic that the church's money found its way back to the church? God works in so many wondrous ways!' He actually chuckled and seemed very happy and jovial. Then he folded his hands and looked at me with his testing eyes again.

"'I've been in Vrapcici once, a long, long time ago, and I may have even met your family and your babalula. From what I hear, she is a remarkable woman and raised you a proud Croatian boy.'

"'Yes, Father!' I said.

"'Here at the Pontifical Croatian College of St. Jerome, we emphasize the importance of tradition, of upholding our culture and language, our national identity, and our religion. We are in contact with other Croatian groups in several foreign countries and provide support and sometimes assistance, if needed. Right now, we have an urgent delivery to make to some good friends in Spain. I have arranged for you to leave tomorrow.'

"For the next hour, he gave me precise and detailed instructions and then we rehearsed the whole scenario twice, until he was completely satisfied.

"'I am putting my trust in you, Vlado, and you have to trust me. Don't double cross me; the punishment will be severe. There is no money in the package; there is nothing of value for you in it. But I tell you what, when you return after the successful delivery? You can make another money transfer to your babalula, I guarantee you that!'

Many years later, I found out that Monsignor Krunoslav Draganovic was a controversial figure. He is alleged to have assisted in the escape of some notorious German and Croatian Nazis to South America and is rumoured to have later also been working as a spy for the CIA. I didn't know any of this at the time. I went on a second delivery mission for him; this time to Greece.

He treated me well and helped me in many ways. He secured political asylum for me. It was a step up from refugee status. Now I could move around freely all over Italy. Shortly after that, I received a passport and my worker permit for Germany.

I was 17 when I went to Germany, and I discovered that I had arrived in paradise. The construction company that hired me looked after me extremely well. They enrolled me in several training and instructional courses and soon I received my operating license for excavators and building cranes. They also sponsored me for mechanical courses and basic understanding of blueprints and introduced me to other building trades. I just loved it.

Chapter XIII

Day Two Begins

"Global representation by population seems fair to us, but I believe it is hardly feasible," said Mr. Singh, the president of India, over breakfast in his whining voice, yet loud enough for everyone to hear him. He turned to Abbasi who was seated next to him. "Excuse me, sir. How large do you propose a global parliament to be? If we, for example, allow only one elected official from every million of the world's population, we will end up with a colossal assembly of some 8,000 members. That is a totally unworkable number, not feasible." He was waving his right index finger. "Not feasible!" he repeated. "Just creating a proper venue to house 8,000 workstations and to accommodate all the elected members would be a utopian project and take years to build. That all takes time—time we do not have! Ergo, not feasible! Ladies and gentlemen, we have to govern effectively and not just fill a sports stadium!"

"Mr. Sadikin tells me that he has played around with some figures and has come up with a viable solution. I don't know the details of his plan, and I am quite anxious to watch his presentation," replied Abbasi.

Singh continued his trail of thought without acknowledging Abbasi's answer.

"Even if we try to reduce that number of 8,000 and send only one elected member from every 10 million of the world's population to the new global legislature, we will still have a remarkably strong membership of over 700, but they would represent a mere 60 countries. It means more than 150 countries will be without a voice and without a vote when it comes to the decision making of global issues in the parliament. Countries like Switzerland, like Israel, like Honduras, and so many more will be side-lined. They, too, are a part of the global community and they do not deserve to be left out and silenced. We have to find a way, a fair solution for better representation and equality in our new government."

"I am sure that Mr. Sadikin has taken this problem into consideration," said Abbasi, a bit irritated.

"America cannot play a dominant role in the world anymore! India has the largest population in the world and it needs to be represented accordingly. India is entitled to receive the leading position to govern the world."

"One of the goals of this meeting is to take down national barriers and not to put more of them up," said Abbasi.

Singh was obviously upset. He threw up his hands in a bold gesture of annoyance and turned away from Abbasi.

Oliver had registered the side swipe of the Indian leader, but decided not to act on it at present. He knew that other opportunities lay ahead of him, and he would choose the right occasion to get back at the Indian. He was not going to forget that Mr. Bigmouth Singh! Instead he asked nobody in particular: "Does this mean that the creation of a global government is a forgone conclusion and a decision has been made already?"

"Nothing has been decided yet, Mr. Oliver. However, there is a strong consensus among the delegates that we need an effective central government to manage the global affairs," said Abbasi.

Mr. Sadikin, the president of SEPA, rose from his chair and began to speak.

"I am a staunch advocate of a global government, and I believe that we, the peoples of our planet earth, will master our destiny. We have to do it together with a combined and a united effort. We need a global decision-making jurisdiction, a capable and determined international body of action in which we all can put our trust and our future.

"I agree with President Singh that we are faced with a very complex and extraordinary undertaking today, and he is also correct in his assumption that we need to explore new and innovative ways in forming a global government. Can we do it fairly, so that it will represent everyone on this planet? I don't think so, not entirely, but I believe we can get pretty darn close to it.

"I have prepared a scale for every country on this globe, detailing their population base and how many elected delegates they may or may not be sending to the new world parliament accordingly. India, of course, the country with the largest population, would post the largest faction of 75 elected members. But then I totally disagree with our learned friend, Mr. Singh. We do not expect the Indian contingent to be a unified bloc that will foremost represent India's interests. On the contrary, we expect of every member in the new global government to be truly independent and not subscribed to and not dictated by national interest groups or political parties."

Sadikin paused and then projected a short version of his proposal on a large screen.

India	1.5 billion	75 elected members
China	1.3billion	65
SEPA	680 million	34
Europe	520 million	26
ULIN	440 million	22
USA	380 million	19
Brazil	275 million	14
Countries with a population of	150-200 million	9
	100-149 million	7
	50-99 million	5
	25-49 million	3
	10-24 million	2
	1-9 million	1
a population less than	1 million	0

"This can be the rough framework to build on. According to my calculations, about 540 elected representatives from more than 150 countries would form the world government.

"Will it be effective and will it have decisive powers at its disposal? My answer is 'yes'! It has to have the ultimate power; otherwise, it will be useless. Yet too much power is dangerous, you will say, and I will agree with you. But I do envision a reformation of democracy as we currently know it.

"In a true democracy, the power one person shall have is the power to vote and the power of the single cast ballot! This shall not only apply to the individual in the street, it shall also apply on the highest level to every individual representative of the new global legislature.

"Now, let me share my ideas of a true democracy and a new political makeup with you. I see it quite differently from the traditional election and governing process. The only political ideology will be the one of the universal democratic world order and its statutes. There is no need for political parties, and as far as I am concerned, they should be abolished. Candidates running for election have to be independent. Pre-election polls, lobbying, and election advertisements will be outlawed. We do not need the media to manipulate the minds of the electorate. We do not need a corrupt mass media to take away the decision-making from the voters. We do not want a mass media that receives bribe money from the multinationals to represent their interests. We do not need spin doctors! We want the voter to form an own personal opinion, watch the interviews and the debates of the candidates, which will be state-sponsored. Personal attacks and smear campaigns will not be tolerated in these televised events.

"Once elected, the approximate 540 new members of the world government will choose a chairman or president and a governing council of 25-30 ministers among themselves.

"Every new proposal before the house has to clear the 300-yes-vote hurdle to become law. The independent members will decide individually and they can vote without being pressured or commandeered by party or partisan policy as is the case in many democracies now. Proposals that receive a simple majority but fail the required 300 hurdle may apply to be included in a yearly plebiscite for a second chance. I am even putting forward the idea of compulsory voting, but this can be brought before the house for a decision at a later time.

"HAY UN CAMINO! Ladies and gentlemen, there is a way to a better world, and we will find it!"

President Sadikin sat down. There was light to enthusiastic applause, again, and this time even Oliver and Maxima Müller joined the approving hand-clapping.

Abbasi went back to the microphone and announced the next speaker. An elegant black man rose and slowly made his way to the podium.

"My name is Dembe Khulani. I am the president of South Africa, and I would like to talk to you about money because I believe that with a new global government we also ought to have a new universal currency and a new global banking system. I also strongly believe that money is the curse of humankind and is the root of all evil. Humankind and its association with money or gold goes back for thousands of years, and history is filled with thousands of stories of good and evil fortunes. When the Lord chased Adam and Eve out of the Garden of Eden, He angrily said to Adam: 'In the sweat of thy face shalt thou earn thy bread!'

"Ever since then ... most people have to work for money, unless they inherited it; most people have to work for money until they are all crippled up or retire; people need money to buy food and drink and shelter, etc.; people use money to pay for bribes and favours; people take death-defying chances for money; people sell their bodies for money; people lie and cheat for money; people kill for money; people gamble with or for money; people make money the honest and fair way; people make money the crooked way; people lose their money and sometimes kill themselves because of money; people hide their money or take it to the bank; people try to swindle you out of your money or even rob the banks. The list goes on and on.

"If money really is the curse of humankind, can money be replaced with something else? Can humankind co-exist without money?

"Who will work, and who will bake bread without compensation? Money is absolutely the greatest incentive! Well, not entirely, because religion can offer promises that money cannot: an afterlife in heaven or paradise, sometimes with or without virgins.

"But we cannot rid ourselves of money. I don't know how, and I don't know of a better alternative. What we can do is implement measures, regulations, and laws to change the capitalistic so-called free market system, where supply and demand are the supreme rulers. 'Supply and demand' has been a proven organizer and manager of world economics, but it fails to deliver when and where there is no profit to be made. Need and necessity never become options, only the demand for the signed and prepaid order!

"Capitalism is solely built on growth. Our economies, our industries, manufacturing or merchandising, our banking system, and even our food producers are desperately trying to show increases in volume, in sales, and in profit. It is asked for and it is expected every year by the shareholders on their annual meetings.

"With the steady population growth, generally there is no problem, because we are breeding daily 200,000 new consumers and customers—that's almost a quarter of a million. Ladies and gentlemen, the appetite of this gargantuan monster called capitalism is enormous and it demands more and more and even more. It will threaten with recession and it will blackmail with fabricated sinister consequences if projections are not met. It will strangle the many to satisfy the few.

"That's why we need to change the banking and the monetary system. We need universal control and a fair distribution of wealth. We need to stop the worldwide financial cyber-gambling craze and shut down the speculative currency trading and the manipulative stock markets. People sit in front of their laptops or hold their fancy ISS pads in their hands, and with just a few clicks, they can make money if they press the right buttons. Others with the larger screens and the super-rich portfolios push bigger buttons and make bigger money! That's not what money was intended for! Not for gambling! Gambling has become the biggest pastime among the overweight humans who cyber-steal from their skinny, malnourished, and overworked slaves half a world away!

"I believe a practise like that is darn right criminal, and I am signalling the end to the opportunists and to the fortune hunters.

"Solutions to the problem are extremely complex, but we can go back to basics and de-complex and re-spool the issues! Humans created the complexity of our existence and humans can unravel it and return to simplicity in solutions. Now, I know that any change will have a reaction, that an implementation of any of my ideas will have a tremendous effect on our daily lives. We must start somewhere, so let's start with a universal currency, a government-owned, and controlled banking system, and the abolition of all stock markets.

"We are nine democratically elected leaders of the world's largest countries and economies. We represent more than 60% of the world's population, and at least 75% of the world's industrial and commercial productivity and consumption of goods. We are the global voice and we have a global responsibility to rescue humankind and save our planet. Changes are imminent. We are the elected representatives of the people and it is our profound duty to make those changes."

The South African president returned to his seat in silence, nobody applauded. You could have heard a pin hit the marbled floor, but no pin was dropped.

They broke for lunch. The sultan and his gorgeous wife were the perfect hosts. They welcomed their important guests into an ornate room, which at first glance seemed lavishly over-decorated, but then upon a closer look, it revealed intricate and precise coordination in very tasteful and artistic arrangements.

Jonathan Oliver was seated between Igor Popov to his right and Mr. Lin, the Chinese president, to his left.

"A very interesting morning," the American started the conversation. "I am deeply surprised and humbled by everyone's sincerity and the urgency to find a fair global solution."

"Only cooperation and unity will lead us to success. We, the nine of us here, have to take the lead and begin the revolutionary process. The rest of the world must follow us. We have to engage our foreign diplomats and send them out on missionary missions," remarked Mr. Lin.

"Well, that sounds funny," said Popov, "but I know what you mean. Russia has many friends; we shall make a list of these countries and instruct our ambassadors to start talks straightaway. Mr. Lin, I know that China also has good relations with many other nations as well. How about America, Mr. Oliver—you must have some friends, don't you?" The sarcasm in his voice was quite obvious.

"Well, of course. We have good friends in Canada, Great Britain, Israel, Australia, New Zealand, Japan, and Taiwan."

"Taiwan has always been Chinese territory; it belongs to China and should become part of our great republic," said Mr. Lin.

"Excuse me, Mr. Lin, please think globally and forget about territorial issues," said Popov. "We must leave territorial issues to the history books."

"Why don't we leave politics and concentrate on our excellent meals," suggested Oliver.

"Okay, good idea. Bon appétit!" said the Sultan and raised his wine glass.

Most of the nine world leaders had brought their own personal chefs. They would oversee the preparation of the meals, but most importantly, they would taste every meal before it was allowed to be served to their masters.

"I can't believe the transformation of Mr. Abbasi," said Oliver. "Either he is a fantastic actor or he truly is the sincere and concerned person he portrays himself to be."

"I know Masoud, he is good people, a deeply devoted family man. Devotion has always been a part of everything he does. I know he never fit into the international scene. He was shunned as an egomaniac, an outsider, and as a critic of Israel. Bad, bad stuff in the eyes of the USA and the West!"

Lin stopped, lifted the soup bowl with both hands and began drinking from it with loud slurping sounds. "Wonderful soup!" he said approvingly and set the bowl back on the table. Henry, Oliver's personal chef, was now serving a curried seafood dish to his boss, while Mr. Popov was receiving his choice, succulent and tender cuts of lamb with rice in a richly flavoured cream sauce.

Mr. Singh put down his fork and knife, wiped his face and mouth with the cherry-red cloth napkin, and said, "The Americans and the Israelis never vacated their biased and hostile opinion of Abbasi, even after they were proven wrong later on. They fabricated a stigma and wanted the rest of the world to believe their lies!"

Oliver jumped to his feet.

"This is completely uncalled for and downright insulting. Why do you always have to pick on the United States?"

"You want to know why? Because you wanted to be world cop all the time and impose your twisted form of democracy onto the rest of the world. You had a disgusting and snotty ignorance and an absolute disrespect for anything and anybody not American. You abused your military power and your monetary dominance over the rest of the world for too long. I am glad our Chinese friends had the foresight and the know-how to finally put a stop to it." Mr. Singh sat down. "I had to get this off my chest," he added.

Abbasi had swiftly moved to the podium and was speaking into the microphone.

"My dear friends, may I remind you, and especially Mr. Singh, that we are gathered here to discuss the global future and not its past. Please refrain from further deviation! Thank you!"

Oliver had been provoked many times in his life before and had often lost his cool, but he didn't this time.

"May I just set one thing straight? America has made great strides in birth control and in human rights, and we are proud of our achievements. Our social programs cover most needs for the poor, the homeless, and the disenfranchised. Surely it could use improvement and we are working tirelessly to make amends, but we have never received any recognition from the international community for our humanitarian work. I think this is long overdue.

"When I look at some other countries, I see a different picture. My information shows that the Chinese and the East Indian races are the most populous on the globe. To credit the Chinese, I acknowledge their effort in curbing reproduction with their one-baby policy in the past. The Indian, Pakistani, Bangladeshi, Sri Lankan, and other governments on the subcontinent have done very little to control the spiralling population explosion, other than, and I have to emphasize 'other than', exporting their people all around the world in record numbers. No other race than the Indo Asians spreads this fast. Your country, Mr. Singh, is out of control. Why should we or any other country subsidize your irresponsible overflow of people?"

This time it was Mr. Singh who jumped from his seat. His face had drained of blood and turned to an ash pale colour. Obviously extremely upset he began to stammer, but then he quickly regained some composure and he answered in a raised and crisp voice.

"Lies! Nothing but lies! I am appalled to hear the president of the USA is completely misinformed. The growth rate in the Indian archipelago has been constant for quite a number of years at 1.58%. The population explosion is happening on the African continent, with rates between 2% and 3%. There the need is the greatest for birth control, for food, for water, for shelter, for medical care, and for education. There the needs are real and require immediate and drastic attention. Get your facts straight Mr. Oliver, before you so freely distribute false accusations!

"I admit that in India we still have a long and difficult road ahead of us to attain the ideal and satisfactory goals. Looking backwards, we have come a long and difficult way already, and we have cleared many hurdles. I am proud of our achievements and I am proud of our skilled administrative people who manage the world's largest democracy, and I must say they manage it extremely well!"

There was some light applause when Mr. Singh sat down and Abbasi returned to the microphone.

"Ladies and gentlemen, there is no doubt that during the last century or so, many parts of the world have seen living conditions improve in general and have experienced a decline in birth rates and in infant mortality. However, the overall picture is not so. We all know that and we have already testified to that. We know the problems humankind and our planet are facing are man-made and self-inflicted as a direct result of overpopulation. The uncontrolled population growth, the consequent uncontrolled pollution and the uncontrolled disposal of our waste are the real threats! These are the real issues!

"We have to stop population growth, economic and consumption growth—generally, any growth in almost every aspect of our lives. We must begin to reduce. We cannot continue to grow and grow! Where and how will it end? Remember, the earth does not grow with us; it remains the same size.

"Ladies and gentlemen, the debate has started with some fervour and some spice! Please, let us finish our wonderful lunch. When we return, we will continue our discussion about the future of humankind and the future of our planet. We might even begin to vote today on some of the proposals and motions already being brought forward."

"Are we really going to vote on these, aah... well, not to offend anybody again—let's say extraordinary, revolutionary, out-of-this-world, and world-shattering proposals?" asked Oliver.

Both, Popov and Mr. Lin nodded their heads.

"I think I am dreaming, this isn't real, this is a movie. You are all very nice people, and I'm waiting for the villain to appear, but when I look around at every one of you, I have a tough time detecting the villain. I am starting to believe there is no villain in this movie."

"This is no movie, this is as real as it gets," said Popov. "My American friend, stop dreaming. The threats to humankind and to its survival are real and very serious. The damage to our planet and its environment is real, and the changes in our weather patterns to more and more extremes are real. The socio-capitalistic end result when all wealth eventually accumulates in one spot is just a question of time and can be mathematically forecast. I think the time is here and now. We do not want a repeat of the social upheaval as it happened in your country, or a repeat of the social and religious turmoil in the Middle East, in North and Central Africa, and many other parts of the world. We do not want anything like that to happen anywhere, not ever again!"

"Voting most likely will take place tonight and tomorrow. The majority decision of this council is binding. You will have to go back to your own country and persuade your government and your people of our decisions. You will also have to send your diplomats to the countries that are friends of the USA, or in your case Mr. Popov, countries that are friends of Russia and bring them onside with persuasion, diplomacy, and pressure, the pressure of reality."

Mr. Lin expressed himself very clearly and left no doubt in Oliver's mind that a vote would bring forth a turning point in the history of the human race.

Oliver was in a daze.

"Is this actually happening?" he was asking himself over and over again. He closed his eyes for a few seconds and his thoughts trailed back into the recent past, ten and twenty years ago.

He remembered many international summits and meetings with foreign leaders, dignitaries, and diplomats in his role as military adviser to the president. In all these meetings, either in the bright focus of the world stage or in the seclusion of a private one-on-one dialogue, he always took charge. He liked to lecture his guests and opponents, and he would bring his agenda forward firmly and unmistakably and do it from a position of power. Some bluntly interpreted his approach as arrogant, but he did not care what they said behind his back. He could do it and he enjoyed it because America was the greatest country in the world and America was the most powerful country in the world.

Back then, America was still the undisputed financial powerhouse of the world. Washington and Wall Street pulled the purse strings in masterly fashion. They could and would dictate terms and conditions, always with the benefit of the "good old USA" in mind. World prices for wheat, which was grown in Canada, Australia, or Kazakhstan, were set in Chicago at the commodities stock exchange. World prices for sugar, cocoa beans, canola, and coffee were dictated in Chicago or its affiliate in New York. When the price for copper and magnesium dropped, mines in Chile, in Indonesia, and in Africa would curtail production and lay off workers.

People said, "When America sneezes, the world catches a cold." The country's economic power was enormous. The mere stroke of a pen or the slightest touch on a keyboard could carry consequences tens of thousands of miles away to the opposite side of the globe.

Equally unparalleled was the military might. The USA, with only 5% of the world's population, tried to control the rest of the world and was quite successful in doing so for numerous years, not without the cooperation of her allied 'friends'. Many of these so-called friends welcomed the American quest of development and of investment and the promise of a rosy economic future. They joined the good cause and pledged to fight communism alongside America and to uphold all the noble virtues of democracy. When the 'friend', by circumstance, happened to be a dictator of a strategically important country or an oil-rich potentate, the noble virtues of democracy were simply dropped in the contract.

If a country with high strategic value for the USA stubbornly refused to join the alliance and the good cause, it was often pushed and pressured into an economic and military dependency. When the sweet-talking and carrot-dangling no longer worked, strong-arm tactics were applied and drastic sanctions were imposed.

America kept a stranglehold on most of the world for a long time by engaging in many conflicts and wars. Always far away from home soil. But the young men and women recruited (or was it Uncle Sam?) did not want to die; marching in flashy uniforms in parades was okay, flying jet fighters and dropping 'precision bombs' or firing a 'precision rocket' was fun and cool, sitting in front of a computer bank and following the images from the spy satellites was okay. Maybe pushing a button and launching a deadly missile from a drone 8,000 miles away was okay because it was like a computer game. But in the morning, when they found out that the missile had hit a wedding party and killed 49 or it had hit an orphanage and killed 28 or it had hit a school or a hospital and killed many more again, then the young men and the young women pushing the buttons felt terrible and ran to the washrooms and puked. They were deeply regretful and deeply ashamed. And many wanted to quit their engagement with the glorious armed forces of the USA, and they cried and many even committed suicide.

Sometimes Oliver entertained these flashbacks into the past and his thoughts wandered off and basked in the glory of days gone by, but they were always followed by dark sentimental clouds. At times, it was regret.

He opened his eyes. Okay, reality check, reality check: Today the USA is ranked #6 or #7 in the world. I have to remember that!

He folded his napkin for a second time. Then he looked straight at the Chinese president and began to speak. "My dear colleague from China. I value your opinion and your deep conviction for the 'cause'. By cause, I mean a united global approach to save the planet and to ensure the survival of humankind. I am generally in favour of seeking a global solution, but we cannot compromise the democratic process. I believe that the people ought to decide what's best for them. We cannot take this democratic right away from the populace."

Mr. Lin smiled. "How do you say in English? You've got to be kidding! I believe or Don't give me that bullshit! Did George W. Bush ask the people if he could attack Iraq and Afghanistan? No, he did not. As a matter-of-fact, Cheney and Rumsfeld helped him make up his mind. They had made up his mind long before 9/11. When Churchill declared war on Germany, did he ask the people in the land of democracy if they wanted war with Germany for a second time? No, he did not! Or Tony Blair when he jumped on the U.S. coattails and sent British troops to the Middle East? Did he ask his people if they wanted to die?"

"These were completely different circumstances, actions of emergency, and defensive measures to prevent a catastrophic consequence," replied Oliver.

Lin raised both his hands. "Please, you are doing it again! We all know what the real motives were, my friend. That's not a secret. Don't try to pull wool over my eyes; don't give me a snow job.

But when you mentioned 'emergency action' you used the perfect phrase because we do have a global emergency. We have to act quickly and decisively. We cannot wait forever and allow the democratic snail-speed process to curtail or, worse, stop the 'cause'. We were elected to give direction to the people, but we were also elected to lead the people into the right direction. You let them choose and they will become confused and run off in all directions. Do they collectively know their way to salvation, and do they collectively always reach the right decision with a majority vote? I actually doubt it.

"The collective mob will take the law into their own hands and they will lynch people! Do you want another collective mob to elect another Hitler? Another Bush or another Berlusconi? They are easily blindsided.

"Democracy is only a theory, believing the common people know what is good for them and for their country. It is only a theory, my friend. I don't think that today's democracy, paid for and sponsored by capitalism, is the right form of government anymore. I do not hear the loud and clear voice of the people any longer. All I hear is a reverberating echo when they mouth or lip-sync the manipulated slogans from their screens or billboards. Then they click a button on their ISS pads and have automatically voted. A swan song for democracy. It too, needs an overhaul!

"We are the leaders and we have to lead the people out of the mess that was created democratically, if I may say so."

"It seems to me you are proposing some sort of domineering style of government over humankind that is based on communist ideas and values. You know that this one ran its course already and failed," said Oliver.

"I don't think communism turned out the way Karl Marx and Friedrich Engels originally envisioned it. Communism failed because of untrained, unskilled, uneducated, and very bribable administrators. It failed because of incompetent managers and incompetence in general.

"However, what we want is to revamp democracy and socialism and come up with a workable solution. We want to find and create the closest form of an ideal government if at all possible. I am quite convinced that we will be successful in our quest!" Lin refolded his napkin and smiled at Oliver but said nothing more.

"You know what? When I return to Washington I will be the only American who will know the details of this plan, and you expect me to persuade not only my own party and my own administration but the rest of the 380 million Americans that this is the right way—the only way to salvation?

"Not only that, to top it all off, I have to convince and arm wrestle a dozen more independent 'friendly countries'. This is a job and a half! A sales challenge of a lifetime!" sighed Oliver.

"So be it, if that's what it takes and no better man than yourself to do the job—that's why we picked you, my friend," smiled Popov. "We all have similar challenges, and after tomorrow our responsibilities will multiply substantially."

Popov and Oliver were receiving chocolate pudding and both of them hastily devoured it as if it were the only thing they had eaten all day. Oliver was looking for more but then he changed his mind and pushed the empty dish away.

"Now I know at least one thing we have in common," laughed Popov.

"Chocolate pudding—that's probably about it," grumbled Oliver.

"You have become a grouchy old man," said Popov. "How do you expect to get yourself re-elected?"

"I could ask you the same question," said Oliver, and then they both laughed out loud.

Chapter XIV

Slipping Away

Three days later, when an anxious proprietor in Chicago checked the offices he had rented to an international charity organization for a "weeklong collection drive", he found a bloodbath and the stinking remains of a headless man.

He called the police immediately and they arrived within minutes. They ushered him out of the stinking room and began the questioning. There was not much he could tell them. No, he never had any prior dealings with this organization, and he had never met the individual before either. That guy had paid the $1,200 rent money upfront in cash and all in 100 bills. Oh, yeah, it was kind of odd that he asked for a freezer and was going to pay an extra $300 just to rent it for a week. I told the guy that I don't have a freezer for rent or otherwise.

"What do you need a freezer for anyway?"

"We need a fucking freezer!" said the creep in a threatening voice. Then I go, if I buy a freezer then I am going to be stuck with it. What am I going to do with a freezer. I don't need one. On the other hand, it will cost me more than 300 bucks to buy one. Sorry, I can't help you."

"Okay, then forget about the freezer. We'll look after it!"

"So, there must have been more than the one person?" said the police officer looking up from his pad.

"I only met this one guy," said the proprietor and gave a general description of Stefanek.

"What else do you remember about this guy? Did you get a name?"

"No, he never told me his name, but he had this heavy accent."

"What kind of an accent?"

"Like a Russian, I think," said the proprietor.

A crackle in the officer's microphone interrupted them. He listened attentively and nodded his head.

"Stick around," he said to the proprietor. "They found the head of the stiff in the freezer. We need you for identification."

"Oh, shit! I already puked today!" Inwardly he prayed to God to spare him from looking at the gruesome find and then the inevitable was postponed with the arrival of the FBI. He was thankful for that. They interrogated him for a second time, and he repeated his earlier story.

"Come with us now," said the older FBI man and he followed him reluctantly to the third room of the office complex. He spotted the freezer right away and shivered. His body was covered with goose bumps. Four other agents were in the room and a young pale-looking woman opened the lid and lifted out a bloody human head by its frozen hair.

"It is him, the Russian," he gagged and threw up all over the floor.

At the exact same moment, Jeffrey and Nadine where leaving the offices of the Motor Vehicle Commission.

"Can you put a spell on people?" asked Jeffrey.

"Sometimes I wish I could!" she laughed.

"It seems to me that the poor guy in there was totally spellbound. He was putty in your hands. You had him completely under your control."

"I guess I can be a bit persuasive at times."

"It was more than that. I think you are a witch!"

Nadine was amused.

"Every woman is a witch, more or less. I even have a broom, but

I don't know how to fly with it! I've been practising and practising, but to no avail. I just can't lift off!" She laughed again.

Jeffrey felt her laugh was invigorating. It was a refreshing sound—the laugh of a woman much younger than she was. He glanced over to her, assuring himself that it was still her who was walking at his side.

He was getting more and more impressed by Nadine. Yesterday she spent most of her time on the telephone and then left the house in the evening only to return later with some official documents.

"It's all legal and official now," she announced. "The judge himself signed and sealed it. Here is your change of name certificate and here is your new revised birth certificate. As of right now your name is Toby Zwosdesky!" She smiled wickedly.

"My name is what? How did you ever come up with a crazy name like that?" Jeffrey raised his voice.

"Very simple—because it is my maiden name," she answered.

"But wouldn't a strange name like that really stand out and attract attention?" he asked.

"Not after I put my kinetic and hypnotic attachment to it. Don't worry, nobody will remember your name."

Today she had fussed about his cut-off earlobe. The bleeding had stopped on the first day and a protective scab had formed to cover the wound, but it was still an ugly sight. She posed as his mother again and they went to apply for a new instant driver's licence.

"Oh my, what happened to your earlobe?" asked the clerk.

"I don't want to talk about it," said Jeffrey, remembering that he used the same answer for the cab driver who disintegrated into small particles together with his earlobe when the taxi blew up.

"Let me get this straight! You want to change your name from Ta... Stefanek to Toby Z... whatever?" stuttered the clerk. He was looking at the old driver's licence and the new birth certificate.

"He already changed his name. This is the document!" said Nadine and tapped at the certificate with her index finger.

"Well, if you ask me, I think it is a step backwards," said the clerk. "I can see changing the first name to Toby, but my God..."

"Nobody is asking you for an opinion!" snapped Nadine. "Toby has a good reason to use my maiden name because his father was a bad dude!"

"Yeah!" said Jeffrey.

"The name change has been legally completed and should be none of your concern, sweetheart. What we need now is a driver's licence for Toby for the State of New Jersey, because he came home to live here with me his mother! I am so happy about his decision. We have great plans together. We want to recapture all those lost years, when he was in the service. Always gone, all over the world and then the time in Houston. I was so scared, so many times. I am so glad you quit the air force and your dangerous job as a test pilot, Toby. Finally, you are home! Come to mama, baby! I love you!" And she embraced and kissed him right in front of the clerk.

"Sorry, Ma'am. Sorry, I did not know. Please, step up closer to the camera, sir. I'll take your picture and an eye scan."

"Eye scan?" asked Jeffrey.

"Yes, as of March 1, every new driver's licence has to have an eye scan. Extra security, you know," revealed the clerk. "Look straight into the camera, sir. Okay, hold still, don't smile!" It clicked a couple of times. The clerk checked the results and was satisfied. He looked at the old licence again. It showed a fuzzy picture of a blond, blue-eyed man, and with some imagination one could even detect a faint similarity to Jeffrey.

"Gee, they sure take lousy pictures in Texas, sloppy work. I've got a much better shot of you. You will be happy with this one, sir!"

He asked for another piece of ID and Jeffrey showed him Ted's visa credit card and social security card.

"Okay, thank you, sir. It'll take a few minutes to process. Please take a seat in the waiting area. It was an honour to meet a real hero, sir!" said the clerk.

That was 15 minutes ago. Jeffrey had now two important pieces of identification in his pocket, a birth certificate and a driver's licence in his new name: Toby Zwosdesky.

His mother saw Nadine's car pull into the driveway. She rushed outside and was so relieved to see both of back safely at her home.

"How did it go? I had the wildest ideas going through my head while I was sitting here waiting for you guys. Thinking all the time you'd be in jail by now."

"We are okay, Mom. Nobody put us in jail. Everything went smooth and slick, thanks to your wonderful friend Nadine," said Toby and hugged his mother.

They spent the rest of the day planning Toby's future and how to disguise and erase the tracks of his past.

"I suggest you leave as soon as tomorrow to get a good head start. Take the bus or the train to Washington and fly from there to the west coast. Go to Portland or Seattle, and if things ever should become dangerous for you, try to slip over into Canada. It isn't far and it's fairly easy to do," said Nadine. Toby's mother started to cry.

"I don't want to lose you again so soon," she wailed.

"It has to be done," Nadine said firmly.

"A bizarre and gruesome beheading took place in Chicago, probably a few days ago. Police were called to a murder scene after the owner of a warehouse complex discovered the headless remains of a male person. Identification of the body will be complex. The security camera at the facility was destroyed and the film was removed. However, police recovered a hidden audio recording device which may be useful to the investigating authorities. No further details were released." They listened to the short announcement during the evening news.

"Shit!" yelled Toby. "They have my voice print; they have my audio profile!"

"Relax, son. Don't you worry, Audio profiling is still in it's infancy and compared with the overwhelming finger printing and DNA databases in the FBI's inventory it is just a trickle," said his mother.

"It has to be done," repeated Nadine. "The sooner, the better! You best leave tomorrow. We will give you $5,000 in cash. When you get there, rent a small apartment and wait for the social security card to arrive. We'll send it out to you as soon as we receive it. Remember, the guy said it'll take up to seven days to have the name change processed and the new card printed. It's a week—that's not bad. In the meantime, lie low, just send short messages on your new ISS pad to your mom, and avoid talking on the phone for awhile. Use some of your cash and the prepaid visa card to do your shopping. I think you are all set."

A couple days later, Toby arrived at Sea-Tac airport. A taxi took him to the La Quinta Hotel in Tacoma.

Chapter XV

The Debate

Masoud Abbasi returned to the microphone.

"Ladies and gentlemen, we all know the United Nations had a mandate, but it failed as a neutral and independent global organization. It failed when it came to issues regarding the environment: reducing population growth, implementing pollution control, stopping unsustainable deforestation practises, creating and enforcing laws governing fishing and harvesting methods in international waters of our oceans. It failed because its financial operating needs depended entirely on the collection of membership fees. A large number of countries were always late with their payments; others never bothered to send a cheque at all to New York.

"Occasionally, even the USA would curtail their commitments, playing political games. Then, when the USA brought up their arrears and the paycheques for the delegates were once again secured, the sympathy swung over and they supported U.S. power-play policies. The members were strongly influenced by national interests and by lobbyists with pockets full of bribe money. The UN was a toothless giant that sent problems to committees and never did act on anything decisively; it deferred and referred, and eventually interest was lost because the problem had become old news and had been replaced by a brand new urgency.

"It failed to prevent or to stop military conflicts and because of its inability to act unilaterally, hundreds and hundreds of thousands were killed.

"The UN became the laughing stock of the world with scandal-ridden affairs. When the membership dues stopped coming in, it had to declare bankruptcy, and the chauffeur-driven limousines were repossessed one by one. The delegates received one-way tickets to return home to their countries and the employees of the UN received their last paycheques, but the paycheques were not honoured by the banks.

"The future of our planet and the future of humankind lies in our hands. We have outlined the severity of the situation and the need for immediate and decisive global changes. Here are some more of my revolutionary ideas for you to ponder over.

"You all know that we humans have the sad knowledge, the capability, and the physical inventory to kill all life on earth, including ourselves. But we lack the material capacity and the will to save all life on earth, often including ourselves. I believe there is absolutely no justified killing of people, no matter what Genghis Khan, Gaius Caligula, Oliver Cromwell, Maximilien Robespierre, Joseph Stalin, Adolf Hitler, Pol Pot, Idi Amin, Saddam Hussein, or G.W. Bush said, or any of the other mass-murderers of the world say.

"Oh, yes! There is self-defence! How do we best deal with this issue? So far there is enough justification to kill, so far there is enough justification to start the ultimate mass murder, commonly known as war. Sadly, not always is self-defence the true reason for starting a war because we can kill the truth and we can fabricate lies.

"We spend horrendous sums of our money on so-called defence budgets, on military equipment and installations, and we train a large number of our young people in the despicable art of killing. Why? Don't you think it is time that we humans grow up and wean ourselves from our ancient animal instincts, when the strongest and meanest killed his opponents, claimed the women, and became ruler until someone younger and stronger came along and killed him. I would like to put an end to this practise and explain my views on disarmament to you."

"Why don't you start with disarming your own countries of the ULIN?" quipped Oliver.

"I have no problem with that." Abbasi remained calm; he smiled and continued with his presentation.

"I have already indicated to you that the ULIN government is prepared to dismantle its entire nuclear power-generating facilities. Contrary to some beliefs, we do not have nuclear weapons. The inspectors of the International Atomic Energy Commission are welcome to search. They may enter our country at any time to do their work. We are also willing to take action in accordance with my following recommendations:

"We believe that an immediate 50% reduction of all military personnel in every country should be implemented. I would like to see further reductions in the future when the role of the military would change to a regional security force and to a first action response team during natural disasters.

"I further suggest that every country should destroy their entire inventory of weapons of mass destruction. 'Weapons of mass destruction' will be redefined to include all bombs, all grenades, all landmines, all missiles, and all automatic weapons. Military equipment and weapon manufacturers will have to close and forfeit their property and inventory to the government. These are some of my suggestions regarding disarmament.

"We need new and innovative approaches in many areas. Illegal drugs are a very serious problem and they cripple society in many parts of the world. I propose legalization of all illicit drugs and their availability in state-owned retail outlets. If they are sold at low enough prices, it will eliminate the current crime problem associated with them. It will not solve the addiction problem; this is a different issue and must be addressed separately by health professionals, not the arm of the law.

"I believe that current worldwide manufacturing capacity of consumer goods is at a sufficient level when combined with the vast inventories we currently carry. I am convinced that we have enough paper manufacturers in the world, that there are enough automobiles, airplanes, tractors, and lightbulb makers on the globe to cover and satisfy our needs, just to name a few.

"That's why I propose the creation of a global industrial watchdog committee, who will establish and impose firm environmental standards for all manufacturing facilities. It will also have the power to limit the uncontrolled growth of new factories or other industrial mega-projects.

"Will we have an unemployment problem? Of course, we will. The economic boom in construction and consumer goods will employ many; mandatory schooling will also need schools, teachers, and learning paraphernalia. I also propose a three-year conscripted vocational training period in combination with a work engagement for young adults in various fields at minimum wages. It could be in social and educational services, in medical care, in environmental restoration; it could be volunteer work in underdeveloped parts of the world, first aid and rescue, etc. This would take many young people off the unemployment roll, improve their skills and their education and become a stepping stone for a future vocation.

"Ladies and gentlemen, we want to build a global universal society where each person has the fundamental right to a decent living, where everyone is provided with adequate food, water, and shelter, where everyone is provided with universal medical care and education. The price is not cheap! Everyone has to forego some liberties, and everyone has to take on responsibilities for the whole of humankind, for our planet, for the ecology, for the environment, for the water and the air. There will be a need for some immediate resolutions."

There was light applause. Oliver looked over to Maxima Müller, who seemed to be concentrating on her notes.

"Now a few more of my radical ideas: Natural resources and their installations in oil, natural gas, mines, and forests will become the sole governance of the new global government. Airplanes will be phased out gradually and replaced with energy efficient airships. Most airports will be reduced in size or will be completely shut down. Large maritime transport and passenger ships will have to convert to a minimum of 50% solar power or the new high altitude wind-sail technology. The prices of crude oil will double in five years and again in 10 years in order to reduce its use when phasing in other energy systems. I am also in favour of a universal carbon tax."

The next speaker was Maxima Müller, the chancellor of the European Federation.

"I support the idea that global issues should be addressed by global representation, with the authority to act quickly, decisively, and effectively. I support, in general, a plan of arms reduction and the elimination of weapons of mass destruction. My definition for weapons of mass destruction is not quite as drastic as my Iranian friend is wishing for."

Oliver cringed. What was the broad just saying? She was calling him her friend? What the hell is happening?

"I further support the idea of humanitarian measures to achieve equality among all people. The idea of basic human rights and the guarantee of basic human services are intriguing. The idea of rewarding birth control with large bonuses has some merit. But how will we overcome the strong influence from the orthodox and the fanatical religious leaders?"

"I was thinking about that," said Abbasi. "Yes, yes, I was thinking about that. You, in the western hemisphere have laws, which despite the free speech guarantees make it illegal for holocaust-deniers to express their views. It is also illegal to spread hatred and discrimination against minorities. We can cover the fanatical and hate sermons with the same law and silence the loud and the screaming voices of extremists and religious agitators."

Oliver looked troubled. "Killing them, you mean? This will not work! These are serious human rights violations you're proposing. I think the plan presented by Mr. Abbasi is more of a childish fantasy and a pipe dream. Get back to reality, ladies and gentlemen. There are 200 or more nations out there who want a say in all this and a universal agreement is impossible; we all know that! Let's not kid ourselves. I know Israel and the USA will never give their consent to a demented idea like this. I am beginning to think that I'm wasting my time by joining a group of lunatics and fantasists!"

"Mr. Oliver, sit down please and listen very carefully!" said the Chinese president. "We invited you to this get-together out of courtesy and we hoped you would have left your arrogance back in America. Frankly, we do not need your support. We can make global decisions with or without you and we can make them for you. We were hoping for your cooperation and for your input of new ideas. If you want to stay for the remainder of these talks, keep in mind that we will not tolerate any more offending outbursts!"

"Do you mean you want to kick me out of this meeting?"

"It may happen if you don't mind your manners and behave respectfully."

Oliver was surprised and speechless for a moment. Then he quietly swallowed his pride and sat down, looking embarrassed like a reprimanded schoolboy.

There was a moment of quiet and everyone was looking expectantly at the American president to respond. He shrugged his shoulders and said, "The floor belongs to the chancellor of Europe, please excuse the interruption, madam."

Müller had remained standing on the elevated podium, waiting patiently for her turn to speak again. She switched the microphone back on and addressed her distinguished colleagues.

"As I said before the entertaining interlude, Europeans would generally support plans for global representation built on democratic principles. They would further support universal arms reduction and the controlled elimination of weapons of mass destruction. But Europeans will be extremely hard-pressed to accept any reduction of personal human rights, which they fought so hard for. These rights are firmly anchored in our society; they have become law and they have changed our way of life. Backscaling them now will be a giant step backwards for humankind!"

"That is exactly right, Frau Müller, we have to stop and go backwards. If we keep on going forward the way we are doing, there will be no stopping and we will fall off the cliff and plunge into annihilation! If we want to prevent the disastrous end, we have to galvanize all of humankind behind our ideas. We need everyone's cooperation and a combined and sincere will to succeed!" interjected Abbasi.

"We have to hear more particulars of these plans."

"Of course, of course! We will have a question period after the delegates make their presentations and declarations," responded Abbasi.

"Thank you, Mr. Abbasi. You all know that I am a German. We Germans are proud of a 2,000-year history of achievements, except for the 12 years of Nazi rule. In that short period of time, the worst human rights violations in the history of humankind took place. The main participants were German Nazis; the main victims were German Jews. Eastern Europe became the main venue of horrendous atrocities, when a rage of racial and religious cleansing swept through the nations like a destructive storm.

"The German name is forever tainted with blood and the acrid smoke from the chimneys of the crematoriums. It is hard to imagine that anything positive could possibly come out of the 12 years of Nazi terror, but it has. It has made the German people stronger in democracy, stronger in the advancement of human rights and in women rights issues. We also excel in the care and education of our children, in the care of our elderly, the sick, and the needy. It has made us tolerant to our global neighbours and the visible minorities in our own country. We look at the rest of the world from a different perspective now with eyes that have witnessed misery and murder, death and destruction.

"Germany has now become in many ways a role model for the rest of Europe and other nations. The good German attributes towards society and positive work ethics prevailed and surfaced in our new multicultural community. They are respect, responsibility and reliability, politeness and punctuality, diligence and dedication, correctness and clarity, accuracy and accountability. There are probably a few more. I can't think of any right now, but this will do. I hope we can instil these attributes into the new global government! What do you think of that?"

She stopped her speech and looked questioningly from one delegate to the next. They shrugged their shoulders and shuffled their feet uncomfortably.

"Ah, I was just kidding a bit." She laughed and continued. "What I wanted to say is that something good came out of something really bad for the Germans. I sincerely hope that something good is coming for humankind out of the bad situation on earth!"

They interrupted her with thunderous applause.

Then Abbasi stood up and said smiling, "I move your list of attributes to be adopted by the new global government."

"I believe with these 'prerequisites' in place, Europeans will be eager to join you and the rest of the world in this monumental task. Let's begin with the salvage operation to save humankind and our planet! Let's do it united! United we are stronger!"

Maxima Müller received the applause gracefully and then she moved back to her seat.

"Thank you Madame Chancellor for your supportive speech!"

Abbasi bowed in her direction and more applause followed.

"May I now present Senhora Isabella Elegante, the president of Brazil to you."

The strikingly beautiful woman slowly made her way to the podium. Her tasteful attire and her noble demeanour truly paid credit to her name.

"Your royal highness and distinguished guests! I am very honoured to be invited and included in this illustrious group of selected participants to this world-level meeting. Ladies and gentlemen, in the last century, humankind has drastically ravaged the surface of the earth and her protecting atmosphere and has entered the new millennium at top speed to continue and to increase its destructive ways. Brazil is no exception. The reckless slash-and-burn deforestation practises in the Amazon basin and the ruthless exploitation of rare and precious natural resources has been highly publicized, but to no avail.

"It all seems to have fallen on deaf ears! Like in many other parts of the world, uncontrolled population growth has created battalions of starving people who in their desperate quest for survival attack the jungle basically with their bare hands. They slash and burn and cultivate a small plot with only primitive tools. Here they begin to grow corn and vegetables, raise a few chickens and maybe even a pig. They will erect a pitiful excuse of a shelter and they will call it a home.

"Those are the lucky ones. In fact, the poor and unfortunate people do not realize that their relatively small and minor individual acts become a monstrosity of destruction, when multi-folded by the millions of their companions in misery around the globe. Their fires burn and smoulder, and when one extinguishes, two new ones will flare up. Yes, those are the lucky ones!

"Others will spend their lives in close vicinity of an urban garbage dump and will search daily for food scraps in the freshly dumped disposals from the rich and well-to-do. I see the children. I always see the emaciated little bodies with the big eyes, crying silently. The big eyes and the muted cries are unspoken accusations to society and to their parents. 'Why did you put me into this miserable world and why can't you look after me?' The parents don't know how to answer. They have no education, so they don't know any better. And for the most part, society turns a blind eye and does not like to be constantly reminded of the problem.

"Uncontrolled population growth and uncontrolled industrial production growth, driven by an insatiable consumer demand for goods, energy, services, transportation, etc., have led to uncontrolled emissions and discharges of toxins into air, water, and soil in such grand proportions that it is incomprehensible for anybody to grasp the full impact and to calculate the long-term damages. Climate change and global warming have become a reality. Extreme weather patterns are on the rise and have become daily occurrences somewhere on the planet, adding to the environmental damage with floods and droughts and wildfires.

"The protective ozone shield has big holes and ultraviolet rays penetrate easier through it; skin cancer is on the rise and the list of extinct species gets longer with every new daily entry.

"I fully agree that we have to stop our destructive practises, and

I fully agree that effective changes can only be achieved through controlled and targeted global action. A worldwide implementation of any binding regulation for fundamental change needs the proper authority. And I don't know of any better authority than a democratically elected global government to represent all of humankind.

"Now, I think it is time to examine democracy itself. We all know that in its present form it has many flaws. The modern over-regulated and constantly legally redefined western democracies have created an emerging society with an oversized appetite for dependency on government. Middle-class and the poor people are not asking for, not begging for, nor soliciting help and assistance any longer. They are now demanding it.

"They are demanding more and more services and handouts. They are demanding the full and prompt implementation of their new rights and privileges. They take and take and they forget to say thank you!

"Other democracies in other parts of the world, often in so-called developing or third world countries, have a much different society. Although, at first glance, we will find the same three categories of society—the poor, the middle-class and the rich—the demographics are so different. At a closer look you will discover there is no comparison between a poor person of a western democracy and a poor person of a developing or third world country. There is not even a resemblance. Human rights are not the issue. Food and water are the issue! The cold and wet weather and the leaky roof are the issue! Survival is the issue!

"At a closer look you will also discover there is a substantial difference between the middle-class of the western world and the rest of the world. You will find huge discrepancies of annual income for civil servants and for professionals, especially in areas of education and health. When it comes to the rich, there is no obvious difference. The rich are rich, no matter what country they live in.

"However, there is an area of despicable human trait that differs enormously between the two hemispheres, and that is corruption. Where the west has made successful inroads in this area for a considerable time already, we in Brazil are still struggling and are unable to get a proper handle on the situation. Every valiant effort is undermined; legislation is largely ignored and the legal system drags its feet. There is no collective will for change. Corruption is a deep-rooted way of life not only in my country, but in most of the poor democracies. Countries with a strong dictatorship, which could forcefully eradicate this practise, usually fail because there the dictator, his family, and his friends steal whatever they can lay their hands on.

"In Brazil, corrupt officials often hinder or sabotage many well-intended environmental initiatives by the government. They issue exploration permits for sensitive areas and collect a fee for that favour, as an example. Control and enforcement are very difficult in the immense and remote wilderness. So much for our problems!

"Now, I want to return to the issue of human rights and I want to share my thoughts with you. Ultra liberal interpretation by the judiciary in some countries has almost granted unlimited personal freedoms. But we just cannot accept a universal blanket guarantee of all human rights because there are limits to personal freedom in a society, there are also responsibilities and civic duties for every individual. It is not good enough to go and vote every two or four years and spend the rest of the time criticizing the government and sucking up the 'freebies'.

"The media has failed to serve in keeping up with main issues. It glorifies in publishing, ah, minor advances? I know, I should not have used this word, sorry. The media will report, for instance, when a mayor of a city did not attend the gay parade or when a police officer misused his authority. Truth be told: distractions! The true and important human rights issues are very seldom covered in the news. They are: equality among races and among males and females; the right to adequate food and water, clean air, and basic shelter; the right to free education; the right to free medical service; and individual human rights may see limitations in the future. I strongly believe in a woman's right over her body, but I object to her right to bear children in excessive numbers, and I object to her right to bear a child if she is mentally or physically incapable to care for the child. In this case, she does not have the right to put a burden on society. I also believe that in every conflict between an individual and society, the individual has to yield to society."

Oliver jumped up.

"Are you proposing the end of democracy with the reintroduction of these old and warmed-up ideas from communism, socialism, and even from nazism? Ladies and gentlemen, we all know what happened to communism and socialism, and we definitely know what happened to nazism. I implore you, let's not go back there! We've been there! It's a very dangerous road."

Elegante replied calmly: "We have bigger problems, much bigger problems, than haggling over some petty issue like who has the right to allow changes in the DNA of human sperm or eggs. We have a planet to rescue; we have to save and ensure the lives of eight billion people, eight billion brothers and sisters.

"We are not abandoning democracy, Mr. Oliver! On the contrary! We are re-examining democracy and we are looking for ways to improve democracy. There is a give-and-take in democracy. We cannot allow a continuous 'take' without receiving the 'give' in return. Look at what we have been experiencing with capitalism: take, take, take, and no give, give, give! We might have to circumcise the role of capitalism in the new democracy or cut its prick right off!"

Boisterous laughter and enthusiastic hand clapping erupted from the delegates, and Mr. Lin, the Chinese president, almost doubled over. He was laughing so hard.

Elegante smiled and continued.

"I never before lowered myself to the level of gutter language and vulgarity, but today I wanted to make a point, a strong statement. I wanted to get your full attention and I believe I succeeded. Ladies and gentlemen, please start to rethink the role of capitalism in a new global society!

"But we are moving away from the main issue of forming a global government. If we cannot agree on its implementation and if we vote to reject it, then any subsequent discussions and proposals are irrelevant. If the main issue of global government is defeated, we can all pack up and go home. Therefore, I am introducing a motion to conduct a vote as soon as possible!"

There was a short discussion and then acceptance of the motion. A clerk was called hastily to fetch the ballots from an adjacent room. He handed one ballot to each of the nine assembled delegates. The voting was conducted by secret ballot and it took only a few minutes. The clerk returned to collect the ballots, verified their validity, and then he declared unanimous approval.

Thunderous applause followed the announcement. Abbasi returned to the microphone.

"Thank you, ladies and gentlemen. This is the first step to a better world. It is the most important step because now we have a platform on which we shall build our future. This concludes the official program for the afternoon. We will meet again for dinner, and afterwards, we will reconvene here and continue our discussion. We are looking forward to your constructive input and your questions. I wish you all a pleasant afternoon!"

And with that, Abbasi left the room.

"Mr. Oliver, would you like to accompany me on a stroll through the palatial grounds? I need to stretch my legs, and I have the urgent need to clear my head with some fresh air," asked Müller.

"With pleasure, Madame," replied Oliver. "With absolute pleasure!"

They stepped outside and descended the marble stairs to a stone-paved courtyard. The bright sunshine and the fragrant-laden air were momentarily overwhelming. They stopped and scrambled for their sunglasses and inhaled the heavy exotic air deeply through their open mouths.

A uniformed servant was instantly at their side, enquiring about their wishes. When told, he suggested a half-hour walking tour and volunteered his services to guide the guests. They declined politely and asked for directions.

Less than a minute later, they reached a lush and overgrown wilderness, which again on closer observance revealed perfect grooming and intricate placement of flowering magnolia, rhodo-dendron, bougainvillea, hibiscus, and oleander. When they round-ed another bend of their path, they entered the rose garden and were immediately overpowered by the lovely fragrance.

"I have to stop and get my breathing under control," said Max-ima laughingly. "I just can't get enough of this heavenly scented oxygen into my lungs. Isn't it wonderful?"

"The enchanting royal rose garden," he said. They found a bench and sat down.

He sighed.

"I did not want to vote against the resolution and stir up more controversy. I knew right from the beginning that I was the odd man in this group. What difference would it have made if the out-come of the vote was eight to one or nine to zero? That's why I decided to stay with it, because deep in my heart and deep in my brain, I know that they are right and you are right. The only way to solve global problems is through a united and universal approach! That's what logic dictates and what my mind accepts! But on the other hand, I know that I will be paying a disservice to my country when I surrender a large part of our sovereignty. That is the part that hurts and it really hurts me very much. I am not a traitor. I am a proud American, and I love my country and my people. What makes me so miserable is that in order to do the right thing, I have to betray my people and my country and give up our freedom, our independence, and our individuality."

"Isn't it sometimes better to let go of certain possessions, rath-er than hanging on to them for too long and then have them taken away by brute force?"

"What exactly do you mean by that?"

"Over time we become accustomed to a variety of things, to certain people, to certain tangible objects, to certain ideals. When your child tells you it is leaving the family home to live on it's own, that hurts! But it hurts so much more when you lose your child in an accident or to a deadly disease. When you have to sell your house because you can't afford the mortgage payments and the upkeep anymore, it will hurt. But it hurts so much more when your house burns to the ground and you lose all your possessions. It hurts when your partner lies and cheats on you, but it hurts so much more when your partner dumps you, takes all your money, and leaves you alone, broke, and disillusioned.

"As a country and as a government, you will have similar problems. When the idea of a European Economic Union was first brought up, we all knew that every single country had to bring something to the negotiating table. None of the European countries was big enough and strong enough to compete on the world market alone. To become a successful economic power, we had to forego some of our liberties, some of our sovereignty. Our national identity changed, demographics changed, when we made way for a multicultural society.

"Look at what we gained in Europe—look at what we received in return! We are enjoying high living standards and a social support system unparalleled in this world. But the greatest accomplishment is the political stability in Europe. Except for the massacre in the Balkans, we have enjoyed peace in Europe since the Second World War-that's a long stretch! Unbelievable! When I look back now, it was all worth it, every damn bit of it!

"Mr. Oliver, please examine the proposal and your options closer; you will discover that you are not giving up total independence, you are not giving up total freedom, and you are definitely not giving up your individuality as Americans! There will be rewards for every human being on this earth, including Americans!"

After another lavish dinner they began to debate Sadikin's diverse proposals. Abbasi sensed a positive mood amongst his colleagues. He used the chance of surprise and put forward a bold motion to adopt Sadikin's plan for a universal government and his scale for representation in principle.

The distinguished world leaders were taken off guard for a brief moment; then they followed the formal procedure and they passed the motion unanimously.

Abbasi was delighted and continued to babble in his excitement, while the delegates regressed to assess the full impact of the approved resolution. They leaned back content; none of the delegates thought that they had made a mistake.

Abbasi pushed forward.

"We also have to make another decision today. We have to agree on a date or a time line for the first ever global elections."

"The enormity of such a grand and complex undertaking is just sinking in," said Oliver. "I am totally overwhelmed. Nothing of this magnitude and scale has ever been attempted before. Estimates for preparation time will be difficult to figure out, even for the experts. I don't think that we can pinpoint a fixed date tonight. What do you have in mind, Mr. Chairman, six months, twelve months, or two years?" he asked Abbasi.

"Ladies and gentlemen, as you all know, time is very precious and time is running out. We called this emergency meeting because we believe that humankind and our planet are in a grave situation and emergency measures are absolutely in order.

"We called this emergency meeting, because we have to act immediately and without delay. I personally would like to see national elections to be held in every country of our globe within the next three months to determine who to send as representatives to the global government. If some countries cannot execute this task in the given time, they may send their elected members at a later date. However, these late members will not be part of the early important decision-making and of the writing of the global constitution."

Maxima Mueller raised her hand and said, "I move that national elections to be held within the next six months. I believe this is a more realistic time frame."

The motion was passed unanimously. Abbasi was pleased and lauded the quick decision of his distinguished audience. Then he continued to outline the importance of reforming democracy, and he also emphasized the significance of independent candidates, the abolition of political parties and the abolition of lobbing tactics.

He talked at great length about the destructive influence of capitalism on world cultures and the decadent lifestyles in the Western

World. He talked about the evils of stress and the rat race, where a throw-away society was already destined and programmed to pursue the unnatural life of maximized consumerism.

A servant approached him with an urgent message and interrupted his flamboyant speech. Abbasi was obviously annoyed, but when he read the text, he began to smile.

"I am just being informed that our secret meeting is not a secret anymore. The international news media has arrived at Muscat Airport in droves, and more chartered flights are underway and scheduled to arrive either tonight or early in the morning.

"Ladies and gentlemen, we have to face the press tomorrow. There is no way around that! I suggest that we prepare a joined and signed communiqué outlining the passed resolutions of this illustrious group. It should also contain the "Principle Ideas and Goals of a Global Government," which include: fundamental rights and equality for all humans; food and water for everyone; shelter for everyone; free education for everyone; free health care for everyone; universal birth control; universal currency and bank reform; English as universal language; and abolition of weapons of mass destruction."

A frenzied discussion started after this announcement and lasted well until midnight. Even a late break with snacks and refreshments did not seem to slow their activity.

Abbasi rose again.

"May I offer one more suggestion before we retire for the night? We already deviated once from the protocol today. I hope you will allow me to do it a second time. I have prepared special suggestion ballots for the location of the global parliament. Each voting member may mark down four cities of their choice in random order. The nominations will be added up tonight and the four most popular choices among us will be announced for tomorrow's final vote. May I see a show of hands if you want me to proceed?"

Abbasi counted eight hands plus his own. The clerk came in and handed out the ballots and voting commenced in complete silence and concentration. It took quite a while. The first two selections were written down fairly fast, but then, the hand went up and cradled the chin and wrinkles appeared on the foreheads. Finally, almost 30 minutes later, Mr. Khulani, the president of South Africa, signalled he was ready.

The clerk collected the ballots and returned 10 minutes later with a prepared list:

Geneva	6 nominations
Singapore	4
Alexandria	3
Vienna	3
Cape Town	3
Baghdad	3

And he kept reading the remainder of the results.

"I beg to be corrected; tomorrow we will choose one city out of six nominations. Very interesting! I wish you all a good night!" And with that Abbasi left the room.

Chapter XVI

Obesity Explained

Angelika is back. She is fussing about the cushion in the back of my wheelchair.

"Are you comfortable now, my dear?" she enquires cheerfully.

I nod my head dreamily.

"Oh, we are a bit tired again, aren't we?" she says.

"I don't know about you, but I am always tired," I say grumpily. I hate it when she calls me, 'my dear'!

"I am never tired because I am young and vital." She smiles at me and caresses my cheek with the back of her hand.

"I hate you!" I groan.

"No, you don't! You love me, Ed, remember?" And she giggles like a little girl.

Vlado disrupts the flirtatious moment and blurts out loud: "I finally have it figured out why there are so many fat people in this world."

"Oh?" I look at him with provoked interest.

"It's an epidemic, I tell you. The majority of people is grossly overweight and the culprit is the car," he states matter-of-factly.

"I am not overweight. I ride a bicycle," chirps Angelika.

"Okay, you are partially right. People drive cars and do not walk as much as they used to," I agree. "But there are many other causes for obesity; lack of exercise is just one of them."

"I am not talking about exercise, I am talking about the fuel cars and trucks and planes and ships are burning. You see, we take the oil out of the ground and burn it up or make tires and plastics from it, and we think that's the end of it. That's where we make the big mistake. It is not the end of the process. The law of physics states that energy cannot be lost or destroyed. It can only be changed into some other form. You see what I mean? It accumulates in people as fat. Imagine seven billion overweight people with an estimated average of 20 kilos of blubber that will go back into the ground and in 150 million years, presto, we will have new crude oil. How many barrels is that? We do not need dinosaurs anymore—just fat people, fat pigs and cows. Hell, we even have fat turkeys and chickens sitting in row after row, stacked on multiple levels and they shit on their fellow creatures below them, day in and day out. Only the birds on the top stay clean. Oh, what a messy world we live in!" He sighs.

"You are insane," I say.

"No, no, just simple logic! Look, the energy wants to get back into the ground, where it belongs to be stored and not in the air. There is too much energy in the air and it is converted into fat, 24/7, day in and day out. We inhale the fat, animals and plants inhale it too and we eat them. A few grams of fat every day and the grams become kilos. That's how it works. It is nature's revenge on us. We are stealing oil from the ground deep below us and nature is punishing us, using the simple rule of physics! That's how it works, the fat is getting back into the ground!" he repeats.

"This is stupid." I am annoyed. "It is not what we inhale that makes us overweight; it is a combination of lack of exercise and the rich, sweet food we eat and drink, which are responsible for the lifestyle changes of our affluent society in recent decades. Our overindulgence in salt and alcohol or other stimulants and our total intolerance for hunger and fasting are also big contributors to obesity. Fasting is historically known to be a body cleanser and some religions have prescribed rituals and times of abstinence for it. In our modern world, it is not fashionable. Among the poor and the disenfranchised it is called hunger. It is not prescribed and it is not fashionable for them; it is a sad reality."

Vlado is undeterred and continues: "You know, they were gonna build flying cars at one time, but they never did. You know why? I tell you why, because people who have the money to buy a flying car are too darn fat and too darn heavy! That's why aeromobiles never took off, because people are too darn heavy! They can't make 'em fly economically! It is just too expensive!

"I have an idea. I have lots of ideas. What do you think of this? Someone should figure out how to turn the 20 kilo of excessive fat we are carrying around into energy to fuel our very own space car, wouldn't that be something! Imagine you could operate on your own useless fat and become healthier to boot. I guess the air would be full of vehicles then, buzzing around like crazy."

"I prefer to keep the traffic on the ground, the way it has been for a long time," I say.

"Tell me, if the old ways were so good, why then did people die so young? Just go to the cemetery in Barkerville and read the inscriptions on the head stones. I dare you to find anybody over 50 years of age, when they kicked the bucket," counters Vlado.

Now I am really becoming frustrated, and I raise my voice. "For crying out loud, this has nothing to do with obesity! You change the subject faster than a whore changes her panties!"

Vlado laughs and laughs. "That is so funny! I haven't heard it for a long time!" And again, the built-up tension is deflating once more.

Angelika returns. "What would you like for your birthday, sweetheart?" she purrs seductively and leans over.

I am getting a good look of her proudly protruding bosom and sigh and I say mischievously: "It's not what you think! It's not lust or carnal desire this time, just plain hunger and thirst. I want two thick slices of fried bacon and a glass of ice-cold Coca Cola! Oh, and I want to smell the bacon when you fry it! Take me to the kitchen, please."

She is shaking her beautiful head fiercely. "Sorry Ed, those are all no-nos. I have to confer with Jason about this." And off she goes.

"Dream on, Herr Kamerad, no cola for you! Coca Cola and Pepsi

Cola are out of business, my friend. They went broke, don't you remember? I am beginning to worry about you."

Vlado is right. The former darlings and undisputed leaders of the soft drink industry had lost a multibillion-dollar class-action lawsuit last year. The harsh verdict crippled both companies financially and forced them into insolvency. The lawyers got rich, of course, and many made enough money to retire after the trial. There must have been a few thousand of them, lawyers from every country in the world where Coke and Pepsi was consumed, even Mongolia. It was the largest international trial ever and it lasted for almost 10 years.

A similar fate befell the fast food giants. Their entanglement in multiple different class-action court challenges caused their blue stocks to tumble down on Wall Street to worthless penny issues. The soda pop giants and the cholesterol giants fell from grace. They were pushed from their high pedestals and were crushed by public anger! The only stable sections of that industry were the pizza empires, which remain on solid financial foundation with an increased consumer appetite.

But not all is lost for hamburger lovers. Now, if you want to eat a decent hamburger, you will find it at the new Daring-to-Eat restaurants. Your first time order is extremely expensive and will cost you $795. It includes a mandatory legal appetizer, a fingerprinting and photo session, receiving legal counselling from an independent source, and then the signing of a waiver in the presence of two witnesses and the company lawyer. After two solid hours of starving, of giving up your legal rights, your money and almost your hope, a pretty smiling waitress will bring you the mouthwatering reward. While you are devouring this calorie and cholesterol laden delicacy, you smile, because now you are accepted into this exclusive club and next week you will receive your plastic membership card. Then you can come back and order another one of this fine specimen for only $45 with a load of yummy, greasy French fries and all the ketchup and gravy you want.

"Do you have a membership card for the new hamburger chain?" I ask.

"Are you insane? Waste my good money on junk food? Besides, I have to look after my girlish figure, you know, and I don't want to add to that stockpile of crude oil in 150 million years from now." He laughs.

Suddenly my wheelchair is in motion and I am frantically grabbing my armrests for support. Now, I can hear Angelika's voice over the intercom.

"Taking you to the kitchen, my dear! Come and get it!"

My short frightening moment turns to joyous anticipation.

"Bacon, bacon, bacon! Tocino, tocino, tocino! Slanina, slanina, slanina!" I am yelling excitedly as Angelika manoeuvres me with her remote control into the kitchen.

"Calm down, calm down! What a silly childish outburst! What are you babbling about anyway?"

"Bacon in Spanish and in Polish. Isn't it slanina what they call bacon in Ukrainian? There are lots of similarities between the Polish and Ukrainian languages," I tell her.

"With bacon the similarity with Polish ends. The Ukrainians adopted the English version and they call it bakon!" she lectures me.

It smells so heavenly in the kitchen. Angelika brings over a plate with the fried bacon slices and places it in front of me on the built-in tray of my wheelchair.

"Here we go! Enjoy, my dear! I am still upset that you prefer the greasy bacon over me, when you could have had me—all of me!" she pouts seductively.

I can't wait any longer. Without a reply I attack the bacon with fork and knife and smack my lips. It's delicious and I savour every morsel of it. Jason brings an ice-cold Coca Cola for me and I take a long refreshing drink right from the can. I smack my lips again.

"Thank you, guys! That was a wonderful treat. The bacon was fried just perfectly, not too crisp and not undercooked, just the way I like it."

"We are trying to please," beams Jason.

"We? What is it with the We? What's going on between the both of you? Are we getting a bit too cozy? You can't fool an old guy like me, I see things and notice the signs, and I know that 'we' are very much in love!"

Angelika is trying to protest, but I lift both of my arms to stop her gibberish and she looks at me bewildered and stunned.

"But it is true!" she stammers. "I love you, Ed, and I wish I had a father like you!"

She has tears in her pretty eyes and in a choking voice I reply, "Thank you, Angelika! You are one of a kind; you are a very special lady! I will cherish these wonderful words until I die!"

There is a moment of awkward silence and then Jason clears his throat and clumsily restarts the conversation.

"I just want to let you know that I took a quick inventory of your private stock. You have 21 cans of Coca Cola left."

"Don't tell Vlado, because I don't like to share my Coca Cola with anybody—not even with him!" I instruct Jason and lean back, momentarily at ease.

Chapter XVII

Separation

The volcanic activity in Puget Sound had slowed after the first week. Red hot magma was catapulted high into the sky in the early days of the eruption. Now it had lost its velocity and spewed only a few metres high. During the day a massive cloud of escaping steam was visible for miles, and steam from the steady flow of lava engulfed the newly created landmass. But during the darkness of the night, the new island appeared to glow through the obscuring mist and the erupting magma sent off spectacular sights of fireworks accompanied by showers of exploding sparks.

The roar that accompanied the initial outbreak had been replaced by an occasional rumble. There were still mild aftershocks registered, but the average person did not notice them. The waters in closer vicinity to the new island had cooled and were not boiling anymore. Fewer dead fish were floating around now and no more human or animal corpses were spotted. The ones that did not get picked up during the recovery operation had sunk to the bottom of the ocean.

The ocean waters were not angry any longer; the terrible tsunamis retracted after they claimed so many lives and after they inflicted so much horrific damage. The seas calmed down for a short respite and it felt like the world was holding its breath. Then it exhaled and nasty autumn storms were streaking over the wide expanse of the Pacific, whipping up the calm waters and crowning every single wave with fresh white froth.

After their dramatic rescue and the exhausting session with the news media, Toby and Lori were totally bushed. They collapsed on the fold-up beds in the shelter and succumbed to a deep and lengthy sleep.

Toby was the first to wake up, almost a full day later. He jumped from his cot and rubbed his eyes. When he opened them fully, he was astounded by the bizarre and unfamiliar surroundings. In the dim light, he could see hundreds of people sleeping and snoring in row after row of folded down beds in very close proximity of each other in this super-sized tent.

He rubbed his eyes again and then he spotted Lori and he focused on her. She was so pretty, blowing little puffs of exhaling air from her half-parted lips. Lips he remembered, full and cherry-red and sensuous, lips he had kissed and lips which had responded so eagerly, so sweet and so hot.

The terrible recent events came back to him slowly. And he relived them first in slow motion. Then the slow motion increased and changed over to high speed. The pictures of destruction, of escaping, of running, pushing, and shoving flew by, and the pictures of love making and the daring rescue by the president came back in a flash.

Toby knew it wouldn't take long. Somebody would recognize him after watching the evening news. He and Lori and the president made the top news story of the day. Millions were following the broadcast on their television sets and their ISS pads last night, and this morning it was back on again. That's for sure!

They were instant celebrities, he and Lori, and he knew the FBI had also been watching. Maybe he was lucky and they would not remember a wanted criminal from 10 years ago. His file must be buried in the archives, and the archives were invisible, hidden in a computer bank. But just one touch on the keyboard could access those archives and some swift finger work could bring up his profile and his past.

Toby became increasingly agitated and stressed. He knew he had to leave this place, the sooner the better. Thinking of 'sooner' scared him because it meant now! One last look at Lori, he blew a kiss and she opened her eyes.

"Where you going, love of my life?" she whispered and smiled.

"Outside, I have to find a bathroom," he answered in a low voice, not to wake any more people.

"I'll come with you!" She jumped from her cot and grabbed her jacket. They had both slept fully clothed and once they got outside, the cold damp air made them shiver.

"Meet you at the cookhouse," he said and pointed in the direction of a long line of people.

She found him in the line, and he almost did not recognize her when she tugged at his arm. She was all bundled up. Her beautiful red hair was completely hidden under the large hood of her jacket. She had tightened the strings of her hoodie and only her cold nose and her red mouth were visible.

"What's gotten into you this morning? You never gave me a kiss!" she complained. She got on her tiptoes and offered her lips to him. He kissed her lightly, just brushing her lips, without an embrace and without passion.

"Something is bothering you," she determined. "You want to talk about it?"

"Not now," he answered grudgingly. "Let's get something to eat first and find a bit of a private place where we can talk."

"That serious?"

"Yes, that serious."

It was cold and damp and windy, really ugly weather. They lifted their feet, they moved their legs, and shifted their weight from one side to the other. They exercised their upper bodies and swung their arms around in a flailing motion just to stay warm. It looked quite dangerous, but they did not hit each other or anybody else. Finally, they received a steaming bowl of nourishing hot oatmeal.

"This is great! Very delicious! It ain't the Hilton, but do you think the Hilton can cook better oatmeal than this?" asked Toby.

They moved away from the crowd and found a secluded spot with a picnic table and discovered that the emergency shelter was set up in the campground of a state park. It was an ideal location. Here was enough space to shelter thousands of people.

"Now tell me, what's eating you, mister?" she demanded.

He sighed.

"This is not easy. I have been an accessory to some serious crimes a long time ago. I was blackmailed and I was forced to commit some despicable acts by a ruthless international crime syndicate that was holding my sister captive and murdered her. When I escaped, I killed our worst tormenter. I've been on the run ever since. I believe the FBI has a thick file on me and is still looking for me, even today, 10 years after the fact. Yesterday's media circus exposed me to the entire country and beyond. Somebody will remember my face and somebody will link me to the past and the hunt will be on again."

She sat there with her mouth open and stared at him with that incredulous look in her eyes.

"No, you are not going to get rid of me that easily. Who do you think I am? A one-night stand? You are the father of my child! Face up to your responsibilities and don't chicken out now. It's a fantastic story, I give you that! When did you dream this up? During your sleep, last night?"

"Lori, please listen to me. I love you very much, and I love you with all my heart. Every word I just told you is the truth, the absolute truth. You must believe me. Our future life together is in jeopardy and my life is in danger. We have to separate right here and right now, and I have to go underground. We cannot have any contact. The FBI will bug your phone and your body. They are ruthless in their pursuit; expect the impossible and the unimaginable, and it will likely happen. They are bloodhounds! They will drug you and they will hypnotize you to extract information. They are not allowed to physically torture you, but there are no limitations on mental torture."

"You're not making this up?" she asked in a squeaky voice. She looked at him through tears. Searching for his eyes, she already knew the answer before he could shake his head.

"What are we going to do?" she sobbed.

"Can you stay with your mother for awhile?"

"I don't know if she is still alive," she wailed.

He handed her his ISS pad.

"Please, call her now!"

"I have my own phone," she replied and started dialling her mother's number and to her surprise she could hear a ringing tone, and then her mother answered. Lori was overjoyed and told her about her ordeal, she mentioned Toby, but her mother interrupted. She had watched the news, and she had seen her daughter and Toby on TV and the president, of course.

"Try to get out of that shelter as soon as you can, my darling. Come and stay with me. I'm not sure if I can accommodate Toby, though," her mother said.

"Thank you, Mom. I will see you soon. Toby will not come with me. He is joining the rescue teams."

"How did you know that I want to join the rescue teams?' he asked a bit bewildered, and before she could answer him, a loudspeaker interrupted her with a public announcement.

"Good afternoon. I hope everybody had a comfortable sleep. The cook shack is open now, so why don't you wander over there and get a bowl of hot oatmeal and a steaming coup of coffee? After you had your breakfast, please report to the stationmaster in Pavilion #1, if you are uninjured and physically sound and fit. Seniors, mothers and children, injured, disabled, and sick people please return to your stations and wait for help and care. You will be looked after soon."

Toby looked at Lori.

"You may have difficulties leaving this place today and getting to your parents," said Toby.

"Why?"

"Because you are healthy and you are fit. They will recruit you for a rescue team."

"No, they won't. I am pregnant, you know," she quipped.

"That might work. Great idea! Listen Lori, we have to separate now. We should not even meet the stationmaster together. It's very likely he will recognize us. You go ahead and leave your hoodie on, but before you leave, let's switch phones. I think we can use them for about four days, then you destroy my phone, and I will destroy your phone. I cannot talk to you, because they have my voice print. I'll have your parent's number and I'll send a message to you from inconspicuous sources and sign out with Jill and a happy face, when everything is okay. If I mention the word coffee, then I am in trouble. Just sit tight and don't reply."

She looked at him again with those incredulous sad eyes and said, "Toby, I'll never stop loving you. I will wait for your return! When the time is right, please come back to me and to your son!" She jumped up, kissed and hugged him, and then she ran to Pavilion #1.

Toby joined the line-up 20 minutes later and when he entered the pavilion of the stationmaster, there was no sign of Lori.

"Hey, I saw you on TV! Yeah, with that girl the president saved yesterday, right? Toby, isn't it?"

"Actually, the news people got it all wrong. It is Tony—Anthony," he replied.

"If I remember right, you have a Ukrainian name. What was it again?"

"The news people mis-spelled that one, as well. My last name is Szwasdelski."

"Easy to make a mistake," laughed the stationmaster. "Okay, what are your qualifications? Have you had any special training in search and rescue, first-aid courses and the like?"

"I am a nurse," replied Toby.

The stationmaster looked him over. "I always figured that nurses looked much prettier than you."

"Not funny, sir!"

Toby received a name tag, it read 'TONY S. Medical'.

He was in a boat with at least 15 other guys and two women and he did not know where it was taking them. The landscape seemed re-arranged, foreign, and alien; nothing looked even remotely familiar to him.

The skipper finally told them that they were headed to a remote northern island community, which no one had been able to make contact with after the disaster. He said that he was completely at the mercy of his instruments, like the forward sonar warning system, which could detect underwater obstructions and shallows up to 500 metres ahead of them. He also had other modern gadgets, but he still relied on his radar and he fully trusted his GPS, because some islands and some landmarks had entirely vanished.

"Right now, right here, there should be an island. We are actually on top of the darn island. Can you imagine that? No, no, no! Nobody can! It is so fucking scary! But we have to keep a cool head and trust the instruments. On a normal day, there would be hundreds of boats out here, today there is only us. That alone is eerie enough in itself."

"I hope the island we are looking for is still there, and I hope we will find a whole bunch of survivors," said somebody.

"We will know in less than one hour," replied the skipper, and he carefully moved along at a safe speed.

They watched the island emerge out of the mist, and soon after, they spotted a fire on shore. Then they saw the first survivors, waving bright fluorescent objects above their heads. The lower lying area of the native fishing village was totally destroyed and every building was turned into rubble. The fishermen had their boats tied up to wooden docks in the small sheltered cove, but it had not been sheltered well enough. The monster tsunami had pushed the boats and the wooden docks way up the hillside, and then it sucked most of them back into the ocean, and with them went the village diesel generator. It was resting now on the bottom of the sea somewhere.

The skipper slowed down and entered the cove. He nudged the boat very cautiously forward until it was no longer safe to go any further. He dropped anchor and deployed the two rubber rafts, the boat was carrying. Three people climbed in each of the rafts. Toby was in the first Zodiak.

"The injured people are in the church," somebody said when they clambered ashore.

Toby had noticed the small wooden church perched on a hillside high enough to be spared by the monster tsunami. It had been abandoned for almost 20 years, after the elders voted not to replace the catholic priest who was removed from their village in shame and disgrace. The wooden pews were the next things to go, right after the priest left the town. The locals vented their anger and their outrage over the dismissed priest by chopping the pews into kindling. Can't get any drier wood than that! Some considered it good therapy, others wanted to go further and burn down the church, but cooler heads prevailed. They were also somewhat scared and superstitious, fearing the Almighty's wrath if they destroyed His house.

"It is a solid building, it will be good for something, and it is still the House of God. If someone wants to pray and to worship, it is the right place to go to."

Toby grabbed the medical kit and rushed towards the small church, not looking behind, if anyone was following him. The rubble-strewn basin was impossible to cross. It stopped him for a second and he broke to the right to circumvent the area and then he forged ahead again.

A little girl opened the door before he reached it.

"Are you coming to help my mummy? My mummy is very sick, you know," she said.

"Yes, I will try to help your mummy."

She led him inside, and he had to adjust his eyes to the semi-darkness. Two women quietly stood up when he approached the little girl's mother. Her hip was a mess. He could see that. She probably had multiple fractures in her right hip and possible fractures in her upper leg. The scrapes and wounds to her face and to her arm, however, were only superficial. In the meantime, the female nurse and one of the first-aid attendants had caught up to him. He instructed the first-aid man to clean the wounds and the abrasions. The nurse and he proceeded to check over the rest of the injured patients. They counted 27 in total; one of them was deceased already. They also determined that two additional patients needed to be hospitalized and airlifted from here.

"Will my mummy be okay?" asked the little girl.

"Yes, she will be fine, but she has to get to a hospital soon. Let's hope a helicopter will come tomorrow. They can't make it today; they are really busy today."

"I will pray for a helicopter to come very, very soon!"

The stationmaster had done a terrific job in selecting this team. Each member was highly qualified and trained in various useful skills and expertise. By the end of the day, a kitchen-tent was set up and hot meals were prepared in it. Six more tents went up with fold-up cots, securing shelter for the night. They had brought two generators with them and schlepped the small one all the way to the church and hooked up lighting in there. The larger unit stayed down at the base, providing light and power to the cook-shack and the other tents.

Communication to the mainland rescue centre in Bellingham was also established and Toby had to seek medical advice several times during the night, when the conditions of the patients in the church worsened. He was particularly worried about the mother of the little girl, whose temperature shot up, and her breathing became difficult and labour-some. She was gasping for air one minute and then she relaxed and drifted off into unconsciousness, just to come back a few minutes later and repeat the same scenario. He administered oxygen, but it did not change the cycle. The other two severe cases were of further concern,; their situations were grave and he had the female nurse and the first-aid man watching them.

The little girl did not leave his side and stayed with him almost until midnight, and then finally overcome by fatigue, she curled up on the floor by her mummy's bed and fell asleep. Toby carried her over to a portable bed. He stayed up all night.

By morning, the whole place was set in heavy fog. One couldn't see further than a hand's width away. The early risers scrambled about, bumping into things and each other, just trying to find a private place to relieve themselves. Somebody started the big generator and the cook-shack lit up dimly, enough to provide a bit of orientation to the temporary lost.

The weather situation in Bellingham was the same. A heavy fog blanketed the entire Pacific North Coast, from places like Victoria to Vancouver, to Abbotsford and Bellingham, and south all along the Washington coast as far as Northern Oregon.

"All scheduled flights and all emergency flights are cancelled for this morning. Check with us again by lunchtime; hopefully the situation has changed by then."

The situation did not change by lunchtime or the afternoon, and by evening it was worse than it had been in the morning. Toby was heartbroken. Overnight he had lost a patient and he sent for a body bag this morning. The little girl was back at his side. He took her to the cook-shack for breakfast; it was quite a harrowing trip to get down there. The only sure guide was the dim light of the tent, but many obstacles blocked their way and it was quite a dangerous undertaking. Pancakes with syrup were on the menu this morning, plus hot coffee and hot chocolate. They were both hungry and filled up their plates and devoured their meals.

"Why didn't God listen to my prayer and send a helicopter this morning?" asked the little girl.

"I can't answer that," said Toby. "Only God himself can answer your question."

"Will he ever talk to me? He never talked to me before, never. I don't even know his voice because I never, ever heard him talk." And then she started to cry. "If God won't help my mummy and the helicopter can't come today, will my mummy die?"

Toby brushed the tears out of his own eyes. Since yesterday's initial examination and early diagnosis, he knew now that her mother had either internal injuries or serious head trauma. Whatever it was, she needed to be in a hospital and the visit was already overdue.

"Your mummy is very, very sick. We are still hoping for the fog to lift, so that a helicopter can come and take her to the hospital."

Light rain began to drizzle and the thick fog did not want to clear out. It stayed miserable like that for the entire day, the next night, and persisted even into the following day. They didn't get the break in the weather they had hoped for, and they didn't get the lucky break they had wished and prayed for either. The little girl's mummy died during the night in her sleep.

"Now I am all alone. I have no mummy and no daddy anymore," she told him in her sad voice, and the accusing look in her eyes made him feel guilty. Toby was totally devastated. There were no hallelujahs heard from the small church above and nobody at the base could hear the muffled cries of the little girl.

The grief counsellor, who had come with the boat and was a member of the rescue team, spent more time with Toby and the little girl, than with any other of the original victims on this island. Other consolation came from Lori's steady flow of short messages, always filled with hugs and kisses and the affirmation of her unwavering love. She had safely arrived at her parents' house.

On the third morning, the fog and the rain miraculously disappeared. The temperature had dropped, and a blue sky and bright sunshine greeted the late risers with the promise of a beautiful day. Toby left the island on the first helicopter with two patients, the only survivor of the three critically wounded, and a young boy who had developed signs of appendicitis over night.

Bellingham rescue headquarters was a busy place, a madhouse of activity. Toby had no time to himself to reflect on the dramatic events of the past four days. He was rushed to the dispatching centre, and 15 minutes later, he had his marching orders. He was assigned to meet an arriving Filipino search and rescue crew at the airport in less than an hour.

"Your job is to help them get set up and coordinate with headquarters. You are the man in charge. There is unbelievable damage and loss of life in the Fraser River Delta on both sides of the border. You report directly to Charlie. Here is his number! Good luck!"

"But I don't speak Filipino, not a single word!" protested Toby.

"You will learn fast, amigo," laughed the dispatcher and sent him on his way.

Chapter XVIII

At The Filipino Rescue Centre

It was much easier than he imagined. The Filipinos spoke Spanish and English, and Toby was fluent in both languages. Communication with the new team was not a problem. He had three four-wheel drive pickup trucks and two quads (ATVs) at his disposal. He arranged to transport them further west, closer to the disaster area, and within a few hours, they had set up an operational and functional rescue depot.

He checked in with Charlie and received praise for the smooth transition.

"Two miles southwest, at the end of Boundary Road, you will find Timothy and his boat. He is waiting for you guys. Punch the coordinates into your GPS.

"We had a piece of large equipment working in that area yesterday. I hope Boundary Road is cleared well enough, so that you can get through. Weather conditions are excellent, put a couple of people into the boat and have them search the shorelines of the river. Let some of them ride around in the pick-up trucks and the quads, and the rest can get out on foot and comb the neighbourhood for survivors and for bodies."

The intentions were high-minded, but there was not enough daylight left to accomplish anything significant. Instead it gave them a chance to familiarize themselves with the terrain and the lay of the land. The Filipinos had already seen the enormity of the destruction from the air before their plane touched down at the airport. Plans and strategies for the following day were discussed, while everyone was hugging a hot coffee mug.

The two crew members assigned to Timothy's boat hadn't returned yet. Efforts to contact them failed. Toby was becoming quite concerned, but he tried to conceal his nervousness. It was pitch dark when he finally spotted a bouncing headlight in the distance, and a few minutes later, the quad pulled up.

Fermin jumped off the vehicle and yelled, "Urgencia, Urgencia! This kid is in very bad shape!"

It only took seconds to lower the unconscious body on a stretcher and rush him over to the medical tent. The three Filipino doctors sprang into action, attempting to save the young man's life.

Meanwhile Fermin told them how he had spotted the injured man. "Just a reflection in the thickets on shore, probably from his wristwatch, and then I saw something yellow. That looked odd and out of place. It was his shirt. He was alive, but he was too weak to move and wave his arms." He paused. "We have to go back and get Timothy and my partner."

The doctors worked wonders overnight and successfully stabilized the young man. This was welcoming news first thing in the morning. Plans and strategies from the night before were changed after the patient revealed there were more stranded people in the area. A dog handler and a search dog were added to Timothy's boat crew from yesterday, and before they headed out, their communication devices were double-checked.

"We don't need a screw up like yesterday!" grumbled Toby.

He dispatched the other three search dog teams and the rest of the available men and women. Only a skeleton crew was left behind, the medical and the kitchen staff, a dispatcher, and a communication specialist.

Shortly before 10:00, the PA system came alive, and then they heard Fermin's frantic voice: "Urgencia, Urgencia! We have found many human bodies. Don't know. Most are dead, some are still alive, but not for long. Very bad situation. We need help, very much help! Please, tell me what you will do."

"Give me your coordinates or your GPS location code. I'll try to get a helicopter to you. Do you have an approximate body count?"

"There is more than 50, I am sure. Maybe even a 100, I don't know."

"Okay, I am coming in. Please send Timothy back to the checkpoint to pick me up," said Toby.

He asked one of the doctors and two of the kitchen staff to accompany him. They agreed and climbed into the only pick-up truck left at the camp and raced towards the end of Boundary Road. Timothy was already there waiting for them.

His jet boat took off with a deafening roar and accelerated like a rocket. The scared passengers were hanging on for dear life. Within minutes, they reached their destination and disembarked a bit unsteady on wobbly legs.

Timothy led them through the thick bush to an open field. It was a grisly sight. Part of the field was still submerged in stale brackish water. Dead corpses everywhere, floating in the shallows or deposited on the muddy shores left by the receding waters and on the higher strip of bush separating it from the river. Then the pesky ear-splitting and high-pitched sound of the birds overwhelmed them. They covered their ears. Seagulls, ravens, crows, and eagles in great numbers were picking at the dead bodies in a virtual feeding frenzy, trying to protect their tiny individual food claims with their aggressive cries.

Fermin was waving his arms and called Toby on his two-way, which actually was a multi-way and recording unit all in one. It connected every member of the Filipino team instantly.

"Bring some stretchers, please and hurry!"

"How many do you need?"

"The many as you can carry, man, and hurry!"

They rushed over to Fermin with four stretchers. He was excited; it was quite obvious.

"So, you saw all the dead bodies, yes? But here are the ones still alive, clinging to their lives. Everyone is an urgencia. I counted over 20 who are still breathing; it's amazing! Yes? You get helicopter?"

"No, no helicopter. They are all busy. There are not enough helicopters in the whole darn world to help every emergency here on the west coast. We have to carry the victims on stretchers to the boat, ferry them to the Boundary Road checkpoint and rush them to our hospital tent by pickup truck or quad, whatever is available. I am calling the other search teams back to assist us in this rescue operation."

The medical doctor went back with Timothy and the first two stretchers of patients. It took 45 minutes for the boat to return and more empty stretchers were on board, which was a good thing. Because the last two stretchers were already loaded with patients and waiting on shore for transport.

From then on it went like clockwork, like a well-oiled machine. The stretchers were loaded and carried to the checkpoint. Timothy took now four of them at a time, two lengthwise and side-by-side in the boat, the other two precariously balanced and strapped down opposite on top of both sides of the small vessel. It slowed him down, but he was back in good time, just in under 60 minutes. The clockwork continued.

Toby walked back to the dead on the muddy shore and looked again at the scene of devastation. He tried to scare off the belligerent birds, but they did not want to give up ground without protest. Toby screamed louder and ran towards them, and eventually they did move further away, to a safer distance.

He started to count the bodies and his wandering eyes became blurry. Oh, my God, there were so many, over 200 for sure. He contacted Charlie at headquarters and updated him on the current rescue operation and he also reported the gruesome find of decaying bodies.

"I'll get back to you on the recovery operation, Toby. As soon, as you can free up some personnel, send them out to catalogue and ID the bodies. Take pictures and secure all personal identification cards of the victims. I will try to get a backhoe over there in a day or two, and then we can start to bury them in a mass grave; there is no other way. I'll let you know on that. Hey, keep up the good work, bud!"

Toby moved to the closest bodies, but the black mud stuck thick and heavy to his boots and hampered his forward motion. The first two victims were older women, and then he saw a younger blond male. He reached into the back pocket of the man's jeans and extracted a soaked and mud-covered wallet. Toby glanced back, there was nobody around, and he shoved the dirty wallet into his own jeans. He was ready to change his identity once more.

The birds had left their horrible marks; the faces were pecked to the bone, some raw flesh, teeth, and hair were still left on the skull. Not much sense taking pictures, he thought.

Just before the early darkness set in, they loaded the last stretchers on the boat and headed back for camp. Toby contacted the other teams and told them to call it a day and return to base. One of the search dogs had led his handler to a partially collapsed farmhouse; inside he found two bodies and a frightened young boy, who was in surprisingly fair condition. There was joy and a proud feeling of accomplishment among the Filipinos that evening.

"It was a good day; we save lots of people," said Fermin with satisfaction. The doctors were busy in the hospital tent. It was filling up fast; they had 27 patients now, and a few of them in very critical condition. Some of the first aid paramedics were recruited for nursing duty, which they didn't mind.

One of the Filipino doctors was at his bedside, trying to wake him up. Toby jumped off his cot.

"What is going on?" he asked, still dazed.

"My patient is very sick, extremely sick, need dialysis, I think. Very urgent matter! I cannot do more help for her here. She will die, maybe has eight or ten hours to live."

Toby called headquarters and surprisingly Charlie answered. "Hey, what's up, my man?"

Toby explained the situation.

"Stay on the line, while I make some enquiries."

A couple of minutes later, Charlie was back.

"Can you take your patient to the hospital in Abbotsford, BC? They are already notified, and they will accommodate your patient. Sorry, Bellingham Hospital is totally swamped and will no longer accept patients until further notice."

"Where is Abbotsford?" asked the doctor.

"It is not far from here, but it is in Canada," said Toby.

"I do not know if our emergency-visa papers will be good for Canada, only good for USA. We cannot go to Abbotsford. Big problem, maybe," said the doctor.

"Okay, I'll go!" said Toby and left his dispatcher in charge.

"See you later, guys!" he waved. But they never saw him again.

Chapter XIX

New World Order

It was early in the morning when the sun rose over Muscat and a soft fresh red flushed over the still waters of the gulf and the cloudless sky. For a short moment, the buildings of this spectacular city were dipped into the soft fresh red and the glass windows and the polished facades would magnify the colour and reflect it onto smaller objects in the streets.

Jonathan Oliver stood on his balcony, but he did not see the transformation as people and cars turned red. He had been standing there for a whole hour. Sleep did not come easily for him last night, and when it came it was deep and dreamless but also very short. His thoughts withdrew him from the present and carried him into the future. Yes, he could envision the rapid self-destructive drive of the human race, and images of the seven-year cycle of rabbits and lemmings entered his mind. Was there a human equivalent to the seven-year cycle? Why not? Entirely possible! Will it soon reach its peak? When will nature act with the inevitable pandemic? When will the big die-off begin? Or can we intervene with a regulated reduction plan like Abbasi is suggesting? Why don't we give it a try?

All of a sudden, uncertainty entered his wandering thoughts and he was torn between a strong loyalty to his own country and a mature and demanding responsibility, that of a universal citizen, for the whole of humankind and the fragile environment of the planet. He had some reservations putting his name under a joined communiqué. Thus not only committing himself, but the entire United States of America. It would be so much easier for him to give in to the nagging reluctance and refuse to sign. If he would take a neutral position, he would maintain a really good chance with the American voter, come election time.

He let go of the balcony railing and returned to his suite. It was time to get ready for the pre-breakfast meeting and the important vote on the future location of the global capital city. And his thoughts wandered again, now from Geneva to Baghdad. Baghdad, oh my God! He won't vote for it. He had been there many times in that Godforsaken city, and he didn't want to return there anytime soon. Already talking like I am a member of the global government, he thought. Baghdad no way, Jose! Its reputation may have changed, but not his horrid memories.

Abbasi was already downstairs in the conference room and welcomed every new arrival with an infectious fresh vitality.

"And how are you this glorious morning, Mr. President?" he greeted Oliver.

Oliver grumbled that he was fine but could have done with a couple more hours of sleep. They exchanged further pleasantries while they waited for the two ladies in their group to make their appearance. That did not take long at all. The men rose to their feet when Frau Mueller and Senhora Elegante entered the conference room.

"Good morning, ladies and gentlemen, please take your seats. We have one important item left on our agenda to deal with before we begin drafting a joined declaration and before we face the international news media. I hope you all had a good sleep, and I also hope that you have come to a decision in what city the new global government will be located.

"There is a simple ballot form in front of you. Just fill in the city of your choice and initial the ballot. As you will remember, there are six cities in the running: Geneva, Singapore, Alexandria, Vienna, Cape Town, and Baghdad. Ladies and gentlemen, please write down your choice. The simple majority shall be the winner."

But it was not simple. When the results were announced, everyone was surprised. It was a three-way tie: Geneva, Singapore, and Cape Town. Abbasi was completely taken aback. He had not expected an outcome like this.

"What shall we do?" he asked almost helplessly.

Maxima Mueller lifted her hand and said: "To get out of this impasse, I suggest each one of us selects two of the three remaining cities." There was uniform agreement right away and without debate. New hastily improvised ballots were handed out to the delegates and they began to write down their choices. In a matter of minutes, Abbasi rose again to announce the results.

"I have the verified count. As you know, we had 18 votes and the results are as follows: Geneva, 4 votes; Singapore, 5; and Cape Town, 9. And the winner is Cape Town, South Africa. Congratulations!"

There was jubilation and also disbelief among some of the members. Over breakfast, Oliver leaned forward and asked: "Is it true that Allah has spoken to you, Mr. Abbasi?" He was seated directly opposite the Iranian.

"Yes, it is very true. Allah appeared in my dream, and He told me to make peace in the lands of ULIN, peace among the Shia and the Sunni and all the other factions of Islam. 'I am your God,' He said. 'There is only one God in this world and I am also the God of all the people on earth, even if their beliefs differ from yours. Islam is a religion of peace and so is Christianity.

"And what have you done? Look what the Muslims have done! Look what the Muslims are doing; there is still fighting and killing going on amongst you. There are misguided suicide bombers who not only blow themselves to pieces, but they also blow up innocent bystanders. I can assure you, there is not a single one of these deranged idiots in paradise. Tell the people of Islam to grow up, Masoud!' He said to me. 'Learn from the Christians! Their past has many dark chapters, just like the Islamic past. They are divided and split into many factions, just like the Islamic faith. But they have reconciled among themselves and now they live peacefully side by side in almost harmonious co-existence. Well, except for the occasional minor flare-ups of some hotheads.

"Remember, Masoud, the Koran, the Bible, the Talmud, and the rest of the Holy Books were all written by good and wise men a long time ago. They meant well, although some of it was self-serving at the time. Over the years, humankind has outgrown a good part of the once wise and adequate quotes, dogmas, rules, rites, and customs. Evolution in religion, you might ask?

"Yes, religion has to undergo the evolutionary process just like everything else. With more awareness, better interpretation has brought more clarity.

"There are too many people on this earth. The planet is over-crowded and has become unsustainable. Get the breeding under control, Masoud. I also want you to make peace with the Americans; they have suffered enough. Make peace with the rest of the world, and work together to save humankind and your planet!' Those were Allah's very own words!" Abbasi said.

They all had stopped eating and were staring in disbelief at Abbasi. Nobody wanted to miss anything and they were glued to every word he spoke.

Oliver was shocked and he thought, I knew it! Boy, this guy has really cracked up, can't they see that? Who is going to believe a cacophony story like that? Maybe a simple and childish mind will? But that's what religion is all about, to either pacify or to whip up the masses. Lead and they will follow like lambs or like stupid cows. "Religion ist das Opium des Volkes!" Karl Marx had said. It is the opiate of the masses, and it will cloud their senses with the sweet smoke of promise. It will enter their brains and find a permanent home and the sweet smoke of promise will make them turn wide-eyed to the heavens and expect to view paradise.'

"Did Allah say anything about the Israelis?" asked Oliver.

"Ah, I was just getting to that part," replied the Iranian. "Actually, Allah did not appreciate me putting questions to Him. 'Use your imagination and your wit, Masoud,' He said, 'and remember, I want peace on Earth'."

"And by applying your imagination and your wit, have you found a peaceful solution for the Jewish state?" enquired Oliver.

"I think so, if Israel cannot live in peace with its Arabic neighbours, maybe then it is time to move. Maybe they should move in with their American friends for awhile. There should be enough territory available in Arizona and Texas where the Jews could resettle among their welcoming friends. I believe that the Middle East has hosted them long enough!"

"I am sorry, but your sadistic remarks about America and Israel have brought on mistrust and a change of heart. I will not sign the joined communiqué. I believe your imagination ran away on you and your wit did not get you very far!" Oliver hissed icily. "You are mad, you are absolutely mad; Israel has a documented historical and biblical right to its territory."

"Bullshit, again!" yelled the angry Lin. "Leave religion and the Bible out of politics. Hundreds and hundreds of nations in this world have lost their identity. They all had historically documented territorial rights. But these rights were trampled upon and completely ignored when the first Europeans set foot in America, in Africa, in Asia, the Pacific, and in Australia; they were trampled upon when the Russians extended their empire into the Caucasus and into Asia. These historical territorial rights were trampled upon and completely ignored when the imperial Europeans wilfully drew borders on the global map and wilfully created new states and nations without any consideration of ancestral rights. Again, they and their American friends dictated new territorial terms at the 'peace treaties' after both World Wars; maybe the Polish people were lucky in that regard and gained a generous settlement of their ancient territorial claim. Regrettably, so many other nations were short-changed. It is plainly preposterous in a progressive world to speak about historical territorial rights. Nobody has these rights! Nobody! We cannot change the past; we can only change the future, and I want everybody in this room to know that changes are coming. Changes are on the way, my friends!"

"You don't want religion in politics, but on the other hand we allow Allah into our debate. How contradictory is that? If you consider just for a minute that the American people will approve the import of the state of Israel into American territory, you are terribly mistaken. It is totally impossible and totally unacceptable. We will do everything in our power to protect the state of Israel and its rightful borders."

"Is this a threat, Mr. Oliver? Who do you want to scare? Remember, we hold the key to stop any of your imperialistic and aggressive intentions, and currently the key is in the 'off position'." Mr. Lin laughed and his floppy jowls bounced happily when they responded to his chuckles.

"You Americans always wanted to change the world for others. Your parochial way of thinking never considered changes for yourself because the American way was always the right way," he added. "I believe time has arrived now for you to make a change for yourself and for America. Actually, you have two choices: sign the communiqué today, or we will start shipping the Jews by boat tomorrow to Texas."

Oliver, despite his dark skin, had turned white. Blood drained from his face. "That's blackmail." He breathed hard and fast.

"No, it's common sense," said Abbasi. "You don't want a Jewish state on your soil and neither do the Arabs on their soil. They have been hosting the Israeli 'presence' for 80 years now. Our Palestinian brothers have all the historical territorial rights to this land, but they have been ridiculed by your propaganda and their claim for nationhood and territory was flatly denied and brushed of the table. Despite all the odds and being labelled terrorists, they have kept up their opposition to the Jewish imperialistic oppressors. That's how we view them! Now you know how we feel and now I hear that America, as one of Israel's best friends, has misgivings welcoming the Jewish people with open arms. What do you want me to think of that, Mister Oliver?"

"So, we do have a problem with Israel, I admit with reservations. But how will the problem go away if I sign the communiqué today? I do not understand your logic, please help me here."

"A convincing endorsement for a global government by all nine delegates is in my view absolutely necessary. We can show to the rest of the world we are united and mean business, if you will. Every country has to adopt the new universal laws and make changes accordingly. Disputes between countries will be ruled on by an elected, international, arbitrary panel and its decision shall be binding. I wager to say that a hearing of the Israeli-Palestine dispute would be one of the first items on the new board's agenda, and I don't think they would export the Jews to Texas," said Abbasi with a smile.

"You have a short fuse," said Popov to Oliver after he had managed to separate the American from the rest of the group. "You know there are people who like nothing better than to irritate you and to get under your skin. It is still the resentment from the past; it filters through occasionally."

"Yes, I know, I know. But I've been under a tremendous amount of pressure lately," confessed a weary Oliver.

Popov put his hand on Oliver's shoulder and said consolingly, "My friend, all of us here are aware of America's enormous recent challenges, and all of us here appreciate your courageous efforts to bring relief and hope and some stability to the destitute people in the stricken areas.

"I have noticed your sincerity and your conviction that our goals are noble and in the best interest of saving humankind and our precious planet. I hope your recent outburst was just a provoked flare-up and not a stubborn refusal of everything you so wholeheartedly supported earlier."

"I admit that I am in a major conflict between my sworn duty to the American people and a newfound global responsibility. Well, and there is also a personal dislike for some of the arrogant members in this room."

"You have to make a decision, my friend. Do you want to please your ego and the American voter, or do you want to be a participating partner of a global team in a global salvage operation?"

Oliver hesitated for a moment before he replied.

"I like the way you beat around the bush, Popov," he finally said and cracked a smile. "Please, tell Abbasi that I want to participate in crafting a joined communiqué, and I will sign it once we all agree on the wording."

Chapter XX

Oliver's Return to America

The summit at the Sultan's palace in Muscat was over and Oliver was on his way back to Washington, seated comfortably on board Air Force One. It had ended with the release of a joint official communiqué to the news media of the world, verifying that the nine world leaders had taken part in a secret meeting and they had unanimously agreed to form a global government with global elections to be held in six months. Further details to follow.

Oliver was in conversation with his two assistants, DeVries and Jackson, and with a group of advisers and a pair of speechwriters who had flown in on Air Force One at the request of the president.

"I had to commit myself; there was no other alternative. I strongly believe it is in America's best interest to go along with the top decision-makers of the world and become part of a new global community and a new responsible global government. We will have to relinquish some parts of our independence in the process for the global good," he told them.

"We are stunned! We are absolutely mystified, and yes, we are stunned. How can you agree to give up American sovereignty and independence at any time? Especially now, in an election year? It's absolute suicide! We were just enjoying the dramatic upswing in your popularity after you rescued that young couple in Seattle. Now, you fucked it all up! Excuse my choice of words, sir, but irreparable damage has been done here. I don't know how to rescue you, and I don't know how to market your brand new mission. I call it: Mission Impossible!" said a very red-faced DeVries.

"What else did you agree upon and what else did you give up, Mr. President? What other concessions did you make? In three days, your distinguished world leaders must have discussed many, many topics and you must have agreed on some of the issues—didn't you, Mr. President?" asked Jackson, the small man with the yellow lenses.

"Well, yes, we did," said Oliver. "We talked about changes to the monetary system, changes to human rights. We talked about birth control and a universal reduction of military personnel and arms. We talked about a ban of all nuclear facilities and of all nuclear weaponry. We also discussed the banning of all weapons of mass destruction and their controlled disposal."

News travels fast!

The president was still over the Atlantic somewhere when his Republican opponent, Mary-Lynn Krocher held a hastily arranged press conference.

"The president has betrayed America!" she began. "On his inauguration the president swore to preserve, protect, and defend the constitution of America, and now he tells us that he has given up some of our sovereignty and some of our independence and some of our freedoms and liberties for the common good. Well, how much is some? 'Just a little bit', he says, but as you all know, you can't get a 'little bit' pregnant. It is the real thing, either you are pregnant or not! It is always the real thing.

"The president sold out America at this obscure meeting. He sold out America without authorization. I am telling you that the president did not act on behalf of the American people. I am telling you that the president overstepped his obligation and his duty because he absolutely did not have the mandate to go out and make those preposterous agreements! We will never, and I cannot emphasize enough, never compromise our sovereignty and our liberty, and that's final. America will always be free and proudly independent! I will see to that!"

By the time Air Force One touched down in Washington, there were demonstrations in every major city of the USA. Hundreds of thousands gathered around federal buildings carrying placards with slogans expressing their profound disapproval of the president's recent actions: 'You sold our Freedom! For what?' 'Impeach the Traitor!' 'Kill Oliver!' 'America will never be ruled by Geeks or Gooks!'

"I believe the president lost his mind and he should undergo immediate medical evaluation. I also call for an immediate temporary impeachment so that the president and his twisted mind can do no more damage to America and to the precious American people. This is the time for the vice president to step in and take over," bellowed a fired-up Krocher through the loud speakers.

Oliver retreated to the White House and went into seclusion. He cancelled all public appearances for the next two weeks.

"Let the bitch have her way," he said, referring to Krocher, his Republican opponent in the election race. He officially appointed the vice president, Dalton Henderson, to take over presidential duties for the time he had sequestered himself.

The impeachment calls grew louder and louder, and the rumours of his alleged mental illness flourished. Hastily fabricated stories stretched the imagination to the maximum and occupied the social media and news networks to the fullest.

Public demonstrations began to turn violent. People were extremely upset and they started to vent their anger in primitive and stupid ways. They were smashing storefront windows, overturning cars and setting them on fire, and there were daily clashes with police and security forces. The public opinion thermometer, measuring political disapproval, climbed into the red, the danger zone, and could have blown at anytime.

But public opinion, which is so often artificially directed even fine-tuned and at other times hotly inflamed, can be changed by unexpected and miscalculated outside interferences or events. It started as a rumour and it was fuelled by more and more rumours, and then it completely reversed and it overturned with a brand new rumour.

Brand new information had leaked out and this new information contained images of 10,000 Euro bills for the simple act of having a vasectomy or having one's tubes tied. The same people who only yesterday were yelling and screaming: "Crucify Oliver!" were out on the street singing and dancing and praising the virtues of the president in hiding. They were calling for him to come forward and show himself, so they could lift him up on the highest pedestal and crown him for another four-year term. Krocher was now relegated to a flash of the past. She had sparked a few times and that was all and no more of it. The mob was back in the streets singing the 'Bye-Bye Blues' and Krocher was covering her ears because she could not stand this chant any longer.

On election day, Oliver won in a landslide victory. It was the largest lopsided election win ever recorded in U.S. history. He had the mandate from the people and his work was just beginning, the enormous task to help form a global government and to integrate the USA into it with dignity. However, he never had the mandate and consent within his government and within his own party. The divisions were just too great, and of course, he only had very little support within the Republican ranks. Political infighting took up most of his energy and most of his valuable and precious time. What a ludicrous waste! Oliver had enough of it and he was fed up!

Six weeks after he was sworn in as president, he resigned in a bold move. Dalton Henderson, the vice president stepped in and took over the temporary leadership of America.

In his memorable abdication speech Oliver said:

"I am a very proud American and I dare to say that I am the proudest of all Americans. I have been honoured to have received your trust twice to lead our country. There is no greater honour bestowed on a man or on a woman than to lead one's entire nation, especially a nation like ours, and I am very, very humbled.

"For my second term as president I campaigned to take America to a new destiny, to take it into the future, and to join the global family of nations. Our world on our precious and overcrowded planet earth has become more and more integrated and intertwined with almost every aspect of our daily lives. Yet, there are huge disparities and inadequacies found in many parts of our world, and the human suffering is so great that it is no longer acceptable. We have to unload this heavy burden from our conscience. We knew about it all along, and it has been there far too long. Let's free ourselves from the silent guilt and begin to share our good fortune with the poor, the hungry, and the underprivileged. Let us become humane! Let us shed the narrow-mindedness, the insular and egotistical attitudes, and invite back the values of brotherhood and family into our thinking and into our lives. Only then will we have matured, only then will we mature to the level of responsible global citizens.

"I was called upon to lead America and I believe I did my utmost best for our great country! You, the people, even chose me for a second term—what a wonderful and great endorsement. I thank you sincerely from all my heart, but I feel that I have a higher calling, the responsibility to take America as a respected partner into a global government.

"I herewith confirm my resignation as president of the United States of America as of tomorrow and declare my candidacy as one of the 19 American members for the new global government. I pledge that I will work to the best of my ability to further the cause of universal betterment for humankind and to preserve our environment in order to save our planet!"

His high profile candidacy sparked a fashionable trend around the world and soon elections were organized all over the globe. Many well-known individuals and many well-known intellectuals threw their hats into the ring. The race was on!

Chapter XXI

Global Elections

May 2029 was the month of global elections for the majority of countries in the world; some of them had held elections already earlier that year. By May 31, all results were in and approved by the respective national supervisory boards.

In the U.S. there were 11,873 candidates vying for the 19 positions of global government member (GGM) and statewide pre-elections sorted through the enormous number of applicants. Finally, in a nationwide run-off, the successful 19 were chosen by the electorate. Oliver was the popular choice and he came in first by a wide margin.

Canada with the much smaller population elected only three GGMs to represent the country in Cape Town: Jennifer Lee, an outspoken environmentalist; Patrick Brown, a well-known scientist and Nobel laureate; and Phil Chingee, a prominent native leader. The French-Canadian and East-Indian communities were disappointed with the performance of their candidates and lamented the loss of their favourites for awhile.

Cape Town had received advance notice since the November summit in Muscat, but it was still under a spell of disbelief. It gradually began to accept the concept and the idea of becoming the capital of the world. Whoa! City council members and city planners took a somber approach and began preparations in earnest to host the first global government.

South Africa is unique in many ways. It has for instance, three capital cities, Cape Town, Pretoria, and Bloemfontein, and 11 official languages, the most in any country. A decision was made to move the seat of Parliament, which is the legislative arm in Cape Town to Pretoria, which in turn is the seat of the president and the cabinet. The vacated premises in Cape Town were to be renovated and used as the temporary site for the new global government.

On July 1, 2029, the first World Parliament was sworn in. The only other order on that historical day was to declare July 1 an international holiday and the order was unanimously approved.

The selection for the elevated position to the Supreme Council took place the following day, and Oliver was appointed to the exalted club of 32 in the first round. The final positions were filled after a lengthy run-off procedure and several rounds of voting that occupied the members for the entire second day. Surprisingly the representatives from the population-strong countries of India and China fared proportionately not that well. They only managed to send two delegates each to the Supreme Council. However, the small countries of Switzerland, Denmark, Costa Rica, and Sierra Leone, did much better; they had their sole elected member nominated. Canada was lucky as well. Patrick Brown, a very popular choice among the delegates, was also elected in the first round to the prestigious circle.

On the third day, the 32 esteemed councillors chose a president among themselves. It was an almost unanimous decision and by noon, Chen Li was declared the winner. The new president went to work right away with so much vigour and determination that by the end of the first week he had earned himself the nickname 'Bulldog'.

The new team in Cape Town was an energetic and dedicated bunch of people, a kaleidoscope of personalities whose common goal was to save humankind and the planet. Their ideas and proposals how to achieve this goal, however, differentiated immensely, just like their own strong individualities.

In his inauguration speech, President Chen Li welcomed the 540 elected members to Parliament. He introduced the 32 honourable councillors without a swearing-in ceremony and explained the position of the Supreme Council.

"As you may know and as documented in the resolution and joined declaration in Muscat, the Supreme Council has the authority to execute emergency orders with a majority approval of at least 25 supporting votes from its 32 members. The council will also be responsible for selecting policy proposals to be brought before the house by importance and by urgency. Each councillor will further receive a specific ministerial resort within the next two weeks, which he or she has to manage to the best of their ability.

"One of the first businesses the Supreme Council has to address will be the drafting of the Charter of Rights and Obligations. It will be introduced to the house for a vote in four days. The council welcomes your submissions and will take them into consideration. Please act on it right away. Other important items high on the immediate agenda will be the nomination of a legal team to draft a new Global Constitution and the installation of a functional international legal system and a Global Supreme Court. Again, your input is important and will be evaluated.

I will meet with the Supreme Council at 14:00 this afternoon and we will discuss a program of priorities, which we will bring before the house in the next days. Be prepared for some surprises, be prepared for some revolutionary proposals, and be ready for a sound judgement when you are being asked to vote. The house reconvenes at 10:00 tomorrow morning. I will see you all then, here and on time!"

It sure sounded like an order. President Chen Li wanted things done. He was a man with a mission. Next morning, the assembly rose exactly at 10:00 a.m., when the president entered the house.

"Ladies and gentlemen, in yesterday's meeting, the Supreme Council and I collectively worked out a schedule of urgent issues, which we will tackle in the house this week. You will find a copy of the schedule on your seat and hopefully on your website, once all the electronic kinks are taken care of. We also unanimously reached two decisions in yesterday's meeting.

"The first was an order concerning a proposed monetary reform: An immediate halt to all financial trading activities for a period of two weeks. This will mean a two-week closure for all stock markets, all commodity and bond markets, all financial brokerage agencies and agents. Furthermore, all banks and financial institutions are ordered to limit cash withdrawals or any other money transactions for their individual clients to the equivalent of 1,000 Euros per day. For small business accounts, the limit is the equivalent of 10,000 Euros per day, medium-sized businesses and institutions have a daily limit of 100,000 Euros. The daily limit for large employers is 1,000,000. Industry and business and of course the banking and finance community have to work with us and obey the new temporary regulations. A violation of this order will result in closure of the violating bank or financial institution and the forfeiture of its assets to the Global Treasury.

"The second order concerns hostile military activities: It calls for the immediate and total stop of all such hostile activities. Representatives of the opposing sides are required to negotiate a settlement within a 30-day period. If they are unable to come to an agreement within the 30 days, starting today, the Governing Council will impose and enforce a binding settlement on them. Intensified pinpoint-satellite-monitoring will record violations and identify violators for a later prosecution date at a global criminal court.

"Ladies and gentlemen, the World Parliament is in full session for the first time today. New proposals will be submitted and debated in the afternoons and in the evenings. Each proposal is limited to a two-hour discussion period, and then the next item on the agenda can be introduced to the house with another two-hour debate limit. Voting on the proposals will always be conducted the following working day between 10:00 and 12:00. Acceptance of any bill requires a minimum of 300 yes votes. Total rejection of a bill occurs when less than 200 yes votes are recorded. Closer outcomes with results between 200 and 299 supporting votes will be included in a twice yearly plebiscite, and if approved then by the people, the proposals will be brought back before the house for reconsideration.

"My honourable colleagues, please consult your schedule and let's get to work! Top item on the list is the election of a Speaker of the House."

President Chen Li did not lose any time on formalities and procedures. He forged ahead with the agenda in parliament. A Speaker of the House was elected after a somewhat lengthy procedure and a 30-day ban on any media and public presence in the house was also passed by a comfortable 360 margin. The ban had become necessary because the construction of a press gallery and a visitors gallery was still in progress. Work crews were busy every night putting on the finishing touches.

The president refused to meet with the news media, and he rigorously turned down all requests for an interview. His press secretary released only details of the previous morning's voting results in a daily and very short news briefing at 14:00. The reporters became quite upset over the press secretary's steady absence of comments and his stoic refusal to answer questions.

The first days of the first business week in the house dealt mainly with administrative and security issues. Then the big hammer fell, when proposals for a new common currency and a bank reform were tabled. Emotions ran high among the members of the global government. Implementing a common currency was revolutionary in itself, but it was an idea that was generally supported. Most members favoured to wait and study the effects of such a move before the introduction of the drastic bank reform the council was pressing for. Stock markets and the banking community were already in uproar and in turmoil over the 14-day trading ban and the limitation on money withdrawals and transfers, which had been ordered by the council earlier.

After a very stormy session in the house, which lasted past midnight, the cooled off heads compromised in the morning hours and voted for the introduction of the denar and the cent as the new common currency. The members also supported the heavily supervised printing and production proposals of the new money in the designated mints and the money-printing houses around the globe. The third bill dealt with a simplified exchange proposal and the establishment of set conversions rates to the denar for every currency in the world. The members also supported this proposal. The last item of the agenda did not deal with a universal bank reform as originally intended. The council withdrew that proposal after they encountered heavy opposition in yesterday's debate and instead they introduced an extension to the 14-day trading ban on stock markets and the daily limits on cash withdrawals and money transfers. The unlimited extension was passed in the morning vote to the dismay of all financial institutions.

Investors and traders were holding their breath, but how long can you hold your breath? Then they were wringing their hands, shaking their fists, shouting, and swearing. It didn't help. They began to plead in public and on television for sanity and enlightening of the honourable members of government. It didn't help. Actually their pleas and their deplorable behaviour only weakened the anti-bank reform group, and popular support for the money men dwindled even more.

There was chaos in the business world all over the globe, not to mention the turmoil and uncertainty in the financial sector. Large industrial giants with enormous budgets, often exceeding that of a midsized country, had to overcome the new financial challenges. CEOs were scratching their heads. 'Work with us!' was the slogan of the president, and most companies followed his invitation for change and innovation.

Every middle-class citizen, who had a nice diversified portfolio of blue-chip stocks, mutual funds, government bonds and deposits in tax-saving retirement programs was having nightmares and sleepless nights.

The larger investors, who had successfully gambled in the past and become filthy rich on paper, were shaking in their boots. They knew now their lucky streak was over, and just like during the stock market crash in 1929, the first suicides were recorded. These desperate people knew their favourite pastime had come to an end. The era of worldwide commercial and government endorsed gambling had closed on them without warning. Some still couldn't believe it; others sensed that the stock markets would never open again and that currency trading had also become a thing of the past.

"I was paper-rich yesterday! I should have cashed it all in! Stupid me!" This phrase was repeated over and over again; no matter in what country, no matter in what city, no matter what skin colour, no matter what denomination.

It became clear to many that the invincible and world-dominating capitalistic monster was mortally wounded. The first blows by the council and by the parliament left deep wounds in the long heralded superstructure. Now it began to crumble after the severe blood-letting was induced.

The next heavy blow occurred after the relatively easy passing of the 'Global Monetary Fairness and Equalization Act', an attempt to distribute the global wealth more fairly and evenly. Detailed proposals were to follow in a separate bill before the house. When the details were released and discussion started in the parliament in Cape Town, a worldwide shudder went through the financial community and through all the well-to-do people.

Finally, after six weeks of turmoil and uncertainty the denar and the cent were ready to take over as the new common currency. Enough coins had been minted and enough banknotes had been printed. The banks were ready for the onslaught, when clients would come crashing through the doors to exchange their old money for the new colourful denar notes. The banks were bound by the strict exchange rules the government had set out earlier:

a) Small cash amounts up to 1,000 of any currency were to be converted at a rate of 1:1.

b) Amounts larger than 1,000 of any currency were to be converted to denar, using a set exchange rate published by the Ministry of Finance. The maximum amount allowed to be converted was 100,000 denar per individual. Amounts from 100,001 to 1,000,000 denar were reduced to 10% of its value and then credited to the account holder.

c) Amounts over 1,000,000 denar became ineligible and forfeited to the global government. Similar regulation applied to all commercial and industrial bank account holders.

Every transaction had to be documented. Applicants needed an existing bank account and two pieces of photo ID; in addition they had to leave fingerprints and a signature for the receipt of the money. Cheating, a duplication or repeat transaction, was almost impossible. For one, the fingerprint ink stuck to the fingers for at least two months. It was just another simple security measure. The access to additional or secret bank accounts was blocked. After 60 days, the global government confiscated all dormant accounts with a leftover balance.

A different set of rules and restrictions awaited the stock and securities holders. They were allowed to cash in their stocks, bonds, and securities papers at the value set on the last day of trading. The first 10,000 converted into denar were exchanged on a 1:1 basis. Amounts from 10,001 to 1,000,000 were converted at a rate of 10%, exceeding portfolios were confiscated by the country where the individual resided in or where the holding company was registered in. Stock markets of the world never opened again; they had simply ceased to exist. Large scale government-sponsored gambling had become a thing of the past.

At the end of the day, there were no more billionaires in the world—period—and there were no more cash-millionaires in the world. Private and commercial property holders were restricted to a maximum of two properties. The rest of their holdings were forfeited to the state. Of course, there were some exemptions for large industrial companies and production and manufacturing facilities.

Other exemptions were granted to registered church organizations but these exemptions applied only to places of worship. All charity organizations were dissolved and their assets taken over by the state. There was no more need for 'private' and often controversial charity organizations. The government had taken over the role of benefactor and caretaker of the needy and the poor, the disabled, the disenfranchised, and the mentally challenged with the creation of the Ministry for Charity and Emergency Relief.

Farmers were restricted to a maximum of 800 acres each. Coops could not exceed the 800-acre limit per active farming member. Excessive property was forfeited to the state and so on, and so on, and so on!

The long-awaited and contentious pension reform with its extreme complexities could not easily be brought down to a universal common denominator. Parliamentary forums and specially appointed committees by the Supreme Council were working tirelessly to find a viable solution they could present to the legislature for discussion and for possible acceptance. Finally, a private members bill was considered and put before the house. Nobody gave it any chance of passing, but to everyone's surprise, it did pass the 300-vote hurdle. Retired teachers in Ohio and in Ontario as well as other high income pensioners were stunned and cried foul. The majority in the house had accepted a plan, where the global government would take over all private pension funds. Pensioners would receive the current government pension payments from their country of permanent residence. All global citizens aged 65 and older would further receive a universal monthly pension of 1,000 denar from the global government.

Luxury items, gold possessions, and jewellery, etc., that were registered with insurance companies had to be fully disclosed by the insurer. Owners were required to file a corresponding declaration with the Department of Financial Re-Alignment and Equalization. A similar regulation applied to bank customers who rented a safety deposit box at their bank. Possessions were restricted to a value of 50,000 denar. Properties exceeding this limit were forfeited to the state and so on, and so on!

Numbered bank accounts, not to be mistaken with bank account numbers, or 'secret bank accounts' in Switzerland, Luxembourg, Liechtenstein, the Cayman Islands, or other tax-free havens were all forfeited to the Global Treasury with no exceptions. There was lots of lamenting going on.

By the end of the day, when the dust had settled, and everything was said and done, there were no more billionaires on the planet. Only a fair number of millionaires were leftover and with them a strong and respectable group of middle-class citizens. Many of the poor and lower income class people experienced a vast and wonderful improvement to their finances. Bank account holders with a balance of less then 1,000 of any currency had their accounts topped up to 1,000 denar. People with no bank accounts and with no cash or only small amounts of cash received a one-time amount of 500 denar. Of course, documentation, fingerprinting, and voice printing were required to make cheating impossible.

It was a good solution. The super-rich were still rich, and the rich remained rich. They all registered losses, but they never left their comfort zone. The middle-class was still well off, and the other 2/3 of the world's population slowly began to rise out of the obscurity of poverty and misery.

Furthermore, all public debt, all private debt, and all commercial debt was cancelled and eliminated. Municipalities, hospitals, counties, provinces, lands, states, and countries were jubilant and breathed sighs of relief. Billions of consumers cut up their credit cards and celebrated for days in euphoria. The new government was very popular. Business and industry were totally taken by surprise. No more debts? Often a very critical and stressful component of running a business was eliminated. But big business and industry celebrated with caution because now they had a majority partner, and that partner was the global government.

The banks were still restricted to the daily limits of cash withdrawals and money transfers the council and the house had imposed on them earlier. Further changes to the bank act were announced almost daily. Percentage limits on savings accounts were firmly set at 3%. New stringent regulations for loans and mortgages were passed and credit cards became illegal and were taken out of circulation. Only bank cards, electronic transfer (with restrictions attached), and cash were allowed for use as payment. The instant-credit-card-debt-transaction was a thing of the past, and the predicted cashless society did not materialize.

Equivalency of values had considerably moved closer. Capitalism had taken a back seat! Free market principles were exercised daily on a micro scale around the corner, where farmers and artisans displayed their goods on makeshift tables. Only the innocence was left. Big enterprises were often strangulated with red tape. At first, the economy stagnated and stood still, but then it surprisingly began to pulse, and slowly it fell into gear, despite the many shortcomings and miscalculations. Small entrepreneurship was first out of the gate and began flourishing early.

By the end of the day, when the dust had settled, and everything was said and done, the citizens of the world were no longer afraid, no longer in total despair; they had regained confidence and hope, and they began to trust the new government in Cape Town and its popular decisions.

"The biggest surprise is the debt elimination," said an enthusiastic man to the interviewer. "I was maxed out on my credit cards. I can say it now. Can you imagine? Almost 50,000 Euros. I was all stressed out and didn't know how to make the next minimum payment. The high interest rate and penalties were killing me, but hurray, hurray, now I am debt free. I do not have to worry about the next credit card payment and I don't have a mortgage payment either. Isn't that fantastic. There will be dancing in the street tonight, mister, and tomorrow night as well, that's for sure. Hallelujah!"

People were dancing and partying in the streets for days. The celebrations did not stop for an entire week. When food and wine and beer finally ran out and the fuzziness cleared from the drowsy heads, the stomach took over command, and life became normal again. Lots of new babies were bred in that week, quite contrary to the wishes of the global government.

News from Cape Town kept dominating the airwaves. Debt forgiveness had a price attached to it. For the careless and carefree consumer, it was the loss of the convenience of credit cards. It brought back old rules, like living within one's means, and it required the simple skills of personal budgeting.

All governments and public institutions had to bring their households under strict financial control and abide by a budget within 80% of their forecast revenue. The expected overages were to be put away into a 'rainy day account' and could be used only in times of extreme emergency.

Next to be announced were wage and price controls for a period of 12 months. It was quite a contentious issue and it was heavily debated in public. The fact that it was to be reviewed after 12 months did not ease any fear or suspicion from the producer, the merchant, or the consumer.

Unlimited travel and movement on the globe was scaled back for 12 months, to be reviewed after that time. The current travel restrictions and visa requirements between the individual national countries remained in place.

Discontent followed the early euphoria. Not everybody was happy. The decision to cut military personnel by 50% worldwide had a devastating impact on the labour market and swelled the unemployment numbers to new highs. Then the global government seized control of all weapon and armament manufacturing and the distribution of all hardware and accessories to military forces around the globe.

A total shut down of all production was ordered for the duration of the six-month transition period and the number of unemployed grew daily. Countermeasures had little effect at the beginning, but seemed gradually to solidify after a lengthy period. The transition took much longer than originally anticipated.

Chapter XXII

After the First 30 Days

When the 30-day deadline passed, only two of the world's hostile conflicts were peacefully resolved. Rebels and government forces in Nigeria and in the Ukraine had put down their weapons and started to talk and listen sensibly and respectfully to each other.

They knew that the chance to reach a satisfactory and lasting agreement with their opponent lay in direct negotiations. Both sides were familiar with the issues and the culture of their neighbour, and both sides knew they had to give up something and share other things equally. None of them wanted an imposed settlement by a faraway and untested new government with no intimate knowledge of the local issues.

The Israeli-Palestine conflict remained unresolved. During the past 30 days, however, a cease fire was observed and bilateral talks were held, but both sides were firm in their demands and didn't move an inch from their rigid positions. No give-and-take at this table and no listening either. They could not even agree on having the global government impose an arbitrary settlement. Both sides remained extremely stubborn throughout the negotiations, and they left the last meeting very angrily and without a promise or a remote chance for a solution.

The Governing Council moved swiftly and introduced a surprising and binding resolution to the house: (a) Palestine would become a sovereign state; (b) Jerusalem would become an independent international city-state and a religious centre, akin to the Vatican; Jerusalem would be governed by an elected council according to Global Law; and (c) Israel had to relinquish 15% of its territory to Palestine.

The next morning, when the noisy house was called to order and the voting on the Israeli-Palestine bill was announced, a ceremonious silence fell over the esteemed members. They knew about the far-reaching consequences of the decision. It could become a precedent-setting day, and a day to solidify the power of the global government. A rejection of the bill, however, would expose a weakness of the law-making process in Cape Town, and it would further be judged as a severe setback for the new reformed democracy.

When the outcome of the vote count was verified, the Speaker of the House announced the bill had passed by a slim margin of 311 yes votes. Israel's reaction was furious. The Palestinians were celebrating what they called a small correction of a very large historical wrong. Two other hotspots on the globe received binding arbitrary ruling from the global government that day as well.

In the afternoon, the assembled house listened to the Council Member from Switzerland. He expressed his personal views in a lecture over the role of religion and the clergy in government.

"There has to be a clear division on this planet between all levels of government and all religious institutions, religious attributes and accessories, religious ceremonies, rites and dogmas, and the clergy in general. Religion and politics are a dangerous mixture and should be practised independently from each other. Religion has no place in government and in politics. Politics has no place in religion or at the pulpit.

"It is my belief that religion is something very private, where the individual can search for the meaning of life and can elect their own way to paradise or to an eternal afterlife. In religion one may also find solace and comfort for the soul. Religion can also become a strong partner in shaping one's moral convictions and standards.

"If an elected member of the global government or any other government has those religious-based moral convictions and standards and finds himself challenged by a certain piece of proposed legislation, he has to make his own decision. It is immaterial if his choice is religion-based or not. What is important is that the choice is reached individually of free will and without external pressure."

Oskar Spruengli, the Swiss council member, went on to say that religion can become a dangerous poison when deliberately administered to the masses by misguided and fanatic preachers or teachers. Fanaticism is just as dangerous a poison as religion. When used in conjunction by skilful agitators, it spells disaster. It is responsible for countless wars and military conflicts, which sadly dominate the history of humankind.

"Generally religion can be recommended for a person's way of life. It is often a hopeful crutch one can rely on for psychological support. Religion distributed en masse can pose a danger.

"Most of the world's religions endorse positive aspects, like kindness, love, friendship, and peace among fellow humans. Some radical splinter groups, however, have found different interpretations of the Holy Scriptures and teachings, and they endorse negative and evil traits. They often seek supremacy by any means, even murder, suicide, or straight-out brutal killings.

"We have to seek a way and a satisfactory solution to stop the misguided and evil minds from spreading their poison among the good people. I welcome suggestions from the honourable members. Thank you very much!"

On the environmental front, small measures to save the planet were introduced early. Plastic bags and plastic containers were banned and its production stopped, unless they were biodegradable and environmentally friendly. Styrofoam was also banned. Coolants had to be environmentally friendly; the application of pesticides was severely restricted and only used if absolutely necessary, when biological methods failed.

Aircraft manufacturers had to stop all new production of jet airplanes and were required to change over their facilities to produce helium airships. The production of jet boats and high-speed pleasure boats was outlawed. Cruise ships, commercial and container ships, oil, gasoline, and liquid gas tankers were required to replace 50% of their energy consumption with solar or high altitude wind energy within the next five years.

All natural resources, including the world's oceans, became the sole property of the global government and became subject to global management and jurisdiction. The oil, gas, mining, and forest giants were a thing of the past. Production of all natural resources was scaled back. Gasoline and diesel prices doubled to discourage the continued excessive use.

It was a start and other radical changes were in the planning stages.

On the labour front, high unemployment was still a major headache for the global government. Even though drastic and revolutionary changes had been executed. Unions were abolished because the government introduced fair and level labour legislation for everyone and also a 32-hour week.

Service jobs were high on the pay scale. People who wanted to do the hard and dirty work got paid exceptionally well. Why not? Garbage collectors and garbage detailers and sorters were some of the highest paid jobs. Eighty huge bulk-carrying transport vessels were taken out of service and were being re-vamped into solar-powered vacuum ships to suck up floating garbage and plastic on the high seas. A robotic SeaVax prototype had been plying the waters of the Pacific Ocean for a number of years. It was a successful undertaking, completely financed by millions of environmentally concerned members of the global civic organization Avaaz.

Then a general cleanup was ordered for all of Central and South America, for all of Africa, for all of Asia, for parts of Europe, for Indonesia, the Philippines, and many islands in the Indian and Pacific oceans. Millions of workers around the globe picked up garbage and discarded materials that littered cities, countrysides, and beaches for many years. The refuse was sorted into four main categories: recyclable, reusable, toxic, and disposable. Toxic included all chemical waste, oil products, and unidentified industrial and commercial waste. Disposable items were burnt at high temperatures in portable incinerators.

Environmental engineering was the most sought after university course. In the first year, enrolment worldwide was measured by the millions. There was just not enough room for all the applicants. Campuses brought in portable housing and portable classrooms to accommodate more students. Retired instructors and professionals were lured back to part-time teaching jobs with attractive compensation packages.

Then the global government announced its most ambitious and most futuristic plan, a plan that would change the energy supply and the transportation system on the planet. In its official statement from Cape Town:

The government approved the construction of 100,000 kilometres of solar-panelled roads and highways per year for the next 30 years. Sturdy interlocking solar panels used as road and parking lot surfaces were originally invented by Scott and Julie Brusaw and promoted through their company Solar Roadways. This fantastic idea never took off. It never gained popularity and never went past a few trial projects. The global government purchased the patent from the Brusaws for the maximum amount allowed under Global Law, which was 10,000,000 denar.

The idea was compelling. Environment and maintenance friendly solar panels would replace asphalt and concrete road surfaces. Hexagonal-shaped solar panels manufactured from a mixture of sand, gravel, and recycled materials, which were abundantly available, were laid on a solid foundation. Each panel could withstand the heaviest loads cars or trucks or any machinery could possibly force on them by a tenfold safety margin. Each panel had interlocking connections on all six sites. In addition to their structural connections, there were electrical power connections and also LED lights and a multitude of sensors connected to strategic computer stations. The computer stations monitored road conditions, traffic flow, and recorded among other data excessive speeders and irate drivers. They also flashed LED warning signs and messages or lane closure to the oncoming traffic.

Easy accessible and covered concrete service channels with impressive dimensions of two metres in height and a width of 180 centimetres ran along both sides of the solar highways and the solar roads. One channel carried the electronic communication wires; the fine fibre optic and ceramic strands were encased in a heavy rubberized plastic conduit. It also carried the LED and other sensory wires and, of course, the cables for the generated electric power, which branched off every few kilometres to join the power grid. All other wires ran to computer monitor stations. Solar roads and solar highways were being built with electric cars in mind. At short intervals of every two kilometres of highway was a pull out with a free electric charging station. The second channel on the other side of the highway would carry rain or melting waters and feed them into rivers, lakes, or man-made catch basins or sewage systems.

When this announcement was made, anti-government labour demonstrations stopped and the unemployed cheered and welcomed the new initiative. Somebody coined a brand new name for this gigantic project and it quickly became popular. It was called: 'Autobahn del Sol'—probably remembering Hitler's massive labour-creating project in the 1930s, the Autobahn. Millions were hoping to land a good and long-lasting job with this enormous global project. They were eagerly awaiting the next announcement, the location of the 100 super factories that would produce solar panels to surface 1,000 kilometres of road and highways per year for the next 30 years. The promise of long-term job security was very important for most of them.

The government's decision to use some of the newly acquired superstructures and convert them into solar panel factories was generally welcomed because most of these facilities were located in the highly populated urban areas of the world with high unemployment rates. Only three new factories were approved for construction: one in Nigeria, one in Egypt, and one in Indonesia. In addition to the 100 super factories, the government granted licences to 200 smaller production facilities, which would service the individual and commercial consumer. There was much interest in the private sector for the application of these special solar panels on driveways, parking lots, schoolyards, airports, and so on. By granting the licences to the smaller manufactures, the government ensured also backup supplies for their own projects, if anyone of the super factories should run into production difficulties or delays.

Maps were finally released and published after thorough consultations with every single country because this project took place in every single country on the globe, proportionally to its geographical size and to its population density. There were plans for a super factory in Puebla, Mexico, and plans for 92 kilometres of highway rebuilding and resurfacing in Costa Rica, for example.

No new road construction was approved anywhere. The rebuilding and resurfacing applied only to existing roadways. The long-term plan, of course, was to eventually return some of the land that was now covered by elaborate road systems to agriculture, forests, and nature.

Chapter XXIII

Social Reform

The barrage of economic changes was regularly interspersed by social announcements. Free basic and advanced education for every child, according to the Muscat Doctrine, was slowly becoming reality. Many schools were being hastily built or temporarily set up in the so-called third world and in the developing countries. Millions of young adults, just recently laid-off from military duty, applied for a variety of educational courses. The short program was flexible and offered a six-month basic course to teach elementary reading, writing, arithmetic, and physical activities for first- and second-graders.

Young students in their first and second year of schooling would attend classes Monday through Friday for four hours each day. They were also required to take part in daily sport activities for an additional two hours, weather permitting if indoor facilities were not available. The new government was very particular in their quest to boost physical fitness among their young citizens.

A further two-year university program prepared the new teachers with English language skills, basic computer knowledge, science, technology, biology, environmental awareness, home economics, and a variety of the muses: art, music, theater, singing, and dancing, both modern and ballroom, etc., for students in grades third to eighth. And again participation in a daily one-hour fitness program or sport activity was mandatory for all students, unless they had a medical excuse not to partake in it. Talent was rewarded and encouraged. Special promotional programs were made available for the gifted children and for young geniuses.

The launch of mandatory basic and universal education with its strictly dictated ground rules was not welcomed everywhere on the globe. Education was regarded by many countries as an integral part of national identity and they demanded it should be kept under national jurisdiction. The global government argued that the imposed measures only applied to primary education covering grades from first to eighth. Secondary, advanced, and higher education institutions would still remain the domain of national education systems. It further went on to criticize most countries for their irresponsible negligence in regard to physical fitness of children.

"It is a world wide tragedy," chastised the council member responsible for global health. "We are raising young boys and girls by the millions, by the hundreds of millions, who are already overweight when they enter the school system. That's why we have decided to include mandatory sports and exercise programs into the ground school curricula. We sincerely hope the early exposure to physical fitness will successfully carry on through the adolescent years and later on through adulthood and will become part of everyone's lifestyle."

Teachers in the westernized part of the world had already been in uproar when labour unions were abolished. They had taken to the street and protested for months. Now, they were upset again and demonstrated their opposition to the new legislation with disruptive work stoppages and protest marches.

President Chen Li's press secretary commented in a rare response to a reporter's question: "Teachers should go back to work and do something useful, like do what they are getting paid for."

The most militant were Mexico's 1.5 million teachers. Until recently, they had been members of the largest union of any kind in Latin America. Even after their union was officially dissolved, a strong bond still remained among the Mexican educators. Their protests and defiant job actions made headlines in the news quite regularly. When the wage and price control act was announced and the Mexican teachers figured out they would receive the same wages as their U.S. and Canadian colleagues for the next 12 months, they were jubilant and praised the virtues of the global government.

Not so their northern counterparts! Teachers in the United States, in Canada, and in Europe were upset to receive a much smaller paycheque all of a sudden and to lose many of their established benefits. Just last week they were shouting and chanting on their protest marches the clear message of 'solidarity forever;, but today they did not want to share their fortunes with their Mexican brothers. Go figure!

Li seemed undeterred by all the opposition and protests and continued to surge forward with his reform policies.

The birth control plan with the monetary rewards had been well publicized at the beginning of the revolution. People were waiting to take advantage of the large monetary incentives. But meanwhile they were still making babies like there was no tomorrow.

The government had to act and it had to act fast. It was already busy behind the public scene creating a whole new bureaucracy to oversee the launch of the voluntary sterilization program. The new Global Birth Reduction Agency worked in close conjunction with the diverse national health ministries and the Global Ministry of Finance to put the necessary infrastructure in place. Smart and dedicated people tried to develop a foolproof system to discourage all attempts of cheating, either by the patients, the doctors, the sterilization clinics, or corrupt civil servants. This was easier said than done! For instance, how could a women verify her status of eligibility (without a doubt), if she was the mother of one child only or if she was the mother of two or more children? It was impossible.

Eventually the Global Birth Control Agency recommended a revised proposal of the voluntary universal sterilization program to the Supreme Council. The new proposal suggested dropping the original requirements and offering instead a one-time bonus of

10,000 denar at the time of voluntary sterilization. Eligible for this plan were all women between the ages of 18 and 45 and all men between the ages of 18 and 50. Every patient was photographed, eye-scanned, and thumb-printed. Cheques for 10,000 denar, bearing the patient's name, photo, eye scan, and thumbprint were available for personal pickup after seven days at the closest administrative government office.

No one was sure how this program would affect the lives of the people in poor countries and what influence it would have on regional economies. Experts with completely different opinions discussed their theories at length in TV interviews. The birth reduction agency used caution and introduced a gradual implementation of the program in selected countries. Their choice fell on South Africa, Nigeria, Haiti, Dominican Republic, Bangladesh, Australia, Greece, and China. The national health ministries were responsible for the proper execution of the program. The reactions in each of these countries were different and were studied with much interest and avid interpretation.

In Hispaniola there was absolute pandemonium. In Haiti, the process of volunteer sterilization had to be stopped even before it began. Long lines formed days before the announced opening of the clinics. Angry and impatient people were steadily jostling for priority positions in the lines and frequent fighting broke out among the unruly people. The police moved in when the violence escalated, but they could not prevent a bloody incident when four people were killed in Port-au-Prince in front of a still vacant sterilization clinic. In the eastern part of the island, in the Dominican Republic, the chaos was similar. Women in line were robbed of their ID cards and their official birth certificates.

Authorities in Bangladesh were also overwhelmed by the onslaught of applicants, but the women there outnumbered the men by a stunning majority. The reason behind this phenomenon was deliberate misinformation distributed among the men. It went from mouth to mouth like wildfire that one could not get an erection anymore and would be unable to have normal sex after receiving a vasectomy. Even after a few brave men had the procedure done and reported no negative effects, the mistrust persisted for a very long time. Wives used all their wits and all kinds of incentives to persuade their spouses to make the trip to the clinic and to collect the reward money for their bravery.

In Nigeria a different problem surfaced after the sterilized mothers or fathers had received their 10,000 denar cheque. Ruthless gangs were targeting some of the 'newly rich'. They kidnapped their children and held them for ransom. The freshly acquired 10,000 denar changed hands quite often, and when this brutal practice took on epidemic proportions, Interpol was called in to help the local police.

South Africa reported no problems, no stampedes, no demonstrations, and no interruptions at the stations. The procedures were carried out in an orderly fashion at all clinics. Participation was high in general with a noticeably low number of white patients.

Australia recorded relatively low participation of the program, whereas in China, all records were broken, millions and millions lined up every morning and waited patiently to be sterilized. The Chinese Health Ministry had expected a large turnout, but was in no way prepared to deal with the vast amount of people who showed up every morning. A hurriedly devised plan to group the applicants into name categories was introduced. People were told to go home and wait for the announcement when their name category was being processed. Even then, authorities estimated the program to take three, possibly five years for completion.

Greece was the poorest country on the old continent and together with England it was not a member of the European Union. Tourism was the number one industry in Greece because it was an inexpensive and attractive holiday destination. The Greeks had welcomed the inclusion into the global government right from the beginning and they also welcomed the benefits of this union. They showed only a casual interest in the sterilization program and participated in their own laid back way.

After three years, when all the government numbers were compiled and analyzed, there were smiles on the officials' faces.

Population growth had been stopped and it began to reverse. CO2 output had been reduced by 40% and the production of fossil fuels had been cut by a whopping half.

"The results are amazing and very encouraging! We knew it could be done and we delivered," boasted a proud President Chen Li in a rare address to his global citizens. "We accomplished a miracle, I agree, but this will not stop us from performing other miracles. One miracle is not enough! That's why we will not stop and bask in our glory when there is work to be done. We will continue in our vigorous pursuit in the salvation of humankind and our beloved planet. That is our foremost and our primary goal."

Chapter XXIV

Vlado's Take

Vlado mumbles a command in his native Croatian and his wheelchair tilts back to a comfortable reclining position.

"That's much better," he says. "I can't keep sitting on my haunches for too long; after a while, I have to stretch out." He remains quiet and I am watching him. He is thinking. I see it on his face. I know it won't take long and he will announce something outlandish again.

"It was not the sterilization that changed the world," he declares. "It was the pension reform. The fact that every senior gets 1,000 denar—that's one grand every month. Imagine! The very fact changed the world! There are millions and even billions of people who have never seen that much money in their entire lifetime. A thousand every month! Whoa! That is something to pull the family together and to start taking good care of the old ones because they have become the new breadwinners. The younger family members soon realized that the granny and the old grandpa have become extremely valuable and they began looking after their elderly very well so that no harm would come to them. The seniors in the poor regions of the world never had it this good before. Now they can enjoy the few remaining years of their life in a newfound dignity and the proffered respect from the younger generations."

"That holds true for two-thirds of the world," I say. "But do these old family members really receive honest respect or is it just a pretend and paid for loyalty? For us seniors in the advanced and rich western world, it doesn't really apply. We actually lost out on the monetary side of things. How can we support our offspring with a 1,000 denar Old Age Pension? Still not feasible! And family, don't talk about family to me. You had a good family and I had a good family; we both know that. But most in our screwed-up society don't even know what family is anymore. They will have a difficult time to find out who their actual grandparents really are. When it comes to caring for them, attitudes change completely and leave little room for compassion. Why should we be bothered and burdened with them? It is the Health Department's duty to look after the old people and not us."

"You can't complain," replies Vlado. "The Health Department is treating you extremely well, sending you this pretty young nurse. I should be so lucky!" He sighs and grins at me mischievously.

"Ah, never mind, but I agree with you that the pension reform did have a positive impact on most of the older population world-wide and that it has brought considerable relief and improvement to the lives of the poor in our world. It has not eradicated poverty, famine, and the freshwater shortages, but the government is working on it. It all takes time, and I believe they are on the right track. People trust the government and they trust Chen Li. Last year they re-elected over 70% of the original members in the parliament. You can't ask for a better endorsement than that."

Vlado does not go into it and ignores what I have just said. His train of thoughts jumps over to another track.

"The revolution had to come from the top, from a few powerful and visionary men with total conviction. And it did come from the top and that was good. It could not have come from the poor because they were too preoccupied with their own day-to-day survival, and they did not have the leadership and the financial resources to organize themselves. It could not have come from the middle-class because they did not want to leave their comfort zone and ruffle too many feathers. The very rich were divided on the issue of climate change and the extreme measures proposed by many of the activists. The very rich were not ready for sudden fundamental changes that would take away their ornate and limitless lifestyle. They favoured a postponement of those drastic measures and adopted a wait and see attitude. I am glad and I am thankful that the courageous heroes from Muscat had the foresight to put in place the bold doctrines needed to change the world."

"Yeah," I say. "I'm happy about that too. There was lots of talk about saving the environment and the terrible effects of global warming. Even heavyweights like the Pope and the Dalai Lama got involved. It made the news for a day and then it was put on the back burner again. A few days later, nobody talked about it anymore, and it was life and business like usual."

"You know, that slavery was actually never abolished until now?" Vlado is jumping tracks again.

"What do you mean by that?" I am completely caught off guard.

"Well, just look back in history. In Europe they had the feudal system as recently as 200 years ago where the Lords owned the people. The 'subjects' lived and worked on their master's property. They were serfs or slaves, subjected to the will and whim of their owner.

"The colonialists generally found their slaves among the local indigenous people. But quite often there were shortages, and then they imported slaves from Africa and even as far away as China. This practice was especially popular in the Americas. Even until very recently slave labour was used in the multinational capitalistic empires to produce cheap merchandise for the already rich masters in Europe and America. Slaves in China, India, Bangladesh, the Philippines, Indonesia, Vietnam, and Africa. Slaves in Mexico, Honduras, and the rest of Latin America worked for pennies an hour, for only a few dollars in a long day to carve out a meager existence.

"In India, they still exercised the caste system as late as the early-21st century, where a certain low classified portion of the population was condemned by birth to do the dirty and degrading work. I am sure slaves were used in other countries and in other societies around the globe as long as humankind has existed.

"Slave prostitutes were brought into the rich enclaves of the world from many exotic places like Thailand, the Caribbean, and Eastern Europe. But prostitution doesn't flourish anymore as it once did. It seems the appetite for sex is on the decline. Why is that? Why don't people want to fuck anymore? The oldest profession is in a crisis, and I am at a complete loss." He sighs and throws up his hands in resignation.

"Yeah, why is that? I haven't heard the mattresses squeak in a long time. These rhythmic squeaking noises in the hotel room next door used to keep me awake quite often in my younger travelling days. I miss that sound now." I am telling him.

"When have you been in a hotel room lately?" he asks.

"Well, it has been a while," I reminisce. "Perhaps they put better insulation into the walls nowadays."

"Or your hearing is not so good anymore?" Vlado laughs. "I tell you what I think. I think somebody is putting something into our cornflakes to curb our sexual desire. Somebody very high up—that's what, I think! It's been done before in the military, a long time ago. Apparently back then, they used saltpeter and fed it to the soldiers. That would make the pecker shrink, just thinking about it."

"But the government has been very transparent. It wouldn't dare issuing secret orders to the food producers and running the risk of being exposed. It can't be the government."

"Higher up," he says and points to the ceiling.

Angelika is back. She has the mysterious ability to suddenly appear out of nowhere.

"What are you two gentlemen talking about?" she asks sweetly.

"Sex! What else could we be talking about?" I say.

"Well, that's a good subject. I hope it hasn't gotten you overly excited because it is time for your nap now, gentlemen. You need a good rest before the guests arrive and the party begins. Vlado, you go home, please. Adrian is already here to pick you up, and I will tuck the birthday boy into his bed."

Angelika wheels me away and in no time she has me transferred from the wheelchair to my bed. She covers me up and blows me a kiss. "Sweet dreams, handsome." She giggles. I close my eyes and doze off. Only for a moment, I think.

It is quiet in my room. I am awake again, and I am trying to rub the sleep and the fuzziness out of my eyes.

"Do you need your eye drops, sweetheart?" Angelika is instantly by my side. I nod drowsily and she skilfully puts one drop of artificial tears into each of my eyes.

"Blink, blink, blink!" she chants. I sit up and reach automatically for my ISS pad to turn it back on. I always have it shut off when I go to sleep, even for my short afternoon naps. The ISS pad comes alive; it lights up and a clear voice emits from the small rectangular device: "Hello Ed, this is Nadine aboard airship Neutron #1207. I'll be landing at your airport at 14:30 hours. Have you arranged a pickup for me?"

"Who is Nadine?" asks Angelika.

"Oh, she is a good friend and an old flame of mine. I invited her to come to my birthday party. We need somebody to run out to the airport and pick her up. Can you please do it, Angelika?"

"Okay, but then I'll have to leave right away." She seems annoyed. "Why didn't you tell us earlier about her visit? How will I know who she is when I get to the airport?"

"Sorry, it must have slipped my mind. By the way, you can't miss her because she will know who you are. Nadine is a top-notch clairvoyant; she is the best of the best. Believe me."

"Oh my, that is so cool and so out of this world. Yes, I will go and fetch your mystery lady. I'm so excited! Oh my, that is so totally awesome, so, so fucking far out, so, so ... incredibly horny!" She rushes from my room and leaves me speechless. What kind of language is that? Coming from a fine girl like her?

I am still baffled when Jason enters. He is obviously very nervous and he has this withdrawn and serious look. His eyes are only slits in his pale face and they dart around from left to right and all over the place. In a trembling voice he asks, "I overheard everything you were talking about. Who is Nadine?"

"You know who Nadine is, Jeffrey. Or should I say Toby?"

I watch for his reaction and my eyes narrow to half-open slits in my face as well. We keep staring at each other for what seems an eternity and then his features collapse in total resignation and he starts to shake uncontrollably. Is he crying? I'm not sure and I do not say anything. Just let him be.

"How did you find out?" he finally manages to ask me between sobs.

"I always knew that Jason was not your real name. I remembered your face from the news telecast when President Oliver rescued you and that girl from the Fidelity Tower. I knew right away that you were that person, when you applied for the homecare job, but I could not remember your name. I searched secretly without success. Then I had the bright idea to send your voice print to the FBI."

"Oh God, no!" He cradles his head with both hands. "This is the end," he says in a weak voice, more to himself than to me.

"It's the end of the run, but it is not the end of your life," I say.

"Do you think I can get a fair trial in Canada?"

"I have reason to believe there won't be a trial in Canada. I received the FBI report already five years ago. According to that report, Jeffrey Brockerhoff was assassinated together with an innocent cab driver in Chicago on June 2, 2025. As far as the FBI is concerned, you are dead my friend, you are very dead for a long time and your file is closed for a long time, that's for sure. The FBI never followed up on my original request from five years ago. Why would they do anything now?"

"But, how did you find Nadine?" he stutters.

"Actually, it was the other way around. Nadine found me. As you must know, I am no computer whiz, but occasionally I have a brainwave and then I return to the darn thing with a different approach. And what do you know? One lucky day, I typed a few key words and bingo, out pops your picture with the president and your name: Toby Zwosdesky.

"Now, I began to look for Toby Z. in earnest. What I found was just a single person by that name, and I traced it to a defunct address in Seattle. No more info—none, nada! Dead end and end of story. Until a month ago that is, when I received a personal message on my ISS pad: 'Do you still want to talk about Toby Z.? Meet me tomorrow at 15:00 hours at Lily's Café. Please arrange to come with your friend Vlado and his caregiver Adrian.' So, I call Vlado and tell him an old flame of mine will be in town tomorrow and I want to secretly meet up with her. 'Can you please phone Angelika and tell her that you and Adrian plan an afternoon out in downtown and would like me to come along? I don't want her or Jason to know I am meeting a former girlfriend. You know, how jealous she can get!' 'You are a hopeless idiot,' he told me, but he did it. He arranged the outing and that's how I met Nadine."

"Did she tell you everything?" he asks hesitantly.

"Yes, I believe so. Yes, I'm pretty sure I do know your whole sad story."

"But how did she trace me to Prince George and to you?" he wonders out loud.

"That my friend, you can ask her yourself in a few minutes."

He has settled down. His eyes are fixed on a spot at the ceiling and are not shooting around from place to place anymore.

"I am a murderer," he finally says. "I killed a man."

"Yes, I know. You killed a very evil man, but you also exposed the entire evil organization to the FBI and you saved many lives with your action."

He is still staring at the ceiling and does not respond to my comment. Then he lowers his head until his eyes are level with mine.

"You must despise me for what I have done. Please try to understand my desperate situation and please try to forgive me," he pleads with me.

"I have no problems with that, young man. I have already forgiven you. The law and God might look at it differently, but I have decided to leave the law out of your affairs. With God you have to deal on your own when the time comes. As far as I am concerned, you have paid your penance."

He comes over and holds me in an emotional embrace.

"Thank you, dear friend," he says.

"It's okay, son. It's all right." And then I say, "Pretty good detective work, eh?"

He smiles. "You are quite a sleuth. I wouldn't want to have you for an enemy. So, what are you planning to do now?" he asks and rubs his hands.

"I want to celebrate my birthday! When is everybody coming?"

"Oh, that! Ah, between four and five o'clock," he replies, obviously relieved. "I have things to do in the kitchen. But before I do that, I better get you dressed and ready for the world."

In no time, I am dressed and groomed and back on the veranda in my wheelchair. I can hear the banging of car doors, the cheery chatter and laughter of women, and the staccato of their heels on the tiled floor. The door flings open and Nadine is by my side. She hugs me and smothers me with kisses. I am trying to stand up but she keeps me pinned down. I am totally overpowered by so much woman.

"You just stay there, my dear. Do not get up on my behalf. Oh, and happy birthday to you, young man!" another hug and more kisses.

"You make me breathless, and my pulse is racing," I tell her.

"Oh, what a charmer," she waves her hand and blows another kiss. Then she pulls up a lawn chair and sits down next to me. She takes me hand and pets it with a familiar intimacy. Her close presence is most exhilarating. Her perfume is discreet, yet intoxicating. I begin to relax.

"Thanks for coming. It's very important for us and it makes my day!"

"Have you been looking after my boy?" she asks and keeps stroking my hand.

"He has been looking after me, and he has been doing a darn fine job of it. By the way, he knows. I've told him a few minutes ago."

I am sure Jason and Angelika are listening in over the intercom. They always do. There goes my privacy, I know, but then it has its perks. A wireless intercom system had been set up for the entire house, including the veranda and my wheelchair. What I didn't know until recently is that Vlado's room and wheelchair are connected to Jason and Angelika as well, and by some mistake, they are also connected to me. For weeks now, I can hear Vlado snore and sneeze and swear, but I don't tell anyone. It is my little secret and I keep quiet about it.

Nadine jumps up when Jason and Angelika step out onto the veranda. She runs to Jason and embraces him. The reunion is heartfelt and very touching. Both of them are fighting back tears. When the emotional hurdle is finally overtaken and left behind, they begin to laugh and start talking a mile a minute. I have difficulties following their fast-paced conversation.

Angelika breaks up the gibberish and produces a bottle of champagne and some slender glasses.

"This calls for a celebration," she announces with authority and pops the cork from the bottle. She fills the glasses and hands them to us. The tiny prickly bubbles burst and tickle the insides of my nose. "Cheers'" says somebody, and we sip the refreshing chilled champagne. I lean back and enjoy the moment.

Now, all three of them are talking at the same time. They are happy and they are laughing.

"How did you find me, Nadine?" asks Jason.

"Oh, that was easy. You know, I possess special powers and I used them to keep tabs on you. I always knew where you were at any given time. I was worried and frightened on a couple occasions, especially during the volcanic eruption in Seattle."

"Hey, whatever happened to that girl President Oliver rescued together with you, Jason? Anybody know?" I ask.

Everything and everyone freezes up again. They are all staring at me, as if I have just escaped from the zoo or dropped in from outer space. What have I done?

"She is sitting right here," says Angelika sheepishly. "It is me. I am Lori."

Now I am the one who is flabbergasted, completely taken by surprise and my mouth stays open. I look at her, scanning her with new eyes, trying to find something on her that I haven't noticed before. I can't find anything. She smiles.

"But, you are still the same!" I finally stammer like an idiot.

"Yes, I am still the same," she laughs.

"That's incredible! You really fooled me. You sure pulled the wool over my eyes. Women!" I mutter grumpily to myself. "Could never figure them out. Still can't."

Chapter XXV

Lori

Lori stayed at her mother's place after she had parted with Toby and left the rescue shelter. Every day was agonizing and filled with an aching longing for Toby, and her thoughts were filled with fear, with worry and so much uncertainty. The nights did not bring the desired easing to her tensed body and to her agitated mind. They were deprived of sleep and filled with horror scenes and nightmares. She had sent several short messages to Toby and was anxiously waiting for a reply from him, but it did not happen. No message, no sign. The daily course of unproductive waiting drove her crazy. She refused to eat and became a nervous bundle, checking her ISS pad every few minutes. Toby had instructed her to cut communications after four days and to destroy her phone device.

This was day five and she still hung on to her phone, feeling guilty for reneging on her promise to destroy it. She was desperately hoping for some news from Toby. She decided to text him one more time and if she did not receive a reply, she would discard her ISS pad the next day.

A slight vibration alerted her. It was him. An electrifying shock rushed through her tired body and she trembled in anticipation.

"Don't worry any longer, my love. I am fine. Just flew in by chopper from a remote island with a load of badly injured and sick people. A grave situation. I am at the Bellingham Hospital. My next assignment is to help setting up the Filipino rescue centre.

You don't have to wait for too long. Over and out. I love you! A thousand kisses!"

She was overcome by a gentle wave of joy. Her anxiety and her frustrations began to draw back and to minimize. She was happy.

"He is alive and he is free and he loves me!" she yelled. Her mother rushed over and hugged her and they were dancing in the room. It was the breakthrough her daughter needed. Lori instantly transformed into a new person, a happy-go-lucky young woman. Cheerful and lively.

She even ate her lunch, skipped out of the house, and went for a walk along the river. Lori knew that Toby's texted news contained a cryptic message. She was analyzing every word, but couldn't find anything unusual, except the short phrase: 'Over and out.' 'Over' must mean the end of communication and the order to destroy the devices.

She took her ISS pad and tossed it into the river. 'Out'? She chewed on it for awhile, and then it dawned on her, Toby was going to leave the country and go to Canada. They had talked about this possibility.

On the tenth day her mother showed her an SMS she had just received. "Hello Connie, how is your love life? I have just met the most amazing guy. Out of this world! I am head over heels. He is a wonderful man, a gorgeous looking Filipino. Fermin and I plan to meet his family on the weekend. I can hear wedding bells. Wish me luck! Hugs, Jill," and it was signed off with a happy face.

This was the signal she had been waiting for. 'Out of this world!' It could only mean that Toby must have left the country already. She made preparations to travel to Bellingham on the weekend to find the Filipino rescue centre and to find Fermin, the gorgeous looking guy! She smiled. It was most amusing to her.

The rescue centre had ballooned into an enormous tent city. The place was bustling with activity and the sheer size of it was stunning. It was totally incomprehensible for Lori to find a pulsating vibrant community cluttered about in the middle of nowhere.

A sign read: 'All Arrivals, No Exceptions! Report to Admissions! Orange Tent #3'.

She stood in line. The first question she was asked: "Are you a volunteer?"

"Actually, I am looking for Fermin."

"Okay, then you must be a nurse. Name? What's your name, lady? I don't have all day."

"Lori Bishop," she stuttered.

"Spell it for me. Okay here is your name tag: Lori B. Nurse. Take your stuff to Orange Tent #8. That's the nurses' tent. Next!" he bellowed.

Lori found the nurses' tent, where she met Angie, a tired look-ing Filipino nurse.

"I am so glad you come to help us. We are totally overworked. Too many hours in a day, too many sick people," she stretched out her hand to greet Lori.

"Pleased to meet you. I start my next shift in 10 minutes, please come with me." Lori tried to explain that actually she wasn't a nurse, but Angie waved her off.

"You are a woman and you care. You want to help and that is important. The rest will come naturally, believe me. I show you."

Ten minutes later, Lori started her new career as a caregiver and a nurse's aide. The workload was overwhelming. After a long first shift, she collapsed onto her fold-up cot. Her sleep was deep and she felt rejuvenated when Angie woke her. Angie was a pas-sionate professional and a terrific teacher. Lori admired her un-compromising commitment for her job and her self-sacrificing dedication to help the sick and needy.

Lori learned how to clean and dress wounds, how to apply and change bandages, check temperatures, blood pressures and blood sugar levels, keep medical charts up-to-date, sponge bathe and dress patients—men and women and children—help them to and from the bathroom or empty their bedpan. There were sev-eral procedures she was not allowed to perform, like stitching up cuts, hooking up an IV or catheter, setting needles or taking blood samples.

The days just flew by, one by one. They were busy days; they were long days. They were days filled with intensity, with interesting and tiring work, with gratifying and rewarding work. Some days were sad because a patient had died.

Whenever she asked for Fermin, she was told that he was busy or simply not available. Well, maybe it was better not to rush things.

"Tomorrow I am going home to my family and to my lover," said Angie. "Do you have a lover, Lori?"

"Yes, I have. But it was only for one night."

"Oh, what a dirty pig!"

"No, no. It is not like that. It is just that we are separated now, and I have to find him."

"Oh my poor little dove," Angie flung her arms around her. "I feel so sorry for you. Don't waste your time on a dream; don't chase a no good guy. Once they are gone, they are gone for good."

Lori cried and went outside. It was raining. It rained every day and it didn't help her gloomy mood.

"I hear you are looking for me, gorgeous."

She spun around and came face to face with a dubious looking character.

"You wish, you creep! Nobody is looking for you, you lowlife," she spat icily at him.

"The borders are still open and you must leave in the morning. I have an envelope from Toby with instructions for you. You must memorize the instructions and destroy the letter. Rip it into tiny pieces and discard them in several different places. Tonight you will exchange identity papers with Angie, including the name tags. We had an expert insert your picture into Angie's passport. She is flying home on a military transporter and won't need a passport. In the morning, you will accompany a patient who is being transferred to Abbotsford Hospital. Abbotsford is in Canada. Good luck, my dear. Say hello to Toby from me."

"You must be Fermin, I am so sorry—" She wanted to apologize for her earlier rudeness, but he had already turned around and disappeared in the dark of the night.

The Greyhound bus maintained a steady speed on the Trans

Canada Highway, en route to Kamloops, a city in the southern interior of British Columbia.

Lori leaned back in her seat and fumbled in her coat pocket for her new Filipino passport. Angie had given it to her last night.

"You are now officially my daughter. It will help your cover. I like to hear from you. Stay in touch, dear friend, and when you call me, don't forget to say 'mother' to me."

She looked at it again. There was her perfect picture and her new name Angelika Brandauer, a birthdate and a street address in Manila. She still had difficulty pronouncing her new name properly. It was not a Filipino name; she was pretty sure of that. There must be a story behind all that, she thought. Maybe one day she'll find out, but now was the end of Lori Bishop and the new beginning as Angie Brandauer. The transformation was complete and she had to get used to her new identity. She was Angie, and that was it! It had to be done. Her future with Toby depended on it.

By the time she arrived in Kamloops, it was already dark and it was raining, rather unusual for the city, which was located in an arid and semi-desert-like region of the province. She had spotted a few houses that were lit up in pretty Christmas decoration. It brought nostalgic sentiments to her and she caught herself wiping away a few lonely tears, but she regained her composure when she climbed off the bus. She checked into a small hotel for the night and continued her travels next day to Edmonton, again by Greyhound bus.

Dawn was breaking when she boarded the bus in the morning. She selected the seat right behind the driver and enjoyed the full view of the highway and the scenery through the large panoramic windshield. The highway followed the winding North Thompson River through a pretty valley with forested hills on both sides. Later on, the hills gave way to imposing mountains in the distance, but after two hours, the sky clouded over and it began to rain. Soon the mountains were covered in mist and disappeared from her view. Visibility worsened by the minute and her interest waned; she became bored and closed her eyes. She had seen enough mountains and trees to last her for a while.

A tap on her shoulder made her jump in her seat. It was the bus driver.

"Lady, we are in Valemount. You have to change buses here. I'm taking this one back to Kamloops. This is my daily run, Kamloops to Valemount and back to Kamloops. I like it. I'm home every night. Let me help you with the luggage, miss. Just follow me, so I make sure you get on the right bus to Edmonton and not on the one to Prince George."

Cold air rushed through the open door into the heated bus. The friendly driver extended his hand to help Lori down the steps.

"Careful! It's a bit slippery, miss," he said.

"Oh, my God, it is snowing!" Angie cried out and pulled her coat tighter around her waist.

"It's been snowing for the last hour or so, ever since we left Blue River. It's early this year. Hasn't snowed this early for ages. Maybe we'll have a white Christmas for a change," he told her and walked her over to a parked bus with the engine idling.

"Your bus won't leave until 1:00 p.m., so you have an hour and 10 minutes to stretch your legs and have some lunch. The café is right over there." He pointed at a yellow building.

Angie was lucky again. There were only a few passengers in the back of the bus and the seat behind the driver was empty. She sat down. Minutes later, a woman in uniform entered the bus.

"Good afternoon," she said. "My name is Cindy. I am your operator of this here coach, and I'm taking you to Edmonton today. There is light snow in the forecast for most of the way, but we are not anticipating any delays along the route. We are on schedule to arrive at 8:30 p.m. tonight. Relax and enjoy the ride!" She laughed and began to back the bus out of the station.

Cindy was a good driver. She handled the huge vehicle with ease and a certain self-assurance. Angie noticed it right away and it was comforting for her to know that somebody competent was behind the wheel.

The bus station in Edmonton was a busy place with many arrivals and departures at this time of evening. There was a coming and a going. Lori took a taxi to the address she memorized. The Lebanese cab driver had no clue where it was, but his GPS told him where to go.

"Without GPS, I can never do this job. So many strange names. Take me years to pronounce and more years to find. But with GPS it's easy. It's kid stuff," he told her. He helped her unload her luggage and she gave him a tip.

"Just wait a minute, please. I'll have to check if they are home," she told him and walked up the driveway. When she knocked at the door, an older lady opened it and said, "Hi, we've been waiting for you for a long time. Come on in." She ushered Angie through the tiny entranceway into a small living room.

"Come in, come in," she beckoned. "Meet my husband Nick, and by the way my name is Lydia. Make yourself a home. You are welcome in this house and you can stay here until Toby says it is okay for you to go. Understand? We are friends of Toby. He such a nice guy and you are perfect for him, just like he told us. Please, sit down. Make yourself comfortable. You must be really tired from the long trip, and you must be hungry. Can I fix you a tea and a sandwich?" she asked.

"Thank you, that would be lovely," Angie said and the older lady rushed off into the kitchen.

Lydia and Nick were a retired couple, who had emigrated from the Ukraine to Canada many years ago. They lived in a modest house in an older part of the city. A white picket fence enclosed a garden in front of their home. Where others usually grew lawn, Lydia and Nick grew flowers and vegetables, herbs and raspberries and sunflowers. But now it was winter. The garden was deserted and covered with a light dusting of snow.

Angie stayed with the friendly and hospitable couple for almost four months. She celebrated Christmas with them, which was extremely depressing. She longed to be with Toby and could not understand why they had to remain separated.

Two weeks later, she celebrated Ukrainian Christmas with them, and they all went to church for the midnight service. There she felt like a child again, bedazzled by the festive setting, the glitter and the multitude of bright shining candles.

Ever since she bought her bus ticket in Abbotsford, she called herself Angie, and that's how Lydia and Nick introduced her to their church friends: Angie, our niece from British Columbia, and Angie called them Auntie Lydia and Uncle Nick.

She registered with the college and enrolled into a nurse's beginner program. She also started work as a volunteer at a senior's care home nearby. These were Toby's instructions. It was easy to get a driver's license, a social security card, a bank account, a credit card, a mobile phone, and such things in those turbulent times. Over a million displaced or frightened people were on the move. They were fleeing the coastal areas of British Columbia, especially the metropolitan hubs of Victoria and Vancouver in search for safer havens in the country's interior.

An estimated 200,000 found their way to Edmonton seeking refuge since the catastrophic day of October 30 when the Big One struck, when the earth opened up and swallowed Seattle. Almost 400,000 converged on the city of Calgary and created chaos and confusion. Municipal services broke down because they were crushed by the overwhelming demand. It put a chokehold on everything. Every single government agency in Western Canada was swamped, totally overrun and buried in applications and requisitions.

The federal and provincial governments reacted fast. In a hastily called combined emergency meeting—the first one in Canadian history—a resolution was passed to cut red tape and to fast track all applications. The Red Cross, the Salvation Army, and other volunteer aid groups were also stretched beyond their limits. It was impossible to feed all the hungry people and to find adequate shelter for all the applicants.

At the same emergency meeting, it was further decided to issue special charity support grants to cities and municipalities affected by the unprecedented influx of refugees from coastal British Columbia. Calgary, for example, received $80 million and Edmonton received $40 million of emergency funds to be dispersed among the local aid groups at their own discretion.

Banks experienced similar problems. Originally banks had been among the first to embrace the new computer age and internet technology. They soon began to streamline their operations to please their profit hungry shareholders. A series of radical cutbacks followed. Personnel were laid off or lured into early retirement; unprofitable and marginal branches were closed. Customers were enticed to use online or telephone banking services and were further persuaded to use ATM machines for cash withdrawals for deposits and for bill payments. More staff were trimmed from the roster. The banks were well on their way to computerized banking and more of the workload was actually shifted to the customer. But being minimal at the beginning, the customers did not notice it. They remained sitting at their desks at home or at the office trying to figure out the new challenge on their computer or iPhone. And when they did so, they proudly submitted the required task to the bank's computer. They did not have to lift their behind off the chair; they did not have to walk or drive to the bank either. It was so super convenient.

The skeleton staff left at the few bank outlets was no match for the sudden deluge of new customers pouring in and requesting personal banking and personal service. Some unfortunate souls had lost their bank records and carried only little or no ID; others experienced memory losses. Many of the claims were legit, but many others were fraudulent. Head offices reacted fast to this crisis and flew in additional staff from the east and with them a number of fraud detection experts.

Angie had over $12,000 in cash, money she had withdrawn from her account while she stayed at her mother's place. She did not wait long. As soon as she received her student card, she took her Filipino passport and $5,000 of her money and went to the bank. It took most of the day to stand in line, but finally she had a bank account, a temporary bankcard, and an approved credit card was on the way.

She had always known that she was pregnant. She was so positive since the night she and Toby made love in the executive suite on the ninth floor of the Fidelity Towers. When she was going through her first morning sickness, she felt absolutely rotten, but she still smiled. My little boy is announcing his presence! she thought and she blew kisses in all directions. Although direct contact with Toby was forbidden, she had to get a message to him.

Angie was desperate. She told Lydia and Nick the good news and also about her predicament that she could not share the happy moment with Toby. Lydia hugged her.

"We are so glad for you. You phone your mother in Manila. You can use our phone. Your mother, she know father of the baby; she will find him and tell him. He better be there for baby, when is born."

Angie had maintained communications with the original Angelika Brandauer in Manila, whom she always addressed as 'mother'. Occasionally she phoned her or exchanged messages with her.

"Don't tell me you are pregnant! I knew nothing good would come of it. He wants to be my son-in-law? Never! I tell him, he better smarten up and start saving money for the baby. Is his responsibility. I cannot pay for a baby. I pay for your education already and that is lots of money—all I can afford. He is no good for you, my dear. There will be no wedding, I can tell you that!"

"But I love him, mother," Angie cried.

"You are both crazy," mother said and hung up.

Two days later, Angie received a short SMS message, just two words: 'Lovely news' and it was signed with a happy face. For the next days, Angie was on cloud nine, happy and cheerful. She knew that all the sacrifices would eventually pay off and lead to the final goal, the unification with her beloved Toby.

It was a sunny and warm spring day in late March. Angie was in a happy mood and very proud. She had just successfully completed her first trimester at nursing school ending up at the top of her class. Every test and every exam she had finished with excellent marks and today she received high praise from all her instructors. She felt like celebrating, but when she arrived at home, she was greeted by Nick and Lydia with reserved politeness. Something was wrong, she sensed it right away. She noticed with concern that Lydia had been crying.

"What's wrong?" she asked, alarmed. "What has happened here?" Nick handed her an envelope and Lydia's eyes welled up in tears again. The envelope was addressed to Nick and it was slit open.

"Look for yourself," he told her. She fingered excitedly inside the envelope and pulled out a bus ticket to Prince George and a short letter. "Congratulations, my love! It's time to move on. I can't wait any longer. I have to be with you. Please get off the bus in McBride tomorrow. I'll be there." It was signed with a happy face.

Angie was delirious. She let out a scream of abundant happiness and she was dancing through the living room and through the entire house.

"Yes, yes!" She was panting. "Yes! This is the happiest day of my life!"

"We are happy for you, Angie," said a tearful Lydia. "But we are also very, very sad that we are losing you and maybe we will never see you again."

"How can you say that? You will come to Prince George, of course, because you are invited to our wedding! And we will come to Edmonton and visit you as often as possible. That's a promise. Yes, and you will come to the christening of our son because you are the godparents. Isn't life wonderful?" She continued dancing.

She remembered Valemount well. Here she had to switch buses. The driver pointed out the connecting bus to Prince George and the yellow café. It was all coming back and familiar to her and she walked over to the yellow café and ordered a small lunch and a Coke. Her excitement was building, her heart was pounding, and she could not help it when she climbed on board the bus. McBride was only an hour away.

What would Toby say? Would he recognize her? Would he still like her?

She was a totally different woman now, much more matured; she had changed her appearance and her mannerism. Her hair was short and blond. She wore baggy jeans, winter boots and a hooded anorak, nothing that would make her look attractive. Her speech pattern had involuntary adopted Canadian phrases and expressions and her name had also changed. People liked to compliment her name. "Angelika? How do you pronounce it?" And when she told them, they would say: "Oh, that is so melodic!"

She stood up and went to the bathroom at the back of the bus, concentrating on each one of the seven fellow passengers and trying to memorize their faces and the obvious details. She had already carefully scrutinized each of them when she boarded the bus. It had become a daily routine to be extra vigilant and always alert after Toby and she went their separate ways into hiding. In all the times, she had never spotted anybody suspicious. Toby must be phobic to put on this charade, she thought.

'Well, he will have time to explain it all to me and I will have time to listen to him. FBI in Canada? I don't think so. Gimme a break, mister!'

"Is McBride a scheduled stop?" she asked the bus driver when she returned to her seat.

"Yes, it is, ma'am," he answered.

"I have to get off there; my boyfriend is picking me up," she told him.

"Boyfriend? I thought you were married!"

"Yeah, sort of. We will be married pretty soon."

She stood on the sidewalk with her bag and a suitcase.

"Looking for a ride, missy?" An ugly dark green car pulled up to the curb. It was him. He got out of the car and she melted in his arms. Their kisses were hungry and passionate. People smiled.

"Who is this happy couple?" They wondered. McBride was still a small town in March of 2029 with a population of less than a thousand; everyone knew everybody. The couple on the sidewalk were definitely strangers, but just the same, they were likable strangers.

"You look wonderful," he said between kisses. "I've been waiting for this moment for a long time."

"You and me both!" she cried.

They checked into a motel along Highway 16. She was trembling.

"Can we make love?" she asked.

"What about the baby?"

"Just be gentle, Toby. Just be gentle and it will be all right!"

And he was.

It had happened before many times in her secret dreams and it was happening now, just as wonderful and sweet as in all of her dreams before.

"Nothing will ever break this love. Nothing," she said breathlessly. "I love you, Toby."

"My name is Jason," he told her. "And what might your name be my lovely maiden?"

"I am a Filipino with a German name." She giggled. "Listen carefully. My name is Angelika Brandauer."

"It's beautiful! It rolls off your tongue as smooth as silk."

"I have practised a lot. It's much easier to pronounce than Toby Zwosdesky."

They both laughed.

Angelika leans back in her chair, lifts her head, and looks coyly at us. She brushes away a lonely tear and tries to smile.

"This is my story. We married two months later. Nick and Lydia came to the wedding and helped us celebrate the marvellous event. I continued my courses at the College of New Caledonia and Jason arranged my employment to this wonderful man." She is pointing at me.

"Incredible!" I am still taken aback by the events of the day and by Angelika's revelations. I am lifting my right finger in an accusing gesture, and with a wavering hand, I begin to speak.

"You have been cleverly hiding your relationship from me for all these years. I feel like an old fool. At times I seemed to notice there was something going on between you two. Something more than just professional friendship. And I thought: 'Why not! They are both young and attractive.' But I never suspected anything like that. Where is your boy and what is his name?"

"His name is Toby, of course, because Toby is the love of my life. We live with my adopted 'mother', the real Angelika Brandauer from Manila, just two blocks away from here. She has been a blessing for all of us and a wonderful friend and teacher to me."

"I'd like to meet her and I'd like to meet Toby," I tell her.

We are momentarily interrupted by a crackling sound in the intercom. I can hear a thud and then the gargled voice of my friend pleading: "Help! Help! Please, help me!"

Jason and Angelika rush out with lightening speed and leave me behind. I can hear the distant wailing sound of a siren, but I do not connect it to the instant medical alarm system that automatically alerts the medics. My blood pressure is up, and I feel an anxiety attack approaching. I am gasping for air and try to bring my breathing under control, but I am not successful. My ears are pounding. The frightening thought that my friend is in trouble and that something very bad is taking place next door claws at me with a terrifying grip and almost chokes me.

"Oh, my God! I think he is gone. He had a massive heart attack!" I can hear Jason's blurred voice. "Hurry, get the paddles. We have to work him hard; you know the routine!"

For the next few minutes I can only hear indistinguishable noises and the pounding in my ears increases. I don't know what is happening. Now I can make out heavy boots scurrying over the tiled floor and loud commanding voices, noisy movements, a muffled sound, and then the slamming of doors and a loud siren as the ambulance takes off.

Nadine takes my hand and strokes it lightly. "He will be all right," she assures me, but I don't believe her and I am scared.

The doorbell rings. Probably guests arriving. Angelika sends them home. The party is cancelled. I don't want to see anybody, but I don't want to be alone either. Nadine stays with me and she whispers encouraging words, soothing words. I still don't believe her. I am so worried for my friend.

A cool breeze is blowing in from the east and the sky is clouding over. I begin to shiver and they move me inside where it is much more pleasant. Nadine is doing all the talking and I listen only with half an ear. I find it hard to concentrate and my mind trails off again and again.

The phone rings. Everyone and everything freezes instantly. The conversation stops in midair; Nadine's mouth is still half open. Then the second ring. Angelika gets up and reaches for the telephone. All eyes are on her.

"Hallo! Yes. Okay. That is good. Thank you, Adrian. Yes, we will pray for him. Thanks for letting us know. Okay. Keep us updated. Thanks again! Yes, I'll tell him the good news!"

"They stabilized Vlado. He is resting comfortably for the night," she informs us.

"Thank you, Lord," I mumble with a big sigh of relief.

Chapter XXVI

Anno Domini 2035

Many changes have taken place since the installation of the global government on July 1, 2029, changes and reforms that altered and affected the life of every human being on the planet.

And when God turned towards earth, He found pleasure in what He saw. The people of the earth had come together under one government. They had adopted the same general rules for everyone and they communicated in a common language for better understanding amongst each other. They had also curbed their animal-like breeding habits and began to spread their semen more sparingly. Education and living standards had improved rapidly among the poor and became the additional factors in reducing the overall birthrate. God also saw that the raping of the environment had stopped, and he noticed with satisfaction the enormous clean-up efforts in all parts of the troubled planet.

Every time, I am reflecting back on the events of the 'Big One', when the earth heaved under the sea and collapsed at another site as the 'super hole' in Seattle, I believe we have been very lucky. It could have been much worse.

On the grand scale of total destruction, this catastrophe was only a minor occurrence, despite its tremendous devastation and the horrific loss of human lives. To put it in perspective on a scale from one to ten, the Big One comes in only as a four.

The 'ones' are the hurricanes, the floods, and the wildfires. The 'twos' are found among earthquakes, volcanic eruptions, super-storms, and tsunamis. The 'threes' represent the nonviolent killers, like droughts, extreme heat waves, and fresh water shortages.

Imagine a colossal incident when an entire continent disappears and a new one rises up at an opposite part of the planet with only a few survivors left in some remote areas. It would be the end of civilization as we know it and a return to an obscure and primitive beginning where survival of the fittest and strongest would triumph. That would be an eight on this scale, and the total annihilation of the planet a number ten.

The Big One was the catalyst. It galvanized humankind together into one authoritative entity, which now has the capability to make universal decisions on short notice, without the hassle and delay of ill-tempered radical elements or short-sighted and ego-minded interest groups. I also suspect a touch of divine intervention here from time to time, and I want to thank the Lord for it.

Fracking is outlawed and has stopped completely after it was linked to several minor earthquakes in areas previously unknown to have tremors. Drilling into the earth's crust past the depth of 2,000 metres is also prohibited. There were constant rumours that fracking was a contributing factor to trigger the events of the Big One, but it was never scientifically substantiated.

Mining experienced huge cutbacks and sweeping changes in recent years. Mining now is state-owned and it is operated exclusively by the individual states, but it is universally regulated by the Global Ministry for Mines and Resources. Underground mining is on the way out, and the first mines to close were the coal mines. Eventually all underground mining will cease operations by the year 2045.

Everywhere around the globe, weapons of mass destruction are now officially destroyed or decommissioned. No more caches and no more stockpiles of biological, chemical, or nuclear weaponry had been found in the past two years. Inventories of bombs and landmines were also destroyed or dismantled, but there are still tremendous numbers of undetected and undetonated bombs and landmines hidden in the ground and in the water. The tedious cleanup continues.

The decimated armed forces in each one of the world's countries took on the role and responsibility of ridding humankind of these evil killing and maiming devices. The armed forces are also being retrained in new skills to become specially qualified first response squads to act on any natural catastrophe.

Most of the navy vessels ended up in scrapyards and so did all the submarines. A few selected aircraft carriers, mainly stocked with helicopters, remain stationed at strategic locations. They are needed to act quickly in case disaster strikes in the area of their immediate operating range.

The possession of firearms and ammunition is only allowed to military personnel and to law enforcement officers. The possession of such firearms and ammunition by any other persons is strictly prohibited. Hunting as a sport is a thing of the barbaric past.

The publication or distribution of literature or instruction material on how to build or make weapons of mass destruction, firearms, and ammunition is punishable with the death penalty. Stupid things like toy guns or other imitation weaponry are outlawed and the manufacture of such items is forbidden. Drones are further apparatus prohibited from being in private hands or being operated by private enterprises.

The sale and possession of alcohol, tobacco products, and narcotics to minors under the age of 18 is prohibited and so is access and exposure to these products.

The sale and possession of wireless electronic communication devices to children below the age of 14 years is also forbidden under Global Law. Furthermore, the usage and the operation of such devices by children under the age of 14 years is not permitted because several alarming studies revealed that over 100 new medical and psychological syndromes can be associated to the usage and exposure of such devices.

There was a public outcry and a short-lived revolt by the youngest of our generations, the global children, when this controversial measure was introduced into law. Chen Li and the Supreme Council were puzzled at first to receive such a hostile reaction. They lost much credibility, even among their own supporters. But then the government put itself back into the positive limelight and passed a much heralded section to the labour law, which simplified the contentious issue of universally paid holidays.

Every employed person age 18 to age 65 is now entitled to a yearly paid holiday. It is based on the age of the employee and it is very easy to calculate: a person age 18 will receive 18 days of paid holidays per year, a person age 19 will receive 19 days of paid holidays per year, a person age 20 will receive 20 days of paid holidays per year, and so on.

People love Chen Li since then and consider him a genius. The global government is encouraging the working population to get away and take the yearly holiday and recuperate from the stress at the workplace. It offers full income tax exemption for travel expenses occurred to and from the holiday destination when using the environment-friendly way of travel by airship, wind/solar powered ships, or by electric trains.

"Capitalism is defeated," declared Chen Li triumphantly in a recent speech. "And we have done it alone, without the bullish advice from the slick Harvard boys and the econo-gangsters from Chicago, who have robbed and ravished every place on earth in the 'sacred name' of democracy without regard for the people and the environment. They were preaching the glorified views of their false democracy, their contorted virtues of privatization, and the highly-praised values of an uncontrolled free market system that allowed them to steal the massive profits and to put a chokehold of misery, poverty, and slavery on every upstart and developing nation.

"Today, the time of misery and enslavement is over. The bells of freedom are ringing and they will be ringing every day from now on!

"Capitalism is defeated and the true democracy is the governance of the day! We govern sensibly, practically, and fairly, and we employ the great talent and know-how that is out there to tackle the enormous challenges facing us. We are working tirelessly at it and we are making progress. Most of our projects are coming along smoothly and will meet the desired schedules, but others are painstakingly slow and require more thorough studies and evaluations, but we are moving ahead, and we know that we are on the right track.

"We are downsizing! Yes, you've heard right. We are downsizing, but we are not cutting jobs to increase profits like the multinationals used to do. We are not elected to lay off employees and to increase profits. No! We are here to downsize on pollution, to downsize on CO2 emissions, and to downsize on the usage of fossil fuels. We are here to downsize the world's population, to downsize poverty and famine, and we are succeeding because we have topped all expectations.

"We are also downsizing the dirty generating of electric power. I am very happy to announce that the last coal-fired generating station in India has been taken out of service. There are no more coal-fired generators on this planet and the last nuclear power generators are limited to the 22 aircraft carriers stationed on important guard duty around the globe. New technology will eventually replace the nuclear power installations on these aircraft carriers with 'clean energy'.

"I am well aware that in many parts of the world electric power supply is not always sufficient and that many electricity grids are underdeveloped and underpowered. We are working on the problem and hope to overcome these shortages with a better distribution system soon. Please be patient.

"In a few years, there will be enough electric power for everyone. We strongly believe that the demand can soon be met. The combination of our declining population with the accelerated construction of 'solar highways', and with the current solar and wind farms, as well as the existing hydro-power dams, virtually guarantees sufficient supply for the future. The long-term goal is to reduce the number of wind farms and to start decommissioning some of of the hydro-power dams and reclaim the flooded lands. We all know that man-made dams will not last forever. We have a team of experts, engineers, and geologists checking the existing structures for safety and for their estimated lifespans.

"Our priorities also focus on the two most important elements in our lives because, frankly, without them there simply would be no life on earth. The two elements are water and air. We do have water and we do have air, so what's the big deal you may think. Yes, we do have water and we do have air, but both of them are heavily polluted and loaded with toxins. We are still releasing untreated wastewater and industrial discharge into the ground, into our rivers and lakes, and into our oceans. Although, it now happens at a much reduced level then at the height of capitalism, it still adds to the overall toxicity and impurity of our waters.

"Our hope and our goal over the next 10 years is to eliminate raw sewage and industrial effluence from entering our freshwater systems and our oceans. The council members and all your elected representatives are working feverishly to introduce a clean water bill to the house for ratification. It will definitely call for mandatory wastewater treatment facilities in all parts of the world and the eventual stop of all untreated discharges.

"The adequate distribution of the world's freshwater resources remains an almost impossible problem for humankind to solve and it is an area of grave concern to all of us. A freshwater pipeline from water-rich British Columbia in Canada to drought-stricken California brings only minimal relief and does not leave a measurable impact. The construction of the experimental pipeline was originally approved by the global government. It met strong opposition in Canada, but eventually the global ideal of sharing one's resources was grudgingly accepted. Yet the results of this megaproject are disappointing.

"Humankind is no match for the awesome powers of nature. But we can take some steps for our protection and small measures to correct the shortcomings. We are increasing the number of desalination plants on the African continent and bringing water to areas of the encroaching desert. With laborious intensity, thousands of dedicated young people plant shrubs and trees and put up intricate irrigation systems to stop the desert from spreading further. These are a tough new breed of shrubs and trees that can survive for long periods of time on a minimal amount of water.

"Four hundred million bottles of drinking water are produced every day and distributed through government affiliates to needy people in the world who are deprived of this precious and life-saving liquid.

"On the other front, dealing with air pollution, we are also gaining quite satisfactorily—mostly due to the decrease of heavy industrial production, the reduced military, a smaller fleet of operating jet planes, a significant drop in the number of uneconomic diesel-guzzling transport trucks, and the complete shutdown of all coal-fired generators. Just to name a few contributing factors for the success. Regulations and policies are in place. We know they are working and we can look ahead to a steady improvement of our air quality.

"I know that some of these measures seem small and insignificant, but they are not because they bring relief to the suffering and they save thousands from dying. We are now in a position to take a bit more of a positive outlook on things and we can brush aside the gloomy days, which led to the emergency summit in Muscat."

Chapter XXVII

Adieu

The UNBC Hospital in Prince George is still in the centre of the city, at the same spot, where it began as a modest medical clinic almost a century ago. Ever since then, it has seen a steady and remarkable growth. Over most of the 100 years, the hospital has been a busy construction site. Many alterations and renovations took place in that time and many new levels and new wings were added to the existing structure. New buildings and edifices sprung up all over the enlarged hospital grounds. Even before the turn of the millennium, PGRH, as it was called then, was already the largest employer in the city. It still holds that important position today.

When the Big One struck on October 30, 2028, it caused a massive exodus of over a million people from the coastal cities of British Columbia. They ran in panic for safety and believed they could find it in the vast interior of the province or in other parts of Canada. In the capital city of Victoria, the politicians debated in the shortest sitting ever recorded in the provincial legislature to move the provincial government to Prince George and make this city the new capital of BC.

The reasons for their decision to relocate in our city were multi-fold. There was the large land base of 318 square kilometres within the city limits housing a small population of only 100,000. Toronto or Chicago have approximately twice the area size of

Prince George, but claim to have an astounding population base of over three million each. Ergo, there is room for growth, lots of growth within our city, plus there are millions of acres of uninhabited bush and forest surrounding it.

Prince George is also the geographical navel of British Columbia and it is appropriately called the 'Centre City'. It is situated at the confluence of two great rivers, the mighty Fraser and the charming Nechako. Two major highways and two railroads cross the city and connect it in all four directions with the rest of the country and the continent and make it an import transportation hub. YKS boasts a large fleet of modern passenger and cargo airships with daily scheduled flights to 42 destinations.

Prince George has the land, the water, the infrastructure, and the power, of course! Electrical power, which is, coming in gigawatts from several Peace River generating facilities and winding its way south along strong thick wires strung high above on monstrous steel stilts. Here, in Prince George at the Williston sub-station, some of the transmission cables branch off to the west while the mainline continues south to eventually join the U.S. grid.

Buried in the ground, just bypassing the city at several points is an array of multiple pipelines. They carry enormous amounts of unrefined oil from the Athabasca tar sands to waiting tankers at the Pacific port of Kitimat; others push enormous amounts of natural gas from British Columbia's northern regions to liquefying plants in Prince Rupert, where again a fleet of tankers is waiting to be filled.

Out of sight, out of mind! People have a short memory! Forgotten are the emotional pleas, the outbursts from passionate pipeline opponents, some 20 years ago, when public hearings were held in towns and cities along the proposed pipeline routes. Forgotten are the loud protests and the strong objections of many native leaders. Luckily there have been no accidents or major spills so far and a guarded acceptance is now tolerated.

But Prince George has never completely lost its bad reputation as a rough and tough frontier's town and a crime-infested place, although the city has made great strides to rid itself of the troublesome slum areas and the vagrant downtown population. The undesirables were secretly shipped back to their towns of origin; others were relocated to Vancouver or Victoria, where there is still a huge inventory of vacated housing. This was all done on orders of the provincial government. Seems the politicians want to live in a peaceful and secure environment, unmolested by panhandlers, pimps and whores, drunks and junkies.

The transformation that took off in recent years is remarkable. They totally rebuilt and redesigned downtown and the bowl area, interspersed with luscious mini parks, smart residential housing, elegant office buildings, small commercial outlets, quaint stores and boutiques and inviting sidewalk cafés, making it an appealing place to visit and to live in.

Other drawbacks in the past that made people think twice before moving to Prince George were its remoteness, the isolation, and the harsh climate. But worldwide climate change benefited the city well. We can now boast four distinct and perfectly balanced seasons and not six months of winter anymore. Vlado jokingly tells everybody that we live in 'Northern California' and that he intends to plant bananas next year.

My friend is in ICU for the third straight day, and we are approaching the elevator to take us up to him.

"Are you okay?" Angelika asks.

"No, I'm not," I say misty-eyed, and I sound like a little boy. Suddenly I feel small and frail. "I'm scared," I whimper.

Angelika reaches for my hand and holds it. It is only a short elevator ride. Jason gets my wheelchair out of the lift cage with ease and pushes me through the long hospital corridor to the nurses' station and I clasp the armrests for support. My caregivers talk to the young nurse behind a solid and high counter, and then she comes out of her cubicle, puts her index finger to her lips, and motions us to follow her.

"Herr Kamerad," his voice is barely audible. His brown eyes have lost their sparkle and are not focused. He looks pale and tired. "Herr Kamerad, you came to say goodbye?" he hisses now with difficulty.

"Oh, no, no, no! No goodbyes!" I protest. "You have to plant bananas next year! I'll teach you how to grow a garden," I promise.

A smile rushes over his pale face and he closes his eyes. I keep on talking, babbling away about trivial things, the lousy wet weather, the neighbour's cat, and what I had for dinner the last three days—piddly stuff like that. Then the annoying beep of a monitor interrupts my monologue and makes me stop in mid-sentence.

"You have to leave the room, please," says the young nurse and repeats with urgency. "You have to leave the room, right now!"

We are already in motion. Jason wheels me hastily out the door, past the nurses' station to a waiting area with some chairs and some old curled-up magazines. People rush by us. Are they running to Vlado's room? Are they doctors? I can hear crackling voices from the loudspeakers, but I can't make out a thing. What is happening to my friend? I am worried and I am trembling. Angelika is reaching for my hand again. Jason just shrugs his shoulders.

"We have to wait and see," he says noncommittally. "Meanwhile, does anybody need something to drink? I am going downstairs to Timmy's."

Tim Horton's is the largest cafe and quick service restaurant chain in Canada and has outlets in every hospital in our country. It is famous for its legendary fresh coffee and doughnuts and has become a very popular meeting place for many, especially the seniors. Vlado and I never frequented the coffee shops much because of his passionate dislike of the 'brew'.

Tim Horton's popularity remains unmatched since its founding days in 1964. Even today, when one puts the ultimate question to somebody in Canada: What is truly Canadian? They will answer: The Maple Leaf (our flag), Tim Horton's, and hockey! Every time, and every time in that same order.

Jason is back with two cups of coffee and a hot chocolate for me. I cannot hold the plastic container. I am still trembling and shaking. Angelika is helping me.

"Take a sip, it will do you good!" she says and holds the cup to my lips.

It might be hot. I am cautious and try to slurp a bit but most of it gets spilled past my sunken chest on the bulging stomach.

"Look, what you have done!" she scolds me now and wipes the brown liquid off with a napkin.

"It was too hot," I reply lamely. I am agitated again. I get that way every time I realize my helplessness and my limited ability to act normally and properly. Then hot anxiety flushes over me and my pulse rate starts to gallop off to new heights. Angelika waits; she watches me and holds my hand. After a while, when my breathing is under control, she says, "Let's try it again. It should have cooled down by now!" This time I take the cup into my own hands and sip the warm chocolate carefully without spilling a single drop.

None of us is talking. I can only think of my friend behind that door in ICU and I don't want to tell anybody what I am thinking. I know that both our long lives are nearing their ends, and I know that Vlado is in deep trouble right now and is hanging onto his life by only a thin thread. Will he come out of this crisis, will he be lucky and victorious again, or will this be the grand finale? I am not afraid of dying, but I am afraid of losing my friend and being alone. I have never done well being alone, I know that.

The grip on my hand tightens slightly and I look up to Angelika. She is reading my thoughts; I can see it in her eyes.

"Vlado is fighting a big battle; he is fighting for his life. We don't know, if he is going to make it, depends how strong his heart is and how strong his desire to live is. But should we lose him, don't worry, Ed. I will look after you. I will always be there when you need me. That's a promise!"

The young nurse walks straight up to me. "Okay, we have him stabilized for now. He wants to talk to you, only to you!" She points her finger at me. Jason puts down the curled-up magazine and gets behind the wheelchair and almost cheerfully he says, "Okay, let's take you to your meeting!"

Vlado is lying on his back, his head a bit elevated. He waits until Jason leaves the room and closes the door, before he begins to speak.

"Did I scare you, Herr Kamerad?" he asks.

"You sure did, big time!"

"This time it really got to me, hit me hard and caught me off guard. Completely surprised me! This is the end, my friend. I can feel it. My hours are numbered. That is, if I have any hours left, they would just be a few. My time is up! That's life, a beginning and an end. It ran its full course. We had some good times together, Herr Kamerad! Such a wonderful friendship for so many years. Remember all the adventures and fishing trips deep into the Canadian wilderness before my accident. Those were great times! And the discussions we had, some darn good ones! Nobody is talking anymore; they are all texting nowadays. What a pity! You and me, we kept the dialogue alive. We always wanted to change the world, but nobody wanted to listen to us."

God is suddenly standing behind him. Vlado gets up and walks over to me.

"I feel good now because now I know that I can walk into heaven on my own. I can walk right through the pearly gates all by myself, unassisted! We can't take our wheelchairs with us when we die; we have to leave them behind. The devil can have them. Why can't the devil suffer for awhile? He brought enough misery to humankind. Goodbye, Herr Kamerad, I'll see you on the other side!"

And he is gone. I am very puzzled and look to God for answers, but He shakes His head.

"Do not ask. I will not answer you. No privileges, you are now like any other human, and most of them don't even know that I exist."

"But I know that you exist!" I protest weakly.

When I open my eyes, God has left and Vlado is dead. And I think: 'There won't be no bananas growing in Prince George. Not for a long time.'

Names, Characters and Events

Names and Characters in 2028

Masoud Abbasi	President of ULIN
Jonathan Oliver	President of USA
Dalton Henderson	Vice President of USA
Igor Popov	President of Russian Federation
Mr. Lin	President of China
Mr. Singh	Prime Minister of India
Isabella Elegante	President of Brazil
Maxima Müller	Chancellor of European Federation
Omar Sadikin	President of SEPA
Stephen Hunter	Prime Minister of Canada
Dembe Khulani	President of South Africa
Edward Doyle	Director of CIA
Hernandez	Chief Operative FEMA, West Coast

Names and Characters in 2035

Megan Prince	Prime Minister of Canada
Chen Li	Global President
Jason	Ed's caregiver
Angelika	Ed's caregiver
Adrian	Vlado's caregiver

Time Table of Events

Katrina	2005 hurricane that devastated New Orleans
Sandy	2012 superstorm that devastated New Jersey and New York
2019	Uprising in USA, 18 months
2021	Establishment of Military Junta, 5 Generals, Oliver
2022 – 2025	Scorcher Years
2024	Oliver elected
2028, August	Fishing with God
2028, Oct. 11	Superstorm Lucinda hits east coast
2028	Election Year planned for Tuesday, Nov. 7, cancelled
2028, Oct. 30	The Big One erupts, Monday, 4:43 p.m., PST
2028, Nov. 1	Abbasi phones Oliver
2028, Nov. 19	Secret meeting in Muscat
2029, May	Global Elections
2029, July 1	First World Parliament sworn in

Quotes

Every bit of evidence I've seen persuades me we are on a course leading to tragedy.
> \- Maurice F. Strong, Secretary General UNCED 1992 Rio

Why are there so many nonbelievers? What's there not to believe? Global warming is not a religion—it is a fact!
> \- Vlado

I declare without a doubt that we have the most beautiful planet in the entire universe and all the other planets envy us. So, why are we out there in full force, hell-bent on ruining it?
> \- Masoud Abbasi

Testimonials

"Is it possible for world leaders to work together to save the planet? Do two elderly nursing home residents hold the key? When a catastrophic event threatens our existence, a drastic plan must be put into action. Author Edmund Arndt offers a plethora of fascinating and, at times, frightening solutions. Against this backdrop, the plot and its cast of characters take the reader to the far reaches of the globe and beyond, culminating in a sweetly satisfying and surprising conclusion!"

- Joyce Rynearson, writer and educator

"I finished reading your book! I am proud of you, Ed! Such good work. It's fabulous! I will read it a second time for sure. My goodness what an imagination you have, but what a well-thought out premise with such a satisfying conclusion. It is also a very thought-provoking theme that, while being intense, did not stop me from attacking the book as a real page-turner!"

- Deanna Lagroix, writer and educator

"I certainly do not endorse all of the author's outlandish ideas. But then, I believe it was never his intention to seek endorsement. His intentions are to ring the alarm bells and to stir up humankind, have them band together globally to confront the serious environmental challenges and the drastic effects from climate change that we humans and our planet are facing.

Bravo Ed! Let the alarm bells ring louder and louder!"

- John Leverkusen, global citizen